TEXT AND CONFUSED

An Accidentally in Love Story, Book 6

WHITNEY DINEEN

MELANIE SUMMERS

For the women out there who have trouble picking the right one.

Love yourself first. Take yourself out on a date; buy yourself flowers; get that gorgeous diamond. The right one will come along at the right time.

XOXO,
Whitney and Mel

The Accidentally in Love Stories
BY WHITNEY DINEEN & MELANIE SUMMERS

Text Me on Tuesday
The Text God
Text Wars
Text in Show
Mistle Text
Text and Confused

Also by Whitney Dineen

Romantic Comedies

The Mimi Chronicles

The Reinvention of Mimi Finnegan

Mimi Plus Two

Kindred Spirits

Relatively Series

Relatively Normal

Relatively Sane

Relatively Happy

Creek Water Series

The Event

The Move

The Plan

The Dream

Seven Brides for Seven Mothers Series

Love is a Battlefield

Ain't She Sweet

It's My Party

You're So Vain

She Sins at Midnight

Going Up?

Love for Sale

Conspiracy Thriller

See No More

Non-Fiction Humor

Motherhood, Martyrdom & Costco Runs

Middle Reader

Wilhelmina and the Willamette Wig Factory

Who the Heck is Harvey Stingle?

Children's Books

The Friendship Bench

Also by Melanie Summers

ROMANTIC COMEDIES

The Crown Jewels Series

The Royal Treatment

The Royal Wedding

The Royal Delivery

Paradise Bay Series

The Honeymooner

Whisked Away

The Suite Life

Resting Beach Face

Crazy Royal Love Series

Royally Crushed

Royally Wild

Royally Tied

WOMEN'S FICTION

The After Wife

Chapter 1

Toni

After pouring an extra dose of bubble bath into the tub, I dip my fingertips into the water to make sure I'm not about to scald myself. The ancient plumbing in my building isn't exactly what you'd call reliable, but since I'm determined to keep up item number four (self-care) on my "New Year, New Me" resolution list, I'm making it work.

Ahh, there. Goldilocks temperature achieved, which means I'll have a good fifteen minutes before it cools down. After sliding into the water, I dry my hands on the cotton waffled shower curtain and pluck my journal off the toilet lid. Journaling is item three on my list, and I've already missed … let's see … nineteen days of it. Since it's January 24th, I'm getting concerned about my commitment to a better me. Well, other than the baths …

I flip the cover open and remind myself of what I'm supposed to be doing to achieve a new and better Toni.

. . .

This Year I Commit to:

1. *Only consume processed sugar on special occasions (and no, Fridays do not count).*
2. *Exercise five times per week for a minimum of thirty minutes per session.*
3. *Write daily journal entries, even if it's just one sentence.*
4. *Set aside time for self-care, including long baths, walks, getting out into nature, and other things my favorite Instagram lifestyle gurus say I should do.*
5. *Find a new apartment without Creepy Hallway Guy and with a bedroom big enough that I can't touch both sides at the same time.*
6. *Find lasting love with a good man. Translation: NO bad boys/grease monkeys/construction workers/unemployed-but-sexy men who want to use me as a crash pad or cash cow. Henceforth a good man shall be defined as an adult human who wears a suit to the job he goes to every day. He will also have an apartment or house he pays for without the help of a roommate, his parents, or the government. He will not ask me to fund his band, finance his sure bet at the races, help his start-up automated vegan hot dog vending cart business, or any other whackadoo endeavor that has failure written all over it. I'm talking to you Dillion, Xander, Taylor, and Bart.*

Number six is obviously my top priority, but according to Kaylie, the Lifestyle Queen, the other stuff must come first. I write today's date, then add: *Took hot bath. Otherwise failing. Must do better.* Sighing, I close my journal and put it back on the porcelain throne, then sink into the water until it's over my head. This time last year, I knew exactly where my future was heading—I was going to marry my boyfriend Joey, buy a house in Flushing, have a couple of kids, and live happily ever after. The old-fashioned American dream.

That was before Joey got fired from his third job in the two years we were together, then proceeded to take out his frustration on me in front of our friends at the Suds 'N' Bowl. After him I went on a slew of crappy first dates that didn't take before waving the white flag of surrender on dating altogether.

My mom didn't take the news well and announced in her Christmas letter she was "learning to be comfortable with having a spinster daughter." *What century is this again?*

In addition, I've been fending off calls, texts, and visits from my well-meaning aunts, who refuse to believe I've given up on love. Here's a sample text conversation of how they view me:

Aunt Jean: Honey, I just read the news. You poor girl. I don't want you to worry though, because Julia Roberts always got the man in her romcoms. If she can do it, so can you.

Me: Um, thanks.

Aunt Jean: Of course, she didn't get hitched in real life until she was in her late thirties, unless you count that weird-looking musician she was married to for a minute (which I don't).

Me: Okay.

Aunt Jean: Although she did have to break up a marriage to get her happily ever after. I'm not saying that's okay, but after a certain age ...

Me: Are you suggesting I start dating married men?

Aunt Jean: I refuse to put that in writing. And don't tell your mom I said that. But it does seem to have worked out well for them, so…

My mom's other sisters have been equally involved in trying to help me find my one true love. Aunt Margie has been sending workmen to my apartment for the last month with false claims of leaky pipes and malfunctioning kitchen appliances. I caved and went out with one of the plumbers, but our relationship only lasted two dates. The guy loved to talk about his work and honestly, there's only so much banter about clogged toilets I can stand. And during dinner, too.

Unbeknownst to me, Aunt Sheila started a Tinder profile in my name. She was swiping right, left, up, and down trying to find me a man. I went out with one guy believing he was my aunt's neighbor. Things were going well until he mentioned a conversation we'd had online about blowup dolls.

That's when I discovered he didn't know who Sheila was and that she'd told him I'd be up for a threesome as long as the third party wasn't human. I'm not sure I'll ever look at her the same way again.

In addition to vowing to *never* go out on another setup, I'm determined to take my dating life into my own hands. I also decided to change my type (see item six on my list). As a lifelong admirer of working-class men—there's something so fundamentally manly about a tight T-shirt covered in axle grease, grass stains, or whatever (I refuse to consider what was on the plumber's T-shirt)—it stands to reason I must now avoid them at all costs.

In a bid to attract a different kind of guy, I decided to

channel Melanie Griffith in *Working Girl*. I'm upgrading from a slick-haired, cheating, lying Alec Baldwin to a sweet, respectful Harrison Ford—à la Jack Trainer (if you've never seen this golden oldie romcom, do so now).

After New Year's, I went out and blew a fortune on clothes I figured a classy woman would wear. No more plunging necklines and tight pants for me. From now on it's modest dresses with conservative heels—no more drag queen shoes. I've also dialed down the amount of makeup I wear, and I've swapped out certain phrases in my vocabulary. My penchant for colorful language has been redirected. I now say things like, "Oh, dear," "my word," and "for heaven's sake."

So far, the only men I've attracted have been a pair of nice young men who wondered if I'd heard about the *Book of Mormon*. But fear not, it's early days. I'm sure there's hope for me yet.

While turning off the cold water tap with my left foot and upping the hot with my right, I decide I can't keep waiting for the man of my dreams to show up out of thin air. If I'm serious about changing my luck—and I am—I have to be willing to go out with someone who doesn't make my heart beat like Ricky Ricardo playing the bongos. (I don't care what generation you're from, if you haven't watched every episode of *I Love Lucy* by the time you're twenty, you haven't lived.)

My luck might be about to change. Tomorrow, Sumner Livingston, the fundraiser my boss hired for the foundation I work for, is going to pop by the office for his first meeting with us. I googled him earlier today, and I have to say the guy's got potential. Clean cut, classic good looks, and a steady job at his family's company. He grew up in Forest Hills, which means he's likely well-educated and probably doesn't catcall women on the street.

I couldn't find any evidence of a significant other, so I'm putting him at the top of my list of potential future life partners. It's a short list, consisting of him and Jack Trainer. Being that Jack Trainer is fictional, let's hope Sumner is single and into me. Oh, and not a complete douchebag.

I turn off the hot water tap when it starts running cold, only to discover another argument has broken out next door. Apparently Jason skipped work again to "manage" his fantasy football team. His girlfriend, Jolessa, has been threatening to leave him since October, as this has turned into a semi-regular occurrence. I'm tempted to get out of the tub, throw on a towel, and go tell her to do it already. I barely know them, except for passing them in the hall, but based on the frequency and content of their fights, Jason is clearly not ready to be in an adult relationship.

Closing my eyes, I try to shut out the familiar pattern of my neighbors' lives. Man-baby screws up for the hundredth time, woman gets angry, blowout happens, followed by hours of woman wondering why she puts up with it. A day or two later, man-baby apologizes, makes promises they both know he won't keep, and they have loud makeup sex until 2:00 a.m. I am never going back to that. Ever.

I don't get out of the tub until the fight is over, and I'm withered like a prune. I'm about to crawl into bed when the phone rings. It's got to be my best friend Holly, because she's the only person other than my mom who calls instead of texts. As it's eleven o'clock on a Sunday night, I know for a fact that my mom is at Gutter Rats bowling alley with her sisters. Together, they form Dolls with Balls and have been the women's champions eight years running. They practice every Sunday night.

"Heya," I say. "You'd better be calling to tell me you bought me a lottery ticket, and I won."

She laughs. "Sorry. I called to tell you Archie and I will be late getting to work in the morning. I wanted to make sure you had your key."

Holly married my boss last year and transformed him from a ruthless investment banker into a full-time do-gooder. It's been an astonishing makeover. Archie retired from his high-powered job and has channeled part of his vast financial portfolio into a new venture called the Faith Foundation, the main purpose of which is to offer services to the homeless. The goal is to get them off the streets and into jobs that will allow them to be self-sufficient.

"Why? Is Archie taking you to Paris for breakfast?" I sound bitter and hurry to apologize. "I'm sorry, that was mean. You deserve every good thing you get." And she does. Holly was single-handedly raising her young niece Faith (whose parents died in an accident when she was two) when she and Archie met. She worked three jobs for years to cover their expenses and was barely keeping the lights on so she could get her gifted niece into the best school. The poor woman's only winter coat was so ratty, you could practically read the logo on her T-shirt through it.

Ignoring my snide comment, Holly tells me, "We're checking out the building site for our first transition neighborhood." The Faith Foundation is building a community of tiny houses the homeless can use until they are employed and able to afford something on their own. How cool is that?

"Well, have fun, and if you pass a Mr. Bagel, I'd love a toasted onion with a schmear."

"You do realize Faith is now addicted to those, thanks to you. She's the only kid in kindergarten who doesn't mind smelling like onions."

I crawl into bed and pull the covers up nearly over my head. "I love that kid."

"She loves you right back."

"Speaking of love, do you know if Sumner Livingston is single? He's been photographed with a ton of women, but I haven't found one that says he's with his wife."

"Are you asking because you've sworn off burly bad boys and assume he's the hot preppy guy you envision yourself with?" She knows me so well.

"I don't need a *hot* preppy guy. Just a regular one. Hot means trouble." I flip off the light on my nightstand. "Also, nearly every article online describes him as classically handsome, which I can confirm, because I'm pretty sure I've seen every public picture ever taken of him."

"I know he's not married, but he might be seeing someone. I'd ask Archie, but he's asleep already."

"That's okay. I can find out when I meet him tomorrow. But if he were single, what do you think? Can you see us together?"

"Maybe. I've only met him a couple of times, so it's not like I really know him." I can tell by her tone she's not loving the idea.

"But?"

Yawning, she says, "I don't know. He's very charming."

"You say that like it's a bad thing."

"He might be a little too slick. Like he's always 'on,' you know?"

"Occupational hazard maybe? I mean, he is a fundraiser. People don't hand you wads of cash unless they're charmed by you."

"That makes sense. The last time I saw him, we were trying to decide if we should hire his firm, so he obviously had to be on for that." Yawning again, she adds, "He seems responsible, so he's nothing like Joey."

"Responsible is my new love language."

Holly clicks her tongue, which is something she does when she's thinking. "I doubt he's the type to sweep you off your feet, but with a guy like Sumner, there wouldn't be any surprises."

"I'm no longer in the market for surprises. I'm perfectly content with the idea of a steady guy with a job." Even though I wasn't a fan of Holly dating Archie, I now think she possibly got the last good man out there, and the thought makes my heart ache.

"You mean, someone who won't steal your Instant Pot," she teases.

"Or my car," I say, reminding her of boyfriend number twelve.

"That too."

"I'm going to sleep now." If I keep thinking about my miserable social life, I might start to cry.

"Sleep tight. Oh, and I almost forgot to tell you. The new contractor is stopping by the office at nine tomorrow to pick up some plans on his way to the site. Archie left them on his desk."

"I'll make sure to point him in the right direction."

"Thanks, sweets."

"You are most welcome. Don't forget my bagel. I'm afraid it might be the best part of my day." I hang up. Closing my eyes, I hope sleep claims me quickly. The last thing I want is another night of lying awake, feeling lonely.

My last conscious thought is that I desperately need something good to happen in my life, and I need it to happen soon.

Chapter 2

Cooper

There are three things I know about women. They want what they don't have, they rarely want what they do have, and unless you see a head poking out, never congratulate them on being pregnant.

Number one and two make me sound like a sexist jerk, but I grew up with three older sisters, so I have insight into the female brain that a lot of men don't. Regarding wanting what they can't have—two of my sisters, Rae-Anne and Willa, have curly hair like our father and wish to God they had perfectly straight smooth hair. The youngest of the three girls, Lily, stares longingly at her older sisters' curls and forever laments having what she calls "horribly boring, poker-straight hair."

When they were little, they were desperate to have a baby brother (wanting what they didn't have), but when I arrived, they acted like I was the biggest disappointment they'd ever shared. I quickly got used to being the black sheep of the family.

My mother is a psychiatrist who somehow managed to get her doctorate while raising four children. My father is a law professor who inspired Willa and Lily to become attorneys (and successful ones at that). Rae-Anne is a surgeon who specializes in neurology. She's literally a brain surgeon.

Imagine my parents' combined disappointment when I didn't go to college. I love being outside more than anything in this world and barely managed to force myself to stay indoors long enough to complete high school. I also love to build things, so working construction during the summers of my teen years was the perfect fit. The second I threw my cap into the air, I picked up a hammer and never looked back.

Driven by my need to prove there is more than one path to success, I quickly amassed enough knowledge to run my own contracting business. I started with a crew of five guys and added on every year until I had three crews working full-time on some of the most expensive houses on the eastern seaboard. Our reputation is such that I have the luxury of being able to regularly turn down work if I don't want the job.

To be honest, I'm doing much better than I ever thought I would. My family would never believe me if I told them what I make—so I don't—but I'm sure it's more than all of them combined. I could retire now at thirty-three if I wanted and never work another day in my life.

I won't do that though, because I love what I do. And if I stopped working, my parents would amp up their nagging about me going to college to make something of myself. They are hellbent on having their only son join the white-collar side of the workforce. Anything would do—

engineering, zoology, a master's degree in interpretive dance—as long as I add some letters to the end of my name. They simply can't fathom that I'm happy in my portable office trailer, moving from job to job.

Picking up the mail on my desk, I release a loud groan.

"Don't tell me they sent you more college admission packages?" my assistant, Yuma Katayama, asks as she shrugs off her wool coat. Yuma has been working for me a little over eight years. She's my accountant/office manager and is enough like family to know all about my real-life family dramas.

"It's that time of year again," I tell her with a wry smile.

"The early admission deadline?"

"My birthday."

"Oh, is it your birthday?" she asks with absolutely no enthusiasm whatsoever. And that will conclude our celebration. Yuma's not a touchy-feely type of person. She's more of a tough-as-nails, don't-mess-with-me type, which is precisely what I need when my suppliers are late delivering materials, and they're *always* late.

"Thanks." I separate the card with my name on it from the brochures it came with, toss the pamphlets into the bin next to Yuma's desk, and go into my office to open my birthday card.

Dear Cooper,

Happy thirty-third birthday!

It's never too late to grow your mind and expand your horizons.

Love,

Mom & Dad

P.S. Check out the mechanical engineering program at Virginia Tech. It would suit you beautifully.

While I'm waiting for my computer to boot up, my

phone rings. Caller ID shows it's Rae-Anne. "Hey there, Brainy Smurf."

"Hey, Handy. How's your birthday so far?"

"Just finished opening my present from our parents."

"Ah yes, the annual gift of shame. I got a one-year subscription to Weight Watchers for my big day."

"Wow. Just wow. You'd think a psychiatrist would know better."

"Eh, it's human nature to have massive blind spots when it comes to your own family."

"A blind spot is one thing. What they've got is more like a black hole. But enough about them. How's the never-ending shift going?"

"Two biopsies, then a decompressive craniectomy that took up most of the night. A guy on a donor-cycle bit it on the freeway. No helmet."

"Of course," I say, wishing she would stop the story here.

"I've never seen such a large bone flap taken before," she says, sounding more excited than you'd think she would be. "If he makes it, it'll be at least three months before it can be replaced."

My stomach churns, making me glad I haven't had breakfast yet. It sounds horrific, but instead of saying that, I go with, "It sounds … thrilling."

"You mean cold-hearted—at least that's how what's-his-nuts referred to me." She's referring to her ex-fiancé, the total waste of air she nearly married. He was fine being with her when she was a lowly pre-med student, but the more her star rose, the uglier his personality got. The final straw was their engagement party, when I discovered him in his car having sex with our parents' maid. Right in front of their house. With Rae-Anne inside, wondering where he was.

It's been over a year, and my poor sister still isn't over it. If I don't say something to head her off, she's going to spiral downhill, talking about him for the next twenty minutes, then thinking about him for the next twenty days.

"You're the last person I'd call cold-hearted. You're a total professional."

"Damn straight I am," she says.

"In fact, if I ever need surgery, I'd want you in the OR."

"Aw, thanks, Coop. That's why you're my favorite."

"Liar."

She ignores me. "What are you doing to celebrate your big day?"

"I'm starting that new project for the Faith Foundation."

"The homeless village?"

"Yup."

"As rewarding as I'm sure that's going to be, it doesn't sound like a celebration."

"I'm thirty-three, Rae. It's not like I need people to make a fuss over me."

"At least pick up some takeout or something. Oh, and if Willa calls, don't answer."

"Why not?"

"She wants to set you up with some lawyer from her firm. Word on the street is she's pretty and has a good sense of humor, but you know, she's *a lawyer* ..." She says it like it's a dirty word.

"Thanks for the heads up."

"No problem. Ever since Willa moved in with that Ted guy, she seems to think no one else can be happy without a significant other. Last week she texted about a client of hers she thought would be perfect for me. As soon as his divorce is final, that is. She wanted me to send a picture she could show him. If I wanted a divorced guy with three kids in my life, I would have married someone and had my own family before kicking him to the curb."

"Think of it this way: you get to have the family without having to go through the whole pregnancy thing."

"That's what Willa said," she huffs. "But I'm not about to complicate my life. Certainly not for a dentist. If he was a stunt man with a six pack and quads like a weightlifter—"

"For the love of God, please stop. I'm getting an image."

"Oh relax, you big baby. I'm not serious," she says before adding, "You and me, Handy. Single for life, right?"

"Absolutely," I say, even though I don't hate the idea of having someone to come home to. Someone down-to-earth and fun, who wouldn't mind going to a baseball game with me once in a while. Someone I could celebrate with when something good happens, like winning a big bid or turning thirty-three …

Chapter 3

Toni

I take special pains today since Sumner will be stopping by the office. I opt for a fifties-inspired shirtwaist dress with a skinny belted waistband and full skirt. It makes me feel powerful and feminine at the same time. Then I pull my hair back in the Marian-the-Librarian bun I've decided will entice the new type of guy I'm trying to attract—hopefully Sumner. After swiping some mascara on and dabbing a light pink gloss over my lips, I'm ready to make the most of the day.

Then I leave my apartment, and everything goes spectacularly to hell.

It rained cats and dogs last night, turning the remnants of snow into puddles of dirty slush. This makes me, and every other intrepid pedestrian, a target on street corners while waiting for the light to change. I avoid all near-misses on my way to the subway entrance and am just about to give myself a mental high five when I'm hit by a tsunami of freezing cold water that sucks the breath out of me. A garbage truck zips past, soaking more than a few victims. I swear I hear maniacal laughter emanating from the cab.

Momentarily forgetting I've given up cursing, I release a slew of foul verbiage in response to the driver and step off the curb into a pothole which causes my knee to buckle. I land on my butt in a river of road filth. After struggling to my feet, I'm frozen in place for a few seconds, trying to process what to do next. I glance at my watch to see if I have time to go home and change. I don't. I'll barely have enough time to get to the office before the new contractor comes in to pick up the plans.

After I get to work and take the freight elevator up to the third-floor loft that's been converted into the Faith Foundation headquarters, there isn't an inch on me that's still clean or dry. I flip on the lights before hurrying into the bathroom to tidy up. One look in the mirror makes it clear what a hopeless endeavor that will be.

The only other clothes I have at the office are a pair of old jeans and a T-shirt I left here the day we moved in. I went out with Holly and Archie for dinner that night to celebrate our new endeavor, so I'd brought evening clothes along.

I'm about to change into my only dry option when I hear the elevator move. I trot out to the reception area in time to see an Adonis in jeans and a snug Pink Floyd T-shirt. He lifts the elevator door with a flick of his wrist (whereas for me, it's a full body effort), before stepping off. There's a tiny crease between his hazel green eyes that's so appealing, I want to trail my fingers across it. He's got a short beard, which looks like he hasn't bothered to shave for a couple of weeks. It's clearly not the kind he spends hours carefully grooming and rubbing with oil. His hair is sandy brown, wavy, and windblown. I want to run my fingers through it. Long story short, I want to touch this guy.

Taking off his black leather jacket, he gives me a quick once-over. "Whoa, looks like you got a little wet."

"Oh, um, yeah, hi …" I sound like an idiot. I'm fairly certain there's a pool of drool forming in the corner of my mouth. When I finally manage to form a sentence, it's unfortunately this one: "Some butt nugget in a garbage truck got me." I groan inwardly, suddenly self-conscious.

"He must have really been gunning for you."

I nod and manage to make a sound that resembles "Uh-huh." *Come on, Toni, pull it together.*

Offering a smile that could instantly melt a pound of frozen butter, he says, "I'm Cooper Flint, the contractor working on the Bedford Falls project." He approaches me like a stealthy jungle cat. "Archie said he was leaving plans here for me."

I hold my hand out, palm facing down as though I want him to kiss my knuckles like a gentleman in some old-timey movie—I want this guy's lips on me. He takes my hand and shakes it up and down a couple of times (you know, like someone who isn't from the Regency era). A warmth flows through me from my fingertips all the way to my toes and back.

"I'm … um … Toni. If you'll just give me a minute, I'll find them for you."

He glances down at the clothes in my left hand and says, "Why don't you change first. I'm not in a huge hurry."

"Thank you. I'm actually freezing."

I hit the bathroom and take off my sopping wet dress, then dry off with a stack of paper hand towels. Two things occur to me as I struggle to pull up my old jeans. The first is that you should never try to put on pants when your skin is damp. The second is that I've definitely gained a few pounds since I started wearing dresses. I can barely get my Levi's up over my hips.

Buttoning them requires sucking in my breath and what I'm guessing would be a rosary worth of Hail Marys. Being that I don't have time to ask the Blessed Virgin for help, I settle with a short plea to the Big Man himself. "Dear God, please let this zipper hold."

By the time my pants are finally on, I'm gasping and sweating from the effort. At some point today, I'm going to have to run home for new clothes so I'm not sporting this camel toe when Sumner arrives. That's not the impression I'm going for. Pulling on my T-shirt with the hot pink lips emblazoned across the front, I look in the mirror and cringe. It's no wonder I used to attract the kind of guys I did, dressed like this.

After unpinning my bun and letting my hair down to dry, I shake my head at my reflection. I look like I've just left an all-night rave and got mugged on my way home.

When I walk out, the contractor looks me up and down. "Wow."

My stomach does this little rollercoaster drop of excitement. I should not be aroused in any way. Cooper Flint is not the kind of guy I'm in the market for. He in no way fits my new definition of the perfect man. I bet he's covered in tattoos under that shirt, and I wonder what they are as my brain spirals into an abyss of lustful thoughts.

Stop it, Toni. You like clean-cut men in suits now. Not men with muscles on top of muscles. I catch myself staring at his torso, and my cheeks burn with feelings that are not suitable for the workplace.

"Do you like what you see?" he asks with what may be the cockiest smile I've ever seen. "Because if so, how about we go out sometime?"

"What? No." My reply is short and rude, but seriously, he's only asking me out after seeing me in my skintight clothing. Had he asked me out when I looked like a drowned librarian, I may not have been able to resist him.

"Oh." He sounds shocked. I'm guessing not many women turn him down. "I thought you might be interested by the way you were looking at me. I didn't mean to offend you."

Busted. I roll my eyes at him. "I was just thinking of all the things you could do with those hours you spend at the gym every week. It's kind of a waste, really."

"Is that so?" He chuckles. "And what are all the things I should be doing with my free time?"

Nuts, I wasn't prepared for *that* question. "So many things … There's learning a new language, reading to children at the library, volunteering at a soup kitchen …" I run out of ideas.

"Which soup kitchen do you volunteer at? Maybe I can meet you there."

Flames of embarrassment flicker across my cheeks. "The one with the soup and the homeless people." I scurry away, mumbling, "I'll get those plans for you."

I practically run to Archie's office, feeling like a complete fool. When I return, I do my best not to look at him. I'm like Perseus avoiding Medusa's gaze for fear of a death scenario (or in my case, fear of falling for another alpha-hole). I hand him the tube of drawings, doing my best to sound uber-professional. "Here you go, Mr. Flint."

Hoping he'll leave if I ignore him, I sit at my desk and turn on my computer. It's an act of God my pants don't split. As it is, I'm relatively certain the strain on my zipper is going to force it to give way.

Instead of leaving, he saunters over to me like he's God's gift. His masculine aura is infringing on my personal space in the worst yet most delicious way possible. "Thanks, Toni. It was nice to meet you. I'm sorry I won't be seeing you outside the office."

"We have a strict no-dating policy for employees," I mutter without looking up from my screen saver.

He looks at me like he can see right through me. "You have a nice day."

"Sure thing," I tell him while my brains screams, "Please, just go!" I'm sucking in my gut as far as I can, and I'm pretty sure I'm doing some serious damage to my internal organs.

When he finally turns to leave, my stupid eyes track his taut butt the entire way to the elevator. He turns and catches me gawking, then gives me a grin that turns my insides to microwaved marshmallow fluff. "By the way, I haven't been to a gym since high school."

Oh. My. Gawd. No gym? "Is that so?" I sound bored, and I'm proud of myself.

"Yes, it is, and I'd appreciate it if you stopped looking at me like an extra-large hot fudge sundae. It's sending mixed messages that my poor man brain can't handle." His eyes are dancing with amusement. I don't know if I want to smack that look off his face or jump into his arms and beg him to take me home.

Making a scoffing sound deep in my throat, I say, "Don't flatter yourself. You're not my type."

"Tell that to your eyes."

I fold my arms across the big shiny lip decal on my shirt. "I don't know what you think you saw, but as shocking as I'm sure this is for you to hear, I'm not inter-ested in you. Besides, as I've mentioned, the foundation has strict rules on these things, and I would never break them."

I'm lying like a dog, but I have to do something to stop this crazy energy we've got zinging between us.

"I guess that makes me forbidden fruit."

"Is that supposed to make me want you more?" The nerve of this guy.

Cooper breaks into a huge smile, and dimples pop up on either side of his mouth. "More? Now that's an interesting word, coming from someone who's so adamant about not being interested."

Why did I say more? *And why did he notice?* I do the only thing a girl can do when she's backed into a corner. I pretend the phone is ringing. I glance at it before picking it up. "Toni Foundation, Faith speaking. How can I help you?"

Well, that's just perfect. Could I make a bigger ass of myself today?

Cooper reaches the elevator door. Once he's inside, he pulls the gate down, presses a button, and salutes me while I tell my phantom caller, "We can definitely do that." As soon as the elevator disappears, I put the receiver down and rest my head on my desk while letting out a loud groan.

I can't remember another time when I've made such a fool of myself. At least I didn't agree to go out with him. I'm drawn to Cooper Flint like a moth to a bonfire, but I *refuse* to wind up with another guy who isn't a keeper—and a keeper he is not. He's cocky as hell and far too hot to be marriage material.

When you think about it, acting like a total nut in front of him probably means he'll lose whatever thready interest he thinks he has in me. It'll be only business between us from now on. No flirting, no gazing, no drooling. Nothing.

Which is a good thing.

So why do I feel like I can't breathe?

Oh yeah, the jeans. I quickly unbutton them and gulp air, then tug my shirt down to cover my wide-open pants.

The next guy I fall for will be an upstanding businessman with his eye on the long game. He's going to be husband and father material, not some contractor who only wants to get me into bed. Been there, done that, canceled my subscription.

Before I can go home and change, the phone rings. My day of fielding calls from an array of building inspectors, architects, and assorted other tradespeople has begun. It's after ten before I even get my first cup of coffee.

When the elevator comes up again, I expect it to be Holly and Archie, but it's Sumner Livingston in the flesh. He's even taller and better looking than the images on my tiny phone screen. He's dressed in a dark gray wool coat, black suit pants, and shiny black shoes that probably cost more than I pay in rent every month.

And I'm in my stupid lips T-shirt with my jeans unbuttoned.

Sumner easily lifts the elevator gate—but not as effortlessly as Cooper. *What is this, a competition?* He's clean-shaven and has a very nice smile with white, even Chiclet teeth. "Hi there, I'm Sumner Livingston. You must be Toni."

I surreptitiously fasten the button on my jeans before standing to shake his hand. My stomach doesn't do flip-flops when we touch. In fact, his skin feels cold and clammy. To be fair, he just came in from outside (where it is, in fact, cold and clammy). "Nice to meet you, Sumner."

"You too." His eyes sweep over my outfit, underlining how unprofessional I look.

"I don't normally dress like this. I got splashed by a garbage truck on my way in and this was the only thing I had to change into."

"I was just wondering if I was overdressed," he says with a hint of laughter.

"Nope, you're perfect. Archie and Holly aren't here yet, but I can take you to the conference room if you want to get a little work done while you wait."

I lead him to the meeting room at the back of the office, realizing there's no way a guy like Sumner will be interested in someone who looks like I do right now. Talk about a horrible first impression.

He takes off his coat and lays it over the back of a chair. He's wearing a crisp white dress shirt, top button open, no tie. He's got the long, lean look of a runner. I wait for attraction to kick in, but there's nothing. I blame Cooper Flint for using up all my "hot and bothered" for the morning.

A quick glance at his left hand confirms he doesn't have a wife, but he could still have a girlfriend. I decide to go on a fishing expedition to find out. "I just put a fresh pot of coffee on."

"Thanks, but I've already reached my limit." He sits at the large table and offers me a friendly grin.

"I'll leave you to it then. Let me know if you need anything," I say breathily, then quickly follow that with, "I hope you don't think I was hitting on you just now. I meant that you should let me know if you need anything work-related."

"I didn't think you were flirting with me," he says and turns his attention to his briefcase, dismissing me.

"Good. I'd hate for you to go home tonight and tell your girlfriend that some woman from work was making a play for you. The last thing I need is for her to storm the office looking for me." I make it sound like that happens to me all the time.

Sumner looks up with amusement. "Yeah, I can imagine you wouldn't want that."

I fidget. "Especially if she's a blackbelt in karate or a gun nut. That would be bad."

His lips curve upward. "It's a good thing I don't have a girlfriend, because I'd hate to see either of those scenarios play out."

Wiping a hand across my forehead, I let out a dramatic, "Phew …"

Cocking his head, he says, "I'm starting to get the impression there *may* be some flirting going on here."

I gasp like a heroine in a Jane Austen novel. Turning, I slowly sashay to the door. "I'd never do such a thing. I'm nothing if not professional."

Back at my desk, I spend the next few minutes trying to talk myself into forgetting about what's-his-name with the muscles. I've followed my hormones far too long, and it's gotten me nowhere. The good news is that Sumner may be a contender for Mr. Right. Eek! That would mean I'd be Mrs. Right (or more accurately, Mrs. Livingston. Mrs. Toni Livingston. A girl could get used to a name like that).

Sumner could be the answer to all my dating prayers. I just have to make him see it …

Chapter 4

Cooper

I smile all the way to the job site. I'd love to say it's because I'm excited about embarking on a project that allows me to give something back to society, but it's not. While I am enthusiastic about the Bedford Falls project, it's the knockout assistant who has me grinning.

Even covered in dirty street water, she's gorgeous. But in those shellacked-on jeans? I almost proposed right then and there. I'm not some conceited jerk who thinks I'm every woman's type, but I have eyes, and I know when someone is attracted to me. The way Toni stared says she's definitely interested in me.

I pull up to the site of the Faith Foundation's first tiny home village, which is an old warehouse with a large shipping yard surrounding it. I shut off the engine as a black Escalade pulls up next to my truck. Time to forget about the beautiful Toni with the tight jeans and get to work.

A cold breeze whips up as I step out of the truck, and I

have to fight to shut the door. After Archie and Holly get out of their vehicle, we exchange quick hellos and hurry inside the warehouse to seek shelter from the elements.

"This is it," Archie exclaims after we walk through the battered steel door. Flipping on the overhead fluorescent lights, he asks, "What do you think, Cooper? Can you envision a small neighborhood here?"

I look around the enormous building. It was built in the 1920s. In its prime, I'm sure it was something to behold—brick walls, enormous wood trusses holding up the tin roof, and lots of windows that must have gleamed in the sunlight before years of grime baked on them.

"Between the building and the yard, there's more than enough space here for your plans," I tell him. "We'll easily be able to fit forty tiny houses, along with sidewalks and green space."

"Don't forget the main office building," Holly says. "We're still waiting on the final plans for that, but I picture using the cafeteria to host community meetings and meals. I'd also like to add a small market, where we sell everything at wholesale prices."

"That sounds amazing." It sounds like my new clients have thought of everything.

"What's your ballpark for demo and removal?" Archie asks.

"My crew could have everything out of here in two weeks." I glance around. "But if it was my money, I'd want to salvage as much of this as possible. They don't make brick in this shade of red anymore, and there's more than enough in the walls to use for the front of each house. The trusses might be reusable as well, but I won't know until I take them down. It would take us an extra week to salvage, but the effort could prove useful for the foundation."

"How so?" Archie asks, folding his arms.

"It would allow us to list the project as eco-friendly. There are grants for that type of thing. We could source windows, doors, and cabinets from secondhand stores, as well. The labor costs for salvaging would be higher, but you'd save on materials and look good to the public."

Holly grins at me and then looks at her husband. "I like the sound of repurposing and lessening our carbon footprint."

Archie nods. "Let's do it."

Walking over to an old metal table, I spread out the plans so the three of us can look at them together. Pointing to one of the house designs, I say, "We'd use the brick here on the front and wrap it around a couple of feet on the sides, then go with regular siding for the rest. The wood could be used for posts holding up a small overhang above each door to give it a classic look. Some of it could be repurposed into window boxes, so the tenants could plant flowers or veggies."

"That's so beautiful," Holly says, her voice catching.

I'm surprised by how emotional she is.

She dismissively waves a hand. "Don't mind me. I'm pregnant, and everything makes me cry these days."

Archie wraps an arm around her shoulders and gives her a squeeze. "It's true. Yesterday, 'Closing Time' by Semisonic came on the radio, and she cried for an hour."

"They were such a talented band." Holly sniffles. "I can't believe they never had another hit after that one." Her face morphs into pure grief. "It's so sad that they were a …" She pats Archie's arm, signaling him to finish for her.

"One-hit wonder," Archie says, giving me a look that says *this is my life now*.

Holly digs in her coat pocket and pulls out a crumpled tissue. "I miss the songs they might have sung but never had the chance to."

Some of my friends have already had kids, so I've been around a lot of emotional pregnant women, but Holly is an extreme case. "That must be awfully hard on you," I tell her, hoping nothing else I say sets her off.

"You must think I'm crazy," she says before blowing her nose.

"Not at all." *Totally.* "It *is* sad. I never thought about it before. Work that hard your whole life and just when you think your career is taking off ..."

Archie closes his eyes, because he clearly knows what's coming. Holly bursts into loud sobs. "I'm so disappointed for them. I'm disappointed for me, for everyone."

Oh, boy. Archie and I wait awkwardly for her to stop. Fifteen seconds in, her phone pings. After she looks at it, she transforms immediately. "That's Toni, wondering where her bagel is. Mmm, bagels. Now that I think about it, I'm starving."

"Toni asked you to pick up bagels for her?" I ask, confused. I've never had a boss I'd ask to do something like that.

Archie nods. "She's Holly's best friend."

"Yup, the best ever," she says. "Toni is why Archie and I are together."

"Well, indirectly," he clarifies. "I did all the heavy lifting."

She rolls her eyes at him.

"You two met through work?"

"We sure did," she says. "Archie hired me to do his Christmas shopping for him and the rest, as they say, is history."

"So you don't have a policy about employees dating each other?"

He shakes his head. "Not at all. It's not like we have that many employees, but if they want to date, it wouldn't bother me as long as it doesn't interfere with the job."

"You met her this morning, didn't you?" Her eyes brighten.

I nod.

"Interesting." Her eyes twinkle in what I can only guess is a matchmaker kind of excitement. Far be it from me to mention that her assistant/best friend shot me down. I'm totally on board if Holly wants to get involved in getting Toni and me together.

She abruptly turns to her husband. "I really am starving."

"That's my cue," he tells me. "We'd better go."

They seem so happy. "I have about an hour before I have to be elsewhere, so I'll stick around and take some measurements—see what we've got for usable materials. Then, if you don't mind, I'd like to take the drawings over to a designer I work with occasionally. I'm sure she'll come up with something special for the project."

"That sounds perfect." Archie reaches out to shake my hand. "Welcome aboard, Cooper. We're lucky to have you."

"Thanks. I'm excited about what we're doing here. It feels a lot more important than my last few jobs, building beach houses for the ultra-rich."

After saying our goodbyes, I'm alone in the quiet warehouse. My thoughts immediately turn back to Toni. It seems a certain beautiful assistant was lying to me earlier.

While that's a bit of an ego hit, I can't help but think there's more going on here. No woman has ever stared at me like Toni did and not been in the market for something more.

Chapter 5

Toni

Archie arrives at eleven o'clock without Holly *and* without my bagel. "Is Sumner here?"

"He's been waiting about twenty minutes. I set him up in the conference room, and he seems to have occupied himself with calls." I pause. "Did Holly get sick again?"

Closing his eyes for a second, he says, "Right into the bagel bag."

"Is she okay?"

He hangs his coat up on our makeshift coat rack—three railroad stakes hammered into the wall. "I took her home to rest. According to her recent schedule, she'll sleep for two hours, then get up and eat enough for a family of five before falling asleep again."

"Growing people is hard work."

"Don't get me wrong. I'm not complaining. I know full-well that if pregnancy were left to men, humanity would be on the verge of extinction."

"You've got that right." I smile. "I feel like I should apologize again for trying to keep you and Holly apart. You really are perfect for each other."

He riffles through the stack of mail on my desk. "No apology necessary. I was a much different person before Holly came into my life. All you were doing was protecting your friend."

"You *were* kind of douchey."

He glances at me in surprise. "I prefer to frame it as being a hard-nosed businessman with no time for a personal life."

"That's what I said. Douchey."

"It's a good thing I like you so much."

"Do you mind if I run out for a bit? I need to change and get something to eat."

"I have a job for you that will help me and feed you at the same time," he says and pulls out his wallet. "Holly can't seem to get enough Italian food these days. Why don't you stop by Ferrantelli's and pick up a bunch of stuff? Take it back to my house, and you and my wife can feast together."

"Yum!" I'm on my feet and grabbing my winter coat with lightning speed. "Do you want me to get you anything?" I ask as I snatch the cash from his hand.

"I would love their lasagna and two cannoli, but you're going to have to hide the latter from Holly. She'll eat them if she knows they're there."

"Poor Archie." I pat him on the arm. "I'll use my key and put your food in the garage refrigerator. Holly will never know."

"Thank you. It's not like I begrudge my beautiful wife anything, but a man has to keep his strength up." He moves his eyebrows up and down like Groucho Marx.

"What time does the bus drop Faith off? I can meet her and let Holly sleep."

"They drop her off in front of the house at four, but Mrs. Firestone usually gets her. Just go, eat, and relax. You deserve it."

"You know, you're nothing like the slightly cruel boss you used to be."

"Cruel? As if. Get going before I change my mind," Archie says with a smile.

I hustle out onto the street, pull out my phone, and call Ferrantelli's, a number I happen to have on speed dial. I order enough food for ten people before catching a cab to Forest Hills.

When I get out at my first stop, I am catcalled by a couple of guys working on the road. "Hey, sweetheart, you lookin' for a date?" one of them yells.

"Depends," I call back. "Are you looking for a black eye?" You don't grow up in New York without learning how to give as good as you get.

The other guy waggles his hips like he's doing a bad Elvis impersonation. "I'm game if you like it a little rough."

He's cute enough, and once upon a time I might have flirted back or maybe even taken him up on his offer to go out, but no more. "Honey, I like it so rough, you'd wind up in the hospital." Then I enter the restaurant, leaving them both in my dust.

After collecting several bags of insanely delicious-smelling food, I get back in the cab to go to Holly's house. She and Faith used to live in a tiny one-bedroom apartment down the street from me, and now they live in a gorgeous mansion Archie bought for her as a wedding gift. I mean that literally. He put the property in her name and handed her the deed.

After the cabbie pulls up at my destination on Herrick Avenue, I give the cabbie a twenty and stroll up the path to the three-story brick home. Mrs. Firestone, Holly's old neighbor and surrogate grandmother to Faith, has rooms on the third floor. As her hearing isn't what it once was, I pull out my key and let myself in. Then I take Archie's food out to the garage.

Back in the kitchen, I text Holly.

Me: I'm downstairs with Italian food if you're awake.

Holly: Did you bring eggplant parmesan?

Me: Yup, and I have a double order of cheesy garlic bread.

Holly: How about calamari?

Me: You know it.

Holly: Ravioli?

Me: Do you want me to bring everything upstairs?

Holly: Please and thank you. You're the best!

I fetch cloth napkins and silverware before running upstairs to her bedroom. Holly is lying under a white duvet, looking like she has the energy of a cooked noodle.

"You brought me food, and after I threw up all over your bagel." She sits up and fluffs a pile of pillows behind her.

"What are best friends for?" I unload the bags on a side table.

She pats the bed next to her. "Crawl in. We can watch a movie while we eat."

"Can I borrow some sweats?" I ask and kick off my shoes. "I got nailed by a garbage truck this morning and had to change. These jeans are so tight, I'm pretty sure I've done some damage to my lady business by wearing them all morning."

She laughs. "You know where the closet is. Take whatever you want." She sighs. "I'm going to have to buy maternity clothes soon. Everything I own is getting snug."

I walk into her closet. "Let's go shopping when you're feeling better. We can take Faith and make a day of it."

"If I can stay awake long enough. All I want to do is eat and sleep."

"Don't forget about watching movies." I return with a soft pink sweatsuit and change into it. "What do you want to watch today?"

"*Baby Boom* with Diane Keaton or *Three Men and a Baby*."

"So, old-school films with babies?"

"I can't get enough of old things lately. Last week I binged every single episode of *Boy Meets World*, then I watched every Doris Day and Rock Hudson film ever made."

"You need to keep a pregnancy journal so Joy can find out what a weirdo you were while you were making her," I joke. "Dear Diary, today I barfed on Toni's bagel—"

Holly throws her napkin at me as I climb into bed next to her. We watch both movies and eat enough Italian to keep me full for a week.

When Faith comes home from school, she crawls between us and digs into the spaghetti I brought for her. With her mouth full, she says, "Kindergarten is a lot of work."

"How so?" I ask. "I thought it would be a breeze for a brain like you."

"The schoolwork is easy. The hard part is having two different boys who keep trying to talk to me. One of them is telling people he's my boyfriend and the other one says he wants to marry me."

"Poor you," I tease. "I can't get one decent guy to ask me out, and you already have two."

Faith giggles. "I bet boys are just afraid of you because you're so beautiful."

"On that topic," Holly interjects, "what did you think of Sumner?"

"He definitely has potential."

"Who's Sumner?" Faith asks, wrinkling her nose, "and why in the world did his parents name him that?"

"He's a new guy at work," I say. "I think his name is a family name."

Holly leans closer and gives me a meaningful look. "And what did you think of Cooper?" She says this like she's asking about a particularly decadent dessert—one covered in hot fudge and cherries.

I scoff loudly. "He's the kind of trouble I don't need."

"Why not?" Faith asks. "Does he eat his boogers or something?"

"Ew, no. I'm hoping neither of your admirers eats his boogers."

She shrugs. "If they do, I haven't seen it. Why don't you like this Cooper guy?"

I don't know exactly how to answer this question so it's appropriate for kindergarten ears. "I don't like the way he dresses." Yet I do, I *really* do.

"That's mean, Aunt Toni. Mom is always saying you shouldn't judge a book by its cover." Faith has recently started calling Holly and Archie Mom and Dad. It's just about the sweetest thing ever.

"You're right. I shouldn't judge Cooper by how he dresses. It's not just that though. I don't like his attitude either."

Faith scrambles out of bed. "Well, they say attitude is everything."

"Is that so, little miss?" I chuckle at her ability to speak in platitudes.

"Yup."

"And what do you say?"

"I say don't go out with him if eats his boogers." She exits the bedroom.

Holly waits until she's gone. "Did you find out if Sumner is single?"

"Yes." My face heats with embarrassment. "Unfortunately, my attempt at getting his backstory was a bit clumsy. I'm pretty sure he suspects I have designs on him."

"Do you?" she asks, looking impressed by what a fast worker I am.

"I could. He checks a lot of boxes: good-looking, responsible, gainfully employed."

"I'm not hearing anything about physical attraction."

"I wouldn't say there's no spark … Just not enough to light the building on fire. But every time I'm wildly attracted to someone, I let the physical stuff rule the relationship, and every single time, I get hurt."

She nods, but I can see she's skeptical. "You may have a point. But come on … Cooper? He could have gotten Mother Teresa's motor running."

I shake my head and laugh. "He's the last man on earth I should be dating."

"I don't know about that," she says with a shrug. "He's a successful businessman—like really successful. None of the other men you've dated owned their own business. They all worked for someone else. *When* they worked, that is."

"I don't care whether or not he owns his own business. I care about him being an upstanding citizen. I'm looking for someone who will be a great husband and dad."

"And you don't think that could be Cooper?" She sounds shocked.

"He is *way too* cocky, whereas Sumner seems nice. I mean, he's got to be a pretty special guy who wants to spend his life fundraising for charities, am I right?"

"That's a good point."

"Damn straight it is. Plus, Sumner's classically handsome. I was thinking maybe I could take things slow for once and see if I have better luck. Like maybe we could text each other for a while, then progress to phone calls, then in-person dating."

"Taking it slow is always a good plan."

The bedroom door opens. Archie walks in, and Holly and I offer him quick waves and continue our girl talk.

"He was really sweet at the office," I tell her. "So who knows? Maybe it'll turn into something."

"What'll turn into something?" he asks before giving Holly a kiss on her forehead.

She smiles. "Toni's thinking about dipping her toe in the dating pool again."

"Good for you." He picks through the remnants of our Italian feast, chooses a piece of garlic bread, and takes a bite. "Based on what you were saying, I know exactly who we're talking about."

I nod. "Do you think it's a bad idea on account of us working together?"

"I could hardly frown on that, considering how I met Holly. Besides, it's not like you'll be working closely together or anything. If it doesn't work out, you won't have to see each other much."

I'm grateful to have such an understanding boss. "I don't suppose you could get me his phone number …?"

"I don't see why not." He pulls out his phone and sends me a text. "I think you guys would make a great couple."

"It's nice to have your support." I roll out of bed. "I'd better get home. I have to stop for groceries. I'm out of coffee."

"Why don't you just stay here?" Holly asks. "God knows we have enough bedrooms, and you can wear anything you want of mine tomorrow."

A sleepover sounds much nicer than going home to my empty apartment to listen to Jason and Jolessa fight. "I would love that. Thanks."

"What you'd love is to take a two-hour bath in the jacuzzi tub in the guest room bathroom."

"Yes. Yes, I would." I return to her closet for jammies and clothes for work tomorrow.

After my bath I'm going to text Sumner and get this show on the road. I don't want to set my hopes too high, but I have a feeling he and I are going to get along well.

Chapter 6

Cooper

I'm watching the Rangers play the Kings while going over the site updates Yuma sent me at the end of the day. Two projects are wrapping up soon, which means dozens of guys on each job site are completing the detail work. It's the most hectic part of any build, but it's also the most exciting. If all goes well, the timing should allow for all three of my crews to be onsite and working on Bedford Falls by the end of the month.

One of our projects is conveniently located down the road. It's a massive eight-bedroom, twelve-bath Georgian mansion in Forest Hills. It's been under construction for nearly two years, because the homeowner, George McMillian, changes his mind about every single detail at least four times before settling on anything. It will be a huge relief when it's over, and I never have to answer another email with the subject line of URGENT ISSUE REGARDING MY FOREVER HOME.

The game announcer's voice grows louder, and I look up in time to see Reaves on a breakaway. He lets a quick one-timer go and ties the game. I release a sharp victory cry before picking up my phone to text Mason, one of my foremen (and a fellow Rangers' fan) about the goal, but I'm distracted by an incoming text from a number I don't recognize.

> 917-555-5225: Hi, it's Toni from the Faith Foundation. I hope you don't mind me texting you. We didn't really have a chance to talk when you were in the office today, and I wanted to remedy that.

Huh, so I was right. She *does* like me. I smile and mute the hockey game. After adding her as a contact, I write back.

> Me: Hey Toni, how did the rest of your day go?

> Toni: It was great, thanks. How about yours?

> Me: Good. I'm excited about the project, so I've spent the evening working on some plans (while watching the Rangers game).

> Toni: I didn't figure you for a hockey fan.

> Me: No? What did you think I'd like?

> Toni: Opera maybe … or antiquing. Oh! I bet you're a museum sponsor.

Ha! She's hilarious.

Me: Do I give off a highbrow vibe?

Toni: Definitely. I'm right, aren't I?

Me: Let's just say I spent my fair share of time in museums when I was a kid. The opera was a one and done thing though. My parents gave up after their first attempt at getting me to become a fan.

Toni: Why do I feel like there's a juicy story here?

Me: Because you're perceptive? I was eight. We were halfway through La Bohème when I told my folks I had to go to the little boys' room. Instead, I left the MET. I found a homeless guy playing his guitar for money and hung out with him for a while.

Toni: At night??

Me: I never said it was the brightest idea. I got lost going back. Luckily, a nice lady figured out I needed help. She walked me all the way back to the opera house, only to find herself being approached by the police. They had a lot of questions about why I was with her. My parents panicked when they couldn't find me, and the show was forced to end midway so the police and staff could comb the building for me.

Toni: That's crazy.

Me: It left an impression, that's for sure.

Toni: I imagine so.

I catch my reflection in the phone screen and realize I'm smiling. Like, a real smile.

Me: I'm glad you texted me.

Toni: Me too.

Me: I knew you were into me. I could tell by the way your eyes were roaming.

Toni: My eyes did no such thing.

Me: Oh, they roamed all right.

Toni: I have no idea what you're talking about. I'm nothing, if not professional.

Me: Speaking of which, I'm surprised you texted me. I thought workplace relationships were usually verboten.

Toni: Not verboten, just not a good idea. For that reason, I suggest we keep whatever happens between us separate from work. Like at the office, we act like we've never spoken outside the office.

Me: Um, okay.

Toni: Also, you should know I want to take this turtle-slow. I've dated my share of not-so-nice guys, and I tend to jump into things too quickly. My New Year's resolution is to learn from past dating mistakes.

Me: Sounds like you've kissed a few frogs.

Toni: You could say frogs have been my type. Which is one of the reasons I wanted to get to know you. You don't seem anything like the kind of guy I normally date.

Me: How so?

Toni: For starters you're employed. And you were interested in working with the charity, so it must mean you have a big heart.

Me: I've been very lucky in my life, and I like to give back.
Toni: See? That right there shows me you're different than my usual pick.

Me: With me, what you see is what you get. If you liked what you saw this morning, maybe we should have dinner this weekend. Just dinner, nothing else.

Toni: …

Toni: …

My heart beats a little faster while I wait for her answer, and it makes me realize how attracted I am to her. Even texting with her is the most fun thing I've done in months. I find myself wincing at the thought of her saying no.

Toni: Can we make it a few weeks from now? When I said I wanted to take things slow, I meant very slowly.

Crap. It's not a no, but it's not exactly a yes either.

Me: Sure. We can definitely take things slow. I'm busy wrapping up two big projects, so this works for me.

Toni: Good, because that's what I need this time around. In fact, let's stick to texting until our first official date.

Me: Okay, deal. Just texting for the next few weeks, then I take you out for a Valentine's Day dinner so great, it'll ruin you for every dinner after that.

Toni: That sounds wonderful. But just because we're getting to know each other via text doesn't mean you jump to fifth date privileges when we do go out.

Me: I was about to tell you the same thing, young lady. Keep your hands off the merch unless you're planning to buy it.

Toni: Bahaha! You're funny.

Me: I'm serious. If you like it, then you better put a ring on it.

Toni: …

I hope she knows I'm kidding. I'm trying to think of a witty way to let her know I'm not serious when she sends another text.

Toni: Okay, Beyoncé. I better let you get back to your game/work. I need to be up early.

Me: Good night, Toni. Sleep well.

Toni: You too.

Me: Wait. If I'm Beyoncé in this scenario, does that make you Jay-Z?

Toni: It might.

Me: Hmm … I'm not so sure about this arrangement. I don't think I'd look as good as you in a skin-tight leotard, but we can sort out the details later.

Chapter 7

Toni

A feeling of pure contentment washes over me as I clutch my phone to my chest. Sumner is funny, and he's not afraid to let me know he's interested in me. I'm tempted to go back to Holly's room and tell her the exciting news—that he most definitely has potential. But I don't do it, because I don't want to jinx anything. This time around I'm playing things cool. That means no daydreaming when I should be working, and no obsessive girl talk about him.

I'm about to crawl into bed when there's a knock on my door. Faith's elfin face peeks in.

"I thought you went to sleep ages ago."

She pushes the door open and shuffles in, looking like a mussed-up angel in her long white nightgown. She's dragging Mr. Buns, her stuffed bunny, in one hand. Climbing into my bed, she announces, "I woke up to go potty and figured you might be uncomfortable sleeping away from home. I thought I'd keep you company."

This is the line she uses every time I stay over. Like I always do, I tell her, "You are so thoughtful. I don't suppose I could persuade you to spend the night with me."

Her eyes brighten, and she slides under the covers. "I'd be happy to. Mom says a good hostess always makes sure her guests are comfortable." Faith yawns loudly. "Speaking of comfortable, I know how much you love making pancakes, so if you want to make them in the morning, I won't mind eating them."

She's asleep before I can reply.

I fondly remember how amazing sleep was when I was a kid and wonder when that started to change. During high school, my anxieties worked themselves out at night, manifesting as the most horrific nightmares. If I wasn't showing up to class naked or taking a test in a foreign language, I was asking out the captain of the football team while sporting a giant zit on the tip my nose. After high school, life got more complicated and so did my ability to get a peaceful eight hours of sleep.

I figure eighth grade was probably my last sound year of rest.

Crawling into bed next to Faith, I close my eyes and tell myself to dream about Sumner. But as hard as I try to push my thoughts in his direction, another face pops into my brain. Cooper Flint's.

He's wearing his tight band T-shirt and form-fitting jeans, and he's standing barefoot at the stove flipping pancakes. Turning to me with a lazy grin, he says, "Hey, babe, I thought you could use some breakfast to recoup your strength."

Then he pulls me into his arms and kisses me with the intensity one might use on a CPR doll they're trying to resuscitate. The contact is hot and heavy, and I wrap my legs around his waist while he carries me back to my bedroom.

He throws me on the bed and is about to join me when the fire alarm starts to ring. "Whoops, I forgot to turn the burner off on the stove." He winks and blows a kiss before saying, "I'll be right back."

Even in my sleep I know this is wrong, and I should make him leave my apartment, but I decide to allow this one fantasy before shutting the door on Cooper for good. Only a few seconds pass before I hear footsteps in the hall. I will my sweatpants and T-shirt to turn into a sexy negligee, the way you can only do in dreams.

Closing my eyes, I lie in heated anticipation for what comes next. The mattress depresses next to me, and I hear, "Did the queen get back to us yet about the tea party?"

What the … My eyes pop open. Sumner has joined me. He's wearing jodhpurs with a pink sweater tied over his shoulders, and he's eating a toaster strudel. He looks like a spoof cover of a bodice-ripping romance novel.

"What are you doing here?" I ask, disappointed.

"What do you mean? I live here. Did you forget we were married?"

OMG. "Um, of course not, but I am a little confused about when that happened."

"Right after we knitted baseball uniforms for the Mets. Don't you remember? You were playing first base, and your uniform tore. I ordered you a nice Irish knit replacement, and it was such a hit the whole team wanted them. Then we said our vows in the dugout." He leans over and kisses me.

This is seriously the worst dream ever. I try to morph Sumner back into Cooper, but it doesn't work. I successfully turn him into a frog, a koala bear, and a tree sloth, but I can't get Cooper back.

I finally get out of bed to splash cold water on my face. It takes me ages to fall asleep again, and just as I'm sinking into oblivion, my alarm rings.

Faith rolls over and opens her eyes, "What time is it?"

"Six. I think you can sleep for a while yet, can't you?"

She yawns. "I get up at six thirty." She goes back to sleep.

I reset the alarm for her and slip into a robe. Tying the sash around my waist, I head down to the kitchen. Mrs. Firestone is sitting at the table, drinking a cup of coffee.

"Toni, hello!" she says enthusiastically.

"Hey, Mrs. F, you're up early."

"That's the life of old people. Once you hit seventy, it's all about the early bird specials and going to bed by eight." She laughs. "I'm not complaining though. It's good to still be alive."

"I thought I'd make pancakes. Do you want some?"

"Oh, no. I ate at four thirty. I'm good until lunchtime." *Which is when, nine thirty?* She drains her cup and stands. "I'm going to get a jump on the laundry while I wait for Faith to come down."

After she's gone, I look around the kitchen and once again marvel at the change in Holly's circumstances. A six-burner Wolf range and a subzero refrigerator are things she never knew existed before she met Archie.

After turning on the griddle, I pull out a mixing bowl and measure the ingredients for my mom's pancake recipe. I'm pouring the first portion of batter onto the sizzling griddle when I hear a knock on the back door. Who in the world comes over at 6:15 in the morning?

I cross to the door and pull the curtain back. *What is Cooper Flint doing here?* He's looking manly, that's what. After dropping the curtain, I hurriedly run my fingers through my hair and unlatch the lock. A blast of cold air shocks my system when I open it. "Hello. It isn't even six thirty."

He's holding the tube of blueprints I gave him yesterday. "I know. I'm actually pretty good at telling time. Just one of my many skills."

There's that grin again. *Look away!* Unable to come up with a witty retort at this hour, I go with a slow, "Ha ha."

"How did you sleep?"

Is he flirting with me? I avoid looking at him. My cheeks burn at the part he played in my dream. "I slept just fine. What are you doing here?"

"I could ask you the same thing." He steps past me into the kitchen.

Closing the door behind him, I remind myself this man is not for me. "I stay over sometimes." I hurry past him to check on the pancakes. "Holly is my best friend."

"You and Holly have sleepovers?" he asks with a crooked grin.

"Well, not with pillow fights or anything." I suddenly feel silly about sleeping over at my married friend's house.

"I'm jealous. I never have sleepovers with my friends." He glances at the griddle. "And you make pancakes?"

Oh, I'm sure he has a whole lot of sleepovers. *Stop it, Toni!*

I pick up the spatula and flip the first pancake, glad when it lands exactly where I want it to. I'm not sure why it matters if he's impressed with my cooking skills, but somehow it does. "I'm quite accomplished in the kitchen," I brag.

"That kind of makes me want to invite you for a sleepover." He rubs his beard, staring at the pancakes.

My knees suddenly wobble. "It seems someone has forgotten that we work together." I punctuate that with a double eyebrow raise to make my point.

"But we're not at work."

I level him with a glare that causes him to raise his hands in surrender. "Right. Totally forgot. We're just two people who happen to work together."

"Exactly."

"Archie told me his nanny would be up, and I could drop these off anytime." He's suddenly dangerously close to me—I can feel the heat from his breath. This is *no bueno*, considering last night's unfinished fantasy.

When I don't respond, he croons, "You look very pretty in the morning."

Oh. Dear. God. This *is* like my dream, only better because it's real. No, it's worse because it should *not* be happening. "Thanks." I push past him to get some personal space back. "I'd offer you a cup of coffee, but I'm sure you have to go."

He sits at the kitchen table. "I'd love a cup of coffee."

Gah! I'd normally tell him to get it himself, but that would mean him getting up and infringing on my sense of calm. You know, the sense of calm I don't have. "How would you like it?"

"I take my coffee like my women—"

"Let me guess, bitter?" My hands are on my hips, like he's a naughty boy, and I'm his teacher about to send him to the principal's office. "Oh, wait, bitter is probably how you leave them, not how you find them."

"Ouch. You've got an edge this time of the day." He drops a faux-hurt look, then grins. "I like my coffee sweet, with three sugars and a big splash of milk." He winks, which makes my head spin.

I lean against the counter for balance, and, you know, to keep from throwing myself into his arms. "That's kind of girly," I mutter.

He laughs. "There's nothing girly about a man who likes sugar in his coffee. How do you take yours?"

"With caution." I'm not talking about coffee, I'm talking about him. I pull a thermos out of the cabinet, fill it, and hand it to him. "You can take that with you."

"Are you kicking me out?"

"I'm sure you have places to be. It's not like the home-less village is finished yet."

"Toni …" His voice pours over me like warm maple syrup, enticing and sweet.

I don't let him finish though. "If you're not going to leave, I'd better go put my clothes on." I practically run out of the kitchen, saying over my shoulder, "Keep an eye on the flapjacks for me."

I hear a deep rumble of laughter, and it's all I can do not to crumple to the floor in a heap.

Chapter 8

Cooper

I cook pancakes while I wait for Toni to return. She's either not a morning person, or between late last night and this morning, she decided she doesn't like me after all. She wants to keep things on the down low around the office, but is it necessary to pretend we aren't interested in each other when there's no one else in the room?

After waiting for a full ten minutes, I start to feel silly. What am I doing making pancakes at my new client's house at this hour, and where is she? I'm checking the latest batch when I'm startled by a child's voice.

"Did my mom and dad hire a chef?"

A little girl with soft-looking brown hair is gazing at me curiously. "My name is Cooper. I work with your parents. You must be Faith."

"Yup." Eying me up and down, she decides, "You don't look like a chef."

"That's because I'm a contractor. I'm building the homeless community your parents are creating."

"It's a worthwhile project," she says, sounding exactly like Archie.

I chuckle. "I think so, too. Hey, you don't know where Toni is, do you? She asked me to watch the pancakes for her, but she's been gone a while."

"She's trying to decide if her outfit is too boring."

There is nothing boring about Toni. She's as far from boring as you can get. "Is it?"

"It's a total snore," she tells me distractedly while looking over the stack of completed hotcakes. "It looks like you don't know how to make bunny cakes, huh?"

"Bunnies might be beyond my scope of expertise. I could give Mickey Mouse pancakes a try."

"Mouse pancakes … hmm." She drums her fingers on her chin. "You know what? Give them a whirl." She climbs on a stool to watch.

I carefully pour three circles of batter so they're just touching. "What grade are you in?"

"Kindergarten."

"It's been a while since I was that young, but as I recall, it was pretty fun." The truth is I hated school right from the start. "Have you learned all your letters yet?"

"In which alphabet?"

"Um, the English one?"

"Mom taught me those when I was two." She peers at the pancakes.

"Two? Wow. I don't think I could even string a sentence together at that age."

"Don't beat yourself up over it. Everybody learns at their own pace. I'm sure you're good at the alphabet by now."

Biting my lip to keep from laughing, I nod. "I … yeah

… I know all my letters. In order, too." I bow at the waist to highlight my achievement.

She glances at the griddle, then picks up the spatula. "When the pancakes have a lot of bubbles in them, it's time to flip. They don't need to cook as long on the second side because they're almost done by then."

"You're a pro. Tell me about your Aunt Toni."

Grinning mischievously, she says, "Why? Do you like her? Do you want to swipe right for her?"

I really burst out laughing. "How do you know about swiping?"

"I'm six. I'm not stupid. Aunt Toni's aunt signed her up for Splinter without telling her."

Splinter? "Do you mean Tinder?"

Before she can answer, Toni reappears with her hair pulled back in the tightest bun I've ever seen. She's wearing a pair of black dress pants and a bulky turtleneck sweater. On anyone else, I wouldn't look twice, but on her … Damn, she looks hot.

"Sorry. That took me longer than I thought it would."

"No problem." Faith lifts her pancake off the griddle and puts it on the serving platter. "I was just getting to know Faith."

She grins back and forth between us. "Cooper was asking about you. And I'm not sure, because I just met him, but I totally think he'd swipe right if he saw your picture on Tinder." She winks at me conspiratorially.

I flush and open my mouth to say something, but since I have no way of forming an intelligent thought, I close it again.

Toni seems determined not to engage in this particular conversation. She hurries over to the fridge. "Maple or blueberry syrup this morning?"

"I'm swiping right on the blueberry syrup," Faith says.

I drink from the thermos and watch Toni dig around for it. Once she's got it, she sets her shoulders back and closes the fridge door. After opening the small jug, she pours a generous amount on top of Faith's pancakes, then she sets it down in front of her. "There you go, little miss. Bon appetite."

Faith looks at me. "Will you cut them for me? I'd ask Auntie Toni, but she knows my parents want me to learn how to do it myself."

I give Toni a surprised look, which she returns with an *I know, right?* face before getting a fork and knife out of the drawer. She quickly cuts Faith's breakfast up for her. "But if anyone asks, this never happened."

"Deal." Faith picks up the fork and stabs a piece. She pops it in her mouth, then chews with her eyes closed. "Mmm, mmm, mmm."

"Faith"—I smirk at Toni—"do you think Toni would swipe right if she saw my picture?"

Faith nods authoritatively. "Oh yeah, you're what she and my mom would call a hottie."

Toni's face turns bright red. "Cooper," she says, glancing at her wrist where a watch would be if she was wearing one. "You must need to be somewhere else by now."

"Is that what your arm told you?"

"Surely you must have a lot to do today, being that you got such an early start," she answers urgently.

I turn to Faith. "It kind of sounds like she wants me to leave, doesn't it?"

"It does," this adorably precocious child says. "But don't take it personally. Aunt Toni can be a real ballbuster."

Toni sputters, then her mouth drops open. "Faith, where did you learn to say something like that?"

"Grandma Firestone said it about you the other night."

"Sometimes the words your grandma says aren't exactly things you should repeat."

"Is this like the sweet buns thing?"

"Exactly."

I want to ask about that but resist. Barely.

I watch their back and forth, riveted by the lovely and feisty Toni and this hilarious child. Part of me wants to pull up a chair and spend the entire day talking to them. Then I remember how busy my schedule is. I take a last swig of coffee before putting the thermos in the sink. "As much as I'd love to stay and eat some of those pancakes Faith and I made, I should probably run."

Toni gives me a strange smile, and I can't tell if she's relieved or disappointed.

"See you around the office," I tell her with a tip of my head. Turning to Faith, I add, "It was wonderful meeting you. I hope you have a terrific day."

"Thanks," she says, suddenly sounding sad. "I probably won't though because my best friend Meghan's away in Fiji for another week, so it's a little lonely at school."

"That's too bad," I tell her, meaning it. "I know how important best friends are."

Shrugging, she says, "It's fine, I guess. It gives Justin P. a chance to hang out with me."

I successfully stifle my laughter. "I wish every child was exactly like you."

"Tell me about it," Faith says, waving off my compliment. "Most kids are total train wrecks."

"Faith, Toni," I say, gazing at Toni longer than I should. "See you soon."

"I hope so," Faith says. "We'll get to the bottom of this swiping business if it's the last thing we do."

"There will be no swiping," Toni says, sounding ultra-stern. Then she says, "Goodbye, Cooper."

I grin all the way to my truck as I plan what I'm going to say to Toni when we text tonight. I just met her, but there's something about her. Whatever this feeling is, it's addictive. Like after the high of initial contact is over, I need another hit.

Chapter 9

Toni

By the time Holly and Archie come down for breakfast, my foot is tapping so fast you'd think I was sending Morse code messages to the inner earth. I'm also on my third cup of coffee.

"You're ready to go early," Holly says. She's still in her nightgown.

"Your contractor brought over your blueprints at the butt crack of dawn," I grumble.

"Cooper's been here already?" Archie asks, pouring himself a cup of coffee. "Why didn't you invite him to stay for breakfast?"

"Because I'm not his mother. He can get his own breakfast."

Archie looks at me with his eyebrows knitted together in confusion. "Okaaayyy." He turns to Holly and changes the subject. "Are you up to coming into the office with us this morning?"

"You know I am. We've got that meeting with Sumner first thing, then Anthony is stopping by to look over our designs."

Anthony—who used to go by Tony until he started working with us (a Tony and a Toni in such a small office can be really confusing)—used to be homeless. Faith and Holly met him last year and got to know him a little. When Archie started the Faith Foundation, he and Holly searched for him and offered him a consulting job.

"I'm so glad you were able to track him down. He's an invaluable resource for us," Archie says. "He's already managed to bring in thirty highly eligible applicants for housing. He assures me he'll probably have another thirty by the time we're ready to break ground."

"How in the world will we ever narrow the list down to just forty? My heart hurts at the thought of turning people away," Holly says.

"I've been talking to the churches in the area," I interject. "I already have two with big enough assembly halls that they're willing to house our overflow. But only at night and when they aren't using the space for church business."

"That's something at least," Holly says. "But they might be there a year before we can get the next housing development up."

"Yeah, but we've already vetted them as being a worthwhile risk. St. Emilion's said they would start a program to teach useful skills, like janitorial work, groundskeeping, and kitchen skills. Some of them might be able to get jobs and their own accommodations before Bedford Falls is complete."

"Speaking of which," Archie says, "I'd love to take you over to the warehouse soon so you can lay eyes on the location for yourself."

"That would be great." I sound less than enthusiastic,

but only because I don't want to run into Cooper again. The man is seriously challenging my vow to change the type of guy I'm interested in.

Holly suddenly stands up, and with no warning whatsoever, throws up on the kitchen floor. I'm super glad I've already eaten.

Archie runs to her side. "That's it, you're going back to bed."

"But I feel so much better now," she insists.

"So you say. But every day you've thrown up has been a real trial. I'd feel better knowing you were resting." He starts to lead her out of the room.

I stare at the floor in disgust. While I love my best friend and would do anything for her, including giving her a kidney if she ever needed one, I am not great when it comes to anything resembling vomit.

Mrs. Firestone appears from the laundry room and clucks. "Oh dear, I'll get a mop."

I grab a roll of paper towels and then drop to the floor.

"No, no, no, no, no ..." Mrs. Firestone says as she comes back into the room. "You go on outside and get some fresh air."

"Are you sure?" I ask as actual bile creeps up my throat.

She shoos me with her hands. "Yes, go! I'm afraid there will be twice as much to clean up if you stay." She's not wrong.

Archie joins me outside ten minutes later. "Holly's already sleeping."

I climb into his Escalade. "I don't want to sound negative, but your wife does not make impending motherhood look glamorous."

"Whatever you do, don't tell her that, or she might start crying and never stop." He pulls out of the driveway.

"You may be married to her, but she's been my bestie since we were kids. Trust me when I tell you I know better than to share anything but good things when she's in the state she's in."

"Too bad you ladies aren't having kids at the same time, so they could grow up together."

I shoot him my nastiest *OMG, you didn't just say that* look, but I don't say anything.

Archie notices the cold shoulder I'm giving him because he mumbles, "I didn't mean that in a bad way."

"I can totally see how pointing out that I don't have a significant other isn't supposed to make me feel bad."

"I just meant that you and Holly would have a great time being moms together." He turns left at the next light.

"No offense, but it feels weird to be having this conversation with my boss."

"I like to think we've become more friends than employer/employee. I mean, you did sleep over at my house last night …"

"Fair point, but if you keep reminding me of my single status, we're not going to be friends for long."

"Duly noted." Archie pulls up to the office building. "Tell you what, I promise not to discuss your dating life unless you bring it up first."

"Which will be never …"

"You're the one who asked me for a certain guy's phone number last night."

I unbuckle my seatbelt. "Now that I have it, we can stop talking about it."

"Uh-huh. I'll drop you at the curb, then park." He veers toward the front door before stopping. His cell phone rings. "You head up. This might take a few minutes."

As I jump out—this vehicle is pretty high off the

ground—I run into Sumner. "Hey, Sumner. How are you?"

He looks up and smiles. "Very well, thank you."

I smile slyly, thinking of our texting conversation last night. "Been to any operas lately?"

"Actually, yes. *Countess Maritza* is playing now. Emmerich Kálmán is such an underrated composer."

He's got to be joking. "That's the one with the lady who wears horns, right?"

"You're thinking of Wagner's *Brünnhilde*," he corrects me and opens the door to the building.

Walking through, I answer, "Actually, I was thinking about Elmer Fudd in those old Bugs Bunny cartoons." I smile at him in such a way as if to say *Aren't I a riot?*

He offers me a light laugh, amusement sparkling in his eyes as he pushes the elevator button. "I can't say I ever watched them. I was more of a *Thomas the Tank Engine* kind of kid."

"I watched a lot of Franklin," I tell him. "There's something about a family of turtles living in the woods that instills a sense of wonder, don't you think?"

"I couldn't agree more," he answers with a wide smile.

When we get to the third floor, I suggest, "How about if I make a fresh pot of coffee and bring you a cup?"

"Why don't I help you?"

Oh my, he really is a gentleman.

Archie, who apparently ran up the stairs instead of waiting for the elevator, blows through the fire door and announces, "I'd love a cup, too."

"Sure." I turn to Sumner. "Thanks for offering to help, but since the bossman has now arrived, I'll let you two get started."

Crossing to the kitchenette in the corner, I grind the Colombian Roast while I mentally replay my recent encounter with my potential future husband. I can picture him thirty years from now, with graying hair and that gorgeous smile still lighting up the room. When the coffee is done, I pour three cups and put them on a tray with sugar and a small pitcher of cream. Then I carry them to the conference room.

Archie and Sumner are already sitting at the table with their laptops open. "The key to arranging a great fundraiser is to have an event slightly out of the ordinary. Everyone has a Black and White ball or a musical event. You want to do something that will stand out," Sumner says.

"What do you have in mind?" Archie asks, opening a sugar packet for his coffee.

"I rented a yacht for the Saturday night before Valentine's Day. A load of guests have already been invited. I suggest we turn the evening into a Faith Foundation fundraiser."

"Wow," Archie says. "Are you sure? I don't want to infringe on your party or anything."

"Everyone's social calendars are booked up months in advance. If we're going to raise money for the build, we need something fast."

"That's really nice of you," Archie says. "Do we need some kind of theme to make it more interesting?"

"I already have one." I don't know why, but *Lord of the Flies* pops into my mind. I don't have a chance to say that because he adds, "Harry Potter cosplay."

What the what? "Harry Potter cosplay? That's pretty *unique*." Translation: weird.

"Perhaps, but let's face it. Almost everyone under fifty has read the series, and I'm guessing those who haven't have seen the movies. My invitations went out six weeks ago, so you can be sure the costumes will be stunning.

No one likes to dress up as much as a bunch of rich people."

"It sounds like fun," Archie says enthusiastically. "Who are you dressing as?"

"Lucius Malfoy," my intended replies.

I have no words. I leave the meeting so the men can finalize their plans. My first outing with Sumner is going to be a Harry Potter cosplay cruise with him dressed as the father of the sniveling Draco Malfoy, worst person in the entire Harry Potter Universe. There is no part of this scenario I saw coming.

I wonder if maybe our entire texting conversation was a figment of my imagination. I'm starting to question my sanity when my phone pings with an incoming message.

New Guy: I just wanted to say that seeing you first thing in the morning was the perfect start to my day.

Me: That's so sweet.

New Guy: You make a mean pot of coffee.

Me: Thanks. You look sharp today.

New Guy: You look lovely yourself. I want to pull the pins out of your bun and watch you shake your hair out. Do you think you might do that for me sometime?

Whoa, this guy runs hot when he gets going. There might just be some potential here after all.

Me: If you play your cards right …

The office phone rings, so I type fast.

Me: I've gotta go, but I'll text you later tonight, okay?

New Guy: I shall wait with bated breath.

I glance in the direction of the conference room as happiness spreads through me. This whole Harry Potter cosplay thing might be a funny story to tell our grandchildren someday.

Chapter 10

Cooper

I grin at my phone.

"Okay, that's it," Yuma says. "You have to tell me what's going on." She's standing at my office door with her arms crossed.

"What do you mean?"

"This," she says, waving her hands in my direction like she's casting a spell. "All this smiling to yourself. It's unnerving. Did you meet someone?"

"No," I tell her, not wanting to jinx it. "Just texting with a friend."

"A woman friend?"

"Is my mother paying you to spy on her behalf?"

"As if I would ever spy for your mother." Her look of disdain is comical. Yuma's not a big fan of my mom. Her opinion is based on dozens of awkward phone calls that usually involve Mom's display of parental disappointment.

As much as my assistant grumbles about me, she's fiercely loyal. "I want to know for my sake."

"Yuma, I had no idea you have feelings for me."

She rolls her eyes. "Dream on, buddy. You know that's not why I'm asking. I just want to know what to prepare for."

"How so?" I ask, thoroughly confused.

"Because if there's a possibility of romance in the air, I need to know about it so I can keep this business running smoothly while you're taking off early to go on dates."

"That has never happened. You're just being nosy."

She gives me a sheepish look. "Well, it could happen if this person you won't tell me about turns out to be 'the one.'"

"I promise you'll be the first to know if that turns out to be the case."

"Thank you." She pauses, waiting for me to spill the beans. When I don't, she sighs heavily. "So? Who is she? And please don't tell me she's someone you met through work."

"What difference does it make?"

"Darn, it *is* someone through work." She purses her lips. "That could get messy. You need to know right now that I am *not* fielding calls from her when it's over so you can ghost her. Also, I'm not going to help you get hold of her if she ghosts you."

"You know that *you* work for *me*, right? Besides, who says we'll even break up? She might be it for me." Before she can comment, I add, "But for now, everything is all very preliminary. It could turn out to be nothing other than some flirty texts. Now, is there anything else, or did you just come in to give me dating advice?"

"There is something else. Natalie said she can fit you in at the end of the day."

Natalie Palmer is an extremely talented designer I work with from time to time. She's usually booked solid, so when I asked Yuma to get in touch with her about the Bedford Falls project, I didn't have high hopes. "Already?"

"Her office, five o'clock," she says before going to her own desk.

She hesitates before sitting. "Unless you're too busy with your mystery woman to go—"

"Tell Natalie that five is fine." I turn my attention back to the spreadsheet I was updating.

"Cooper, great to see you." Natalie gets up from her desk to greet me. She's always well-put-together, and today she's in a high-waisted black pencil skirt with a white button-down top. Her four-inch heels make her almost as tall as I am.

Looking around her office, I'm once again reminded that Natalie's office is an ever-changing display of her skills. Last time I was here, it had a jungle feel, with hunter green walls and potted tropical plants everywhere. Today it's an ultra-modern all-white space with a single black chandelier hanging above her desk. She's big on focal points.

After exchanging a quick hug, she strides back to her chair, sits, and crosses her legs. Gesturing at the room, she says, "What do you think?"

"It's terrific, as usual."

"Be honest, you hate it. It's too stuffy and formal for you."

"I was a pretty big fan of your jungle office."

"Jungle office?" she asks and laughs. "You make it sound like a bedroom for a three-year-old."

"Sorry." I grimace. "What did you call it? Bohemian chic?"

"Close enough." Natalie's gaze grows a little too intense. "It makes sense that was your favorite. You hate being inside."

"That's the truth," I say and steer the conversation to the reason I'm here. "Speaking of being inside, have you had a chance to look at the first set of drawings for the Bedford Falls project?"

"I did, and I have some big questions, starting with how are you possibly going to make any money building houses for homeless people?"

She's most likely wondering how she's going to get paid. "The project is being funded by one of the Harringtons."

"*The* Harringtons? The family that owns half the eastern seaboard?"

"That's the one. Archie retired from the family business last year, and he and his wife Holly started a foundation. They decided to go all-in on creating small villages to help people get back on their feet."

"That you want to be a part of this is like single-woman catnip," Natalie says, giving me a flirtatious look. "I'm pretty sure I just dropped an egg."

My eyes widen as my brain scrambles for a witty reply. My first impulse is to feel flattered, which is swiftly followed by an image of Toni's face and a wallop of guilt (which is crazy, because all we've done is text).

"Relax," she says. "I'm not serious about the egg thing." Her expression says otherwise. "Now, what can I do to help?"

Grateful that she's changed the subject, I explain Holly and Archie's vision for the village. I show her photos of the warehouse and the yard, as well as the materials I want to salvage. She listens intently and takes notes. Everything seems normal, except I can't shake the feeling that I want to get out of here as quickly as possible.

After I finish filling her in on the details of the project, I lean back in my chair. "So? What do you think?"

Her eyes light up. "Honestly, Cooper, I'm inspired. I envision lots of materials donated or heavily discounted by my regular vendors—flooring, linens, textiles … Each house will have a unique feel. Everything coordinated, cozy, and calm. Totally inviting. A real home."

"So you're in?" I ask, even though part of me oddly hopes she'll say no.

"Definitely. My schedule is hectic right now, but I'm going to squeeze this in anyway. It's too wonderful a project to turn down."

"That's great." I stand and gather the plans off her desk. "Archie and Holly will be thrilled. You'll love them, by the way. Great people. Salt of the earth."

She stands and leans on her desk in such a way that I could look down her blouse—which I am not going to do. "I look forward to it," she purrs.

I force myself to look away. "Excellent. I'll let you get on with your evening. I didn't realize how late it was."

She glances at her watch. "I'll walk you out." She holds the door open for me. "You wouldn't want to grab a bite to eat, would you?"

We've eaten together before, but this doesn't feel like a business invitation. "As much as I'd love to, I have plans this evening, and I'm running late." Even though my only plan is to go home and text with the most confusing woman I've ever met, I don't mind if Natalie thinks there's something more going on.

Her face falls for a nanosecond, but she quickly recovers. "Maybe another time then."

"Sounds great." I suddenly wonder why I never asked her out. She's my typical type.

"I'll be in touch in the next few days with some drafts. I'd also love to visit the site before demo so I can see what kind of material we can upcycle."

"Great minds think alike," I say. "I already have my eyes on some bricks and wood."

"Why don't I stop by tomorrow sometime?"

"Sure. Yuma will be there if I'm not. Give her a list of things you want salvaged."

I hightail it out of there before she can nail me down on a time. I shouldn't be avoiding my designer, but I also don't want to flirt with her when my attention is focused on the highly disorienting Toni. Speak of the devil. Immediately after shutting the door to my truck, I get a ping, notifying me I have an incoming text.

Toni: Hey you, I thought you'd want to know, I just took my bun down and shook out my hair.

Me: Whoa! Are we at that stage of this texting relationship already? If so, what are you wearing?

Toni: Fleece pajama bottoms and an oversized sweatshirt with a picture of a unicorn on it. The caption reads, I wish I could be a unicorn, so I could stab people with my head.

Me: Interesting, if not a little scary.

Toni: I like to keep people on their toes. That's a good thing, right?

Me: Absolutely.

Toni: What are you up to?

Me: Just leaving a meeting. Can I text you when I get home?

Toni: I'll be here.

Chapter 11

Toni

I'm not sure how I did it, but I dropped my phone into a sink full of soapy water. I've washed dishes a million times, and I've never done that before. Crap, now I can't text with Sumner, and I have no way of letting him know. I suppose I could email Holly on my laptop and have her contact him, but I really want to keep this budding relationship private until I know there's something there.

I spend the whole night worried Sumner is going to be upset I'm not answering his messages. Trying to keep my mind off things, I take a bubble bath, then curl up on the couch for a *Ted Lasso* marathon. Instead of laughing the whole way through, like I normally do, I obsess over the fact that I can't even call 911 if there's an emergency.

This must be what it was like growing up in *Little House on the Prairie* times. *Those poor people.*

I finally crawl into bed an hour early, so I can stop by

the Verizon store as soon as they open and pick up a new phone.

I have the most sinfully delicious dreams, and once again Cooper is the star of the show. I don't want them to end, they're so good, but I finally force myself to fixate on something else. Turns out that's turnips. Don't ask.

My alarm rings for ages before I finally reach over and throw it across the room. Even though I didn't drink any alcohol last night, I feel hungover. After dragging myself out of bed, I literally jump when I pass the full-length mirror. The woman in the glass looks like she's been in a bar fight. And lost.

Grabbing my hairbrush, I try to get through the knots that have formed. Then I dab extra concealer under my eyes before starting a pot of coffee. I'll leave the cover-up there to soak in before blending it. Hopefully that will make me look less frightening.

After putting on one of those super Amish-looking dresses that are all the rage this year, my intercom buzzes, alerting me that someone is here. "Yes?" I ask cautiously. No one comes over this early.

"Toni, it's Archie. Where are you?"

"What do you mean? I'm obviously in my apartment." *Why is he here at this hour?*

"I texted that I'd pick you up this morning at eight to take you to the job site. I told you to meet me out front."

"I dropped my phone in the sink last night. I never got your text." Panic floods my nervous system, and I feel like I'm being simultaneously stung by a thousand bees. I *need* to get a phone today.

"Come on down."

"I'm not ready yet."

"Toni, we're going to a construction site. Come down, and I'll take you to get a new phone when we're finished."

"You're pretty bossy."

"Which is fine as I am your boss."

I don't bother responding to that bit of snipe. I grab my coat and purse before sliding into my winter boots, then pour another cup of coffee to take with me. Archie is beating his hands on the steering wheel, matching the rhythm of the music blasting out of the passenger door.

He turns down the radio and looks at me. "Wow, look at you."

"What's that supposed to mean?"

"Nothing. Just, you know, wow. You look different today."

"You're the one who stopped by my apartment without notice. What did you expect?"

He flips on his turn signal before pulling out into traffic. "I *did* give you notice. You just didn't get it. It wasn't a mean wow, just a wow, you look different kind of wow."

I decide to ignore him. It's not like Sumner is coming into the office today. I'm going to a building site. The only person there, that I once upon a time might have been trying to impress, would be Cooper. But since I'm not going down that road, I don't care what I look like.

When Archie pulls into the Bedford Fall site, I finally ask, "Where's Holly?"

"She's still feeling nauseated. I didn't want to risk her yacking in the car."

The thought alone is enough to turn my stomach.

Cooper must have seen us pull in, because he exits his trailer and heads in our direction. The expression on his face morphs from friendly to closed-off when he spots me. He immediately focuses his attention on Archie. "I'm glad you could stop by this early. It turns out this is the only time Natalie could make it today."

"No worries," my boss says. "I brought Toni along so she can stay in the loop."

Cooper doesn't even look at me. *Seriously, what's his problem?*

I follow behind them like a lost dog as they go into the old warehouse. The first person we see is a woman so tall and gorgeous, I'm pretty sure she's a runway model, or, you know, a movie star.

"Natalie," Cooper greets her. "This is Archie Harrington. He started the Faith Foundation and is the reason we're building this community."

Archie shakes her hand as she gushes, "Mr. Harrington, I know you by reputation, of course. It's an honor to be working with you."

"Thank you," Archie says and gestures at me. "This is my assistant, Toni."

Natalie gives me the briefest of glances before dismissing me entirely. She turns to Cooper. "I've only got an hour, so let's get this show on the road." She strides toward the far wall on shoes that look more like stilts than heels.

I love them, and the old me would have bought them in six colors if they were available.

"Coop said there will be forty homes. We should also add a centralized garden area. It'll look great in pictures for the press."

"Why do pictures in the press matter?" I ask.

She turns her intimidating self in my direction. I love her dress, too. It's form fitting and super sleek, while still maintaining a high level of sex appeal. "Because the press has the power to bring in additional funds from businesses that want to up their image by doing charitable work."

Well, duh. Of course that's why. I am so off my game this morning, I might as well be playing ping-pong while everyone else is at Wimbledon. "That's a good point," I say reluctantly.

She wraps a hand around Cooper's arm. "Coop and I have worked on lots of projects together so I'm confident we'll knock this one out of the ballpark for you," she tells Archie.

Archie, bless his heart, seems to be cognizant of the fact that Natalie is treating me like a pariah, because he pulls me closer. "Toni has been with me for six years. She knows what I like, so I'm going to make her your contact person."

Natalie glances at me with a distasteful expression— like she's just taken a giant gulp of spoiled milk. Cooper won't even look at me. It's like being in grade school all over again and getting picked last for kickball. At least in grade school, they had good reason. I'm horrible at sports.

"No offense to Tori," Natalie says, "but does she know enough about style to make those kinds of decisions?" She stares down her nose at me like I'm a rogue cockroach, and she's a giant can of Raid.

That's it. I don't care how glamorous and sophisticated this woman is, she's a class-A bitch. "It's Toni, and trust me, I know enough," I practically spit. "The only reason I look like this is because Archie showed up at my apartment to pick me up without letting me know first. I didn't have time to finish getting ready."

"I texted you—" Archie says.

"I told you I dropped my phone in the sink last night and didn't get it," I snap.

Cooper finally enters the fray. "You dropped your phone in the sink?"

Why does he care? "Yeah, so?"

"You didn't see Archie's text? Or any text?" he asks, all lit up.

"That is correct, Cooper." *Weirdo.*

The look on his face suddenly softens. He looks so yummy, I want to jump into his arms and declare my wild attraction for him. I can't do that, so I make a point to avert my eyes. You know, in case I lose my resolve and decide to go back to my old, wicked ways.

I spend the next forty minutes listening to Natalie prattle on about focus walls and subtle but sophisticated soffits while I want to pull off one of my frumpy grandmother boots and hit her with it. I do not want to work with this awful woman.

When she starts rambling on about how the green space should have a feature fountain, I ask Cooper, "Do you have a bathroom I can use?"

"In our work trailer out front. I can show you the way."

I wave him off. "I've got it." I practically run out of the warehouse, mumbling under my breath the whole way. "'Coop and I have worked together on a lot of projects.' *Blech.* I just bet you have. And a feature fountain? Yeah, great idea, genius. 'Cause that's what's missing from every homeless person's life. Water squirting whimsically through the air."

When I get to the trailer, a pretty Japanese woman looks at me with wide eyes. "Whoa, looks like you forgot to blend."

What is she talking about? That's when it hits me—I never wiped off the extra cover-up I slathered under my eyes. Holy hell. "Can you point me to the bathroom?"

She does so, and as soon as I walk into the tiny space, I look in the mirror and nearly fall over in a dead faint. I look like a raccoon mated with a Puritan. Why didn't Archie tell me? Oh wait, he tried, but I got all snippy with him.

I wipe off the cover-up, then open my purse and finish

putting on the rest of my makeup. In an attempt to sexify myself, I take my hair out of the bun and run my fingers through it, hoping for that freshly-tumbled vibe.

When I finally feel somewhat presentable, I leave the bathroom. The woman who greeted me smiles. "I get it now." I have no idea what she's talking about.

"I'm Toni. I work for the Faith Foundation."

"I'm Yuma. I didn't think it could be you when you first walked in here, but I see now I was wrong."

I have no idea what she's talking about, and before I can find out, the door opens and Cooper walks in with Natalie and Archie in tow. Natalie, the narcissistic nut (that's right, I've given her a highly alliterative nickname), rushes over to Yuma, arms wide. "It's been too long. How are you?" She's clearly trying to mark her territory in case I have designs on Coop (or his assistant).

Yuma stiffens at her embrace before pushing her away. "I've been fighting a nasty cough, but otherwise I'm fine." Natalie jumps back like Yuma's a forest fire, and she's wearing a gasoline dress.

Latching onto Cooper's arm again, Natalie grins broadly. "The old gang's back together again, but this time, we've got a billionaire along for the ride. Isn't this fun?"

Archie shoots me a look of disgust. If there's one thing he hates, it's when people bring up his money. His eyes soften. "I see that wasn't a new look you were trying out."

I'm equal parts grateful and humiliated that he brought it up. "Not exactly."

"Thank God!" Natalie says with a phony laugh. "I simply couldn't understand the aesthetic you were going for there. I mean, the dress says cottage core, but the makeup and hair was indie pale, and those two do not blend well." Lowering her voice a touch, as though trying to make it seem like she's not trying to embarrass me (while she is *obviously* trying to embarrass me), she adds, "But it turns out you just forgot to blend. Huge relief."

I open my mouth to tell her how happy I am that *she's* relieved, but Archie saves me from myself. "Toni, we should run. I've got that meeting with the folks over at Empowerment Social Enterprises in an hour, and I really need to get your thoughts on their program before I go."

"Right," I answer, walking past Cooper and his cling-on. "Thanks for your help, Yuma. I'm looking forward to working with you." I don't include Natalie for obvious reasons.

Yuma gives me a warm smile. "You too, Toni."

I continue to pretend that Natalie isn't present while Archie says goodbye.

When we walk back out into the chilly morning air, I can finally take a real breath. Neither of us says anything until we get to his vehicle, where he turns and looks at me. I expect him to ask me what the hell that was all about, but he doesn't. "Sorry I rushed you this morning."

"It's fine." I put on my seatbelt.

"Natalie is pretty awful, isn't she?"

"You could say that." I sit back while he pulls out into traffic. "You realize that a year ago, you would have chastised me for being anything less than pleasant to someone you were doing business with."

Narrowing his eyes, he says, "I would not have."

"You may not know this about yourself, but you used to be on the demanding side of the spectrum."

"I was tough but surely not in an unreasonable way."

"You were definitely unreasonable."

He's quiet for a full block, and I worry I might have crossed a line. Then he says, "In that case, thanks for sticking with me. This whole foundation thing is new. I need someone solid by my side."

"Between Holly and me, we've got you covered."

"That means a lot, Toni. I hope you know I'll always have your back, too."

"I do."

My mind floats to Cooper and how oddly distant he was with me when we first arrived at the job site. He must have something going on with Natalie, and she's clearly the territorial type. He was probably trying not to rock the boat, but something about that whole scene bothers me far more than it should.

Why do I care if he's dating a harpy? I don't want him. Or more accurately, I'm not going to let myself have him.

Even if he were available.

Chapter 12

Cooper

I'm sitting at my desk, finishing the turkey sub I picked up for supper, when I get a text from Toni.

> Toni: I'm so sorry I left you hanging last night. I dropped my stupid phone in the sink while I was doing dishes, and I've been so busy all day, I couldn't get a replacement until now.

Weird. Doesn't she remember I already know that?

> Me: Don't worry about it. I didn't have a lot of time last night to text anyway.

That's a total lie. I basically sat on my couch sipping beer and watching sports updates while keeping an eye on my phone the entire time. I must have checked to make sure the sound was on at least a dozen times. Okay, a hundred.

> Toni: Were you on a hot date with some woman who isn't insisting on texting for three weeks?

> Me: Nothing that thrilling, believe me. But, while we're on the topic, are we texting exclusively or are you also sending messages to a bunch of other guys? #asking-forafriend

> Toni: You're funny. And no, you're my one and only trial texting guy.

> Me: Wow, that's a lot of pressure. I'm not sure I'm ready to text just one woman. Kidding. You're the only one. How was your day?

> Toni: It was one of those days when I wish I actually was a unicorn so I could stab people.

I'm pretty sure I know who she means, although bringing Natalie up seems like a bad idea. The last thing I want is for Toni to think there's something going on between me and my designer.

> Me: I thought unicorns were supposed to be gentle and magical.

> Toni: Unicorns are badasses. Don't let their rep fool you. New topic: Want to try something fun?

> Me: Always. What do you have in mind?

Toni: I found a list of twenty-five questions online that you should ask people when you're dating them. (Or, in our case, considering dating them.)

Me: I'm in. I love games.

Toni: Question one: Does your family have a motto (written or otherwise)?

Me: Not written, but if it were, it would be Stay in School.

Toni: Smart. My family's motto would be "Well, that escalated quickly."

I chuckle, wishing I could stare into her eyes and get lost in their depths. Although I'd settle for talking on the phone so I could hear her voice. I start to type: What if I call you? Then I remember I promised we'd take this as slow as she needs to. I delete the message and replace it with:

Me: Ha! Your family sounds fun.

Toni: You'd think, wouldn't you? All right, number two: What motivates you to work hard?

Me: I love what I do, so it never feels like work.

Toni: Good answer. For me, it's money. I need it, and I don't have enough. Not that I'm complaining, mind you. I know I'm better off than a lot of people.

Me: Money is good. It's even better when you make it yourself.

Toni: How else would you get it?

Me: Some people marry for it.

Toni: Ew. Moving on … Who was your least favorite teacher in school and why?

Me: Mrs. Garcia, seventh grade.

Toni: What happened?

Me: She told me my baking soda and vinegar volcano was uninspired and looked like it had been "thrown together that morning."

Toni: Was it?

Me: Yeah, but I got up really early to make it. She also told me I was never going to get anywhere in life if that was all the effort I was going to put into my work. I'll never forget that moment as long as I live.

Toni: Yet look how you turned out.

Me: Pretty amazing, huh?

Toni: Gah! Can we talk later? My mom is calling, and if I don't answer, she'll send out the Coast Guard. Or the cops. Or even worse, one of my aunts.

Me: Good luck with that.

Toni: Thanks. Have a great night.

Me: You too.

After she signs off, I read over our conversation. A warm feeling washes over me that once again makes me wish Toni was right here in my living room in her farm girl dress from this morning, weird makeup and all. According to Yuma, Toni forgot to "blend," whatever the hell that means.

Yuma guessed that Toni's the woman I'm interested in. Nothing gets past her. Oddly enough, she was in favor of us as a couple. She said she thought we "probably wouldn't kill each other," which in Yuma-speak is a shining endorsement.

After shutting off the TV, I turn off the lights in my living room and go upstairs to my bedroom. There are nineteen days until Toni and I officially go out on a real date. Suddenly going turtle-slow doesn't sound at all good to me. In fact, it's sort of making me hate turtles.

Chapter 13

Toni

"Hey, Mom, what's up?" I raise my voice so she'll be able to hear me over the rush hour traffic zooming past. I'm hurrying along the sidewalk toward my apartment, glad I'll soon be out of the cold and into a nice hot bath, where I can soak while texting with a nice hot man.

"Your Auntie Jean threw her back out. We need you to be a doll with a ball for the evening."

My heart sinks. "Mom, no. You know how awful I am at bowling. What about Hadley? It's *her* mother who can't make it. Shouldn't she be the substitute?"

"Hadley's got a date tonight. With a stock analyst," she says pointedly. "Whereas I'm guessing you're on your way home to spend the evening alone in your little shoebox. Probably with big plans that involve a long bath and watching *Grey's Anatomy* for the fifth time."

"You make my life sound pathetic." I deftly dodge a guy who suddenly stopped to look at his phone.

"It's not me that makes your life sound pathetic. You do that all by yourself."

"Thanks for the support. Now what were you calling me for again? Oh right, to ask me for a favor I don't want to give."

"Is it so bad that I want to see my only daughter happy?"

"I am happy," I lie. "I have a job I love and wonderful friends. I also may have met someone."

"Someone who?" she asks hopefully. I can picture her in my mind's eye, sitting up straight in her chair at the kitchen table.

"Just a guy from work. He's a fundraiser."

"I thought a fundraiser was an event, not a person."

"It's both. Turns out rich people don't set up a bake sale and do all the organizing and baking themselves. They hire the job out so they can pull in some serious bucks."

"Huh, so he raises money for charities for a living?" She sounds somewhat skeptical.

"That's right. It's a great job, too. The foundation is paying him a small fortune, so he must be doing well for himself."

"I suppose that's impressive."

"It is." I'm oddly happy that I've managed to impress her—when it really shouldn't matter because I'm an adult, etc.

"I want to hear all about him tonight at the alley."

"Mom …" I say in a tone that sounds whiny and warning at the same time. I finally get to my building and dig in my handbag for keys.

"Please? Do it for the woman who refused pain meds while giving birth to your enormous head. If you don't say yes, Jean is going to take a muscle relaxant and show up. Last time she did that, she almost went home with the guy who sprays the shoes. I had to call Uncle Ricky to pick her up. *And* we lost."

Unlocking the front door of the building, I sigh inwardly. "Fine. I'll be there at seven."

"Yay! Thanks, sweetie. Come early so we can get you warmed up. You know, 'cause you're not that good at bowling."

She hangs up before I can tell her to forget it. I trudge up three flights to my apartment, no longer excited about the evening. Once I'm inside, I flick on all the lights, then put the kettle on for tea. While I wait for the water to boil, I put leftover mac and cheese into a bowl and pop it in the microwave, then pull out my phone.

> Me: Hey, you! You'll never guess what I'm doing this evening.

> New Guy: Coming over to my place to surprise me? I'll send you my address, and I promise to act surprised.

> Me: I wish. I'm going bowling with my mom and her sisters. One of my aunts threw her back out, and they need a backup.

The microwave signals my dinner is ready, so I pull it out and sit at the table while waiting for a response. After blowing on my first forkful, I shove it in my mouth and let the hot cheesy goodness improve my grumpy pants mood.

> New Guy: SO many questions. You wish you were coming over? I'm totally cool with us taking this to the next level. Also, bowling? I bet that would be sexy as hell to watch.

Me: When I said that, I meant I wish I were doing anything other than bowling. We should stick to our original plan. As for the bowling thing, I'm TERRIBLE at it. But they can't find anyone else, and they'd have to forfeit without a fourth teammate. Question for you – how exactly is bowling sexy? I've watched it on TV, and I gotta say it pretty much has the opposite effect on me. Total turn-off.

New Guy: Imagine you're me, imagining you bowling. All that bending and then jumping for joy when you get a strike.

Me: Trust me, there's no celebrating when I bowl. Only deeply disappointed relatives. I better finish eating so I can get going.

New Guy: Have fun and maybe text me when you get home, so I know you made it safely.

My heart flutters. Like seriously flutters. He wants to know I got home safely. In all the dating I've done, never once has a man asked me to check in with him like that. Not once.

Me: Are we at the checking-in-on-each-other stage?

New Guy: Maybe. Which is strange considering we haven't kissed yet.

Is it hot in here? Because my inner temperature just reached the molten lava stage.

∼

I show up at the bowling alley at 7:15, only to find my mom, Aunt Sheila, and Aunt Margie already practicing. They're in their pink bowling shirts, with their bowling nicknames across the back. Since it's league night, everyone else here has their own shoes, so I'm the only one doing the whole "rent a foot disease" thing. After collecting my rentals, I trudge to their lane, serenaded by their shouts of delight.

"There she is! Our savior!" Aunt Sheila pulls me in for a big bosomy hug. When she finally releases me, she says, "So? We hear you found a man. He sounds like a good catch."

"Yup." I think of how he wants me to let him know when I've made it home. "And he's not looking for a three-some." I give her a pointed stare. "You took that Tinder profile down, didn't you?"

Before she answers, my mom grabs me for a quick hug. Margie does the same and then Sheila thrusts the Dolls with Balls spare shirt at me. It has the phrase Sparing is Caring on the back in big letters, whereas Mom's says Ace, Margie's reads Killer, and Sheila's is Strike Queen.

I pull the shirt on over my tee, and Margie hands me a ball off the shelf. "Let's hear about this new guy. What's his name? How old is he? Has he ever been married?"

Taking the ball, I heave it up against my chest. "Sumner, not sure about the age, but I'm guessing mid-thirties. I also don't know much about his dating past, other than seeing some photos online of him with various women. Most were taken at formal events, so I'm not sure if they were dates or clients or what." Which reminds me, I should find out.

She raises an eyebrow. "You haven't asked him if he's been married?"

"No."

"You'd better do that. What if he's got a bunch of ex-wives he pays alimony to?" She gestures for me to take a practice shot.

"I'll make sure to ask him." Hoping to stop the inquisition, I move to our lane and center myself before releasing the ball. It bounces down the lane with embarrassingly loud thuds, then makes a beeline for the gutter. I cringe and turn toward my teammates, fully expecting to see disappointment on their faces. They're not even paying attention to me. They're huddled over a phone, whispering to each other.

Wait a second. That's not just any phone. That's my phone.

Mom looks at me. "He says he's never been married."

"You texted him?!" I say, grabbing the phone from her. "Give me that!"

She shrugs. "What? I told him who I was."

Glancing at the screen, I see that she's written: Hello, young man, I'm Toni's mom. I understand my daughter is interested in a possible future with you. For that reason I need to know if you've ever been married, if you have any children from previous relationships, and while we're at it, how old are you?

New Guy: No, no, and I'm 33.

I quickly type a response: Sorry about that. My teammates (who I shall murder) grabbed my phone while I was taking my turn. I had NO prior knowledge that those questions were being asked.

New Guy: No problem. It's nice that your family's looking out for you. It's also nice to hear that you're quite interested in me.

"Aww, that's sweet," Sheila says over my shoulder.

Tucking my phone against my chest, I say, "I can't believe you three. Talk about meddling in someone's love life."

"We were just spurring things along," Margie says.

"We wouldn't have had to do that if you'd already known the answers," Mom says huffily. "These are things you should have found out right away."

"These are things I would have found out in due time, thank you very much. Stay out of it," I tell them.

"Look, sweetie, it's only natural we'd want to be involved," Sheila tells me. "Your poor mother has been waiting for her first grandbaby for over a decade."

"What?" I wrinkle my nose. "You expected me to get pregnant at nineteen?"

Mom shrugs. "It wouldn't have surprised me. The boys you used to go out with didn't exactly scream 'responsible guy who uses protection.'"

I blink a few times, wishing I could be anywhere else. "They may not have been responsible, but I sure as heck was. You wanted me to have a baby when I was a teenager?"

"Not *wanted*, but let's say I would have loved being a grandma so young."

"It's true. She would have loved it," Sheila says, turning to her. "That's the beautiful thing about you. No ego. Most women wouldn't want to be a grandma in their early forties, but with you … it's all about the babies."

"It really is," Mom says. "Speaking of which, does this Sumner person want to have babies? Because if not, you can't invest any more time in him."

"We should ask him," Margie says, reaching for my phone. "There's no way Toni would have done that yet. I mean, if she didn't know whether he'd been married or not—"

"That's true," Sheila agrees. "She didn't even bother to find out how old he is."

Clutching my phone tightly, I yell, "Can you please butt out of my love life and get back to bowling?"

All three of them stare at me with matching shocked expressions. "Well, fiddle-de-dee," Margie says.

"No need to raise your voice," Mom adds with a sniff.

"We're only trying to help," Sheila tells me.

"The last time you tried to help, I wound up having dinner with a sicko who wanted me to go back to his place to meet his blow-up doll," I hiss. "So stay out of it, or I'm leaving, and I promise you, I'll never be your back-up again."

Sheila scrunches up her face. "No offense, dear, but that threat isn't as scary as you think it is."

Nice. See if I ever help them out again.

Chapter 14

Cooper

It's almost midnight when my phone pings. I swipe it off the nightstand.

Toni: I'm finally home. You still up?

Me: Just getting into bed. How'd it go?

Toni: Awful. The lowlights have probably been posted on some Bowling Fail YouTube channel by now.

Me: So there's a chance I could still see you doing all that bending and releasing?

Toni: Dream on, mister.

Me: Oh, I will.

Toni: I'm sorry about my nosey relatives. They can't help themselves. My mom is devastated that I haven't provided her with a brood of grandkids yet.

Me: I understand interfering family members. I have three sisters. One of them wants to set me up with a lawyer at her office who is apparently a "real ballbuster." Like I'd want that.

Toni: Are your parents after you to settle down and have a family too?

Me: Not before I get my PhD in something. After I've fulfilled my educational destiny, I'm sure they'd like some grandkids. But I can promise you, that's never going to happen.

Toni: What, the PhD or the kids?

Me: The PhD. I love kids. Where do you stand on the whole bringing little humans into the world thing?

Toni: I'm highly in favor of it. With the right man, of course.

Me: Same here. I wouldn't even consider it without the right man.

Toni: Bahahaha!

Me: Can I make a confession?

Toni: Okay …

Me: I'd really like to spend time with you in person.

Toni: We will. Soon. The whole point of a texting-only relationship is to get to know each other, and as much as I hate to admit it, my mom/aunts may be on to something. There's some pretty basic information I should know about you.

Me: I'm an open book. Fire away.

Toni: How many children do you want?

Me: Enough for a baseball team.

Toni: …

Toni: …

Me: You can stop freaking out now. I was teasing. 2 or 3 would be nice. Maybe 4 if my wife was into it.

Toni: I'm a two tops kind of lady. You need to think of having four teenagers living with you and ask if you'd really want that.

Me: Good point.

Toni: Speaking of teenagers, what were you like at that age?

Me: I was your basic nightmare. Sneaking around trying to get booze and girls. Putting in the least amount of effort at school to pass.

Toni: That surprises me. I picture you as being uber-responsible. You know, captain of the debate team, National Honor Society, class president, polo player.

Me: Really?

Really?

Toni: Yeah. You have that upper crust kind of look about you.

Me: Really?

I suddenly wonder if she knows who she's texting. It sounds like she thinks I'm the man my parents wish I was and not the guy I am.

Toni: You sound surprised.

Me: I kind of am. I see myself as way more down to earth than you seem to. What about you? I have a feeling you were a bit of a handful when you were a teenager.

Toni: What makes you think that?

Me: Because you're a bit of a handful now. I wish I'd known you back then.

Toni: Pervert.

Me: Only when it comes to you.

Toni: Be still my beating heart.

Me: Not too still though. I like the thought of making your heart race.

Toni: Do I have that effect on you too?

Me: I feel like I've just run a 5K when I'm in the same room with you.

Toni: I'm flattered.

Me: You should be. You're so beautiful I can hardly look away. I'm even happy to be texting with you when I should be sleeping.

Toni: Me too, but it is getting late. I'm just crawling into bed.

Me: I'll try not to picture that.

Toni: Picture away.

Me: I can't. I was recently accused of being a pervert.

Toni: If the shoe fits.

Me: I guess I'll have to wear it. Good night, Jay-Z. Sweet dreams.

Toni: Good night, Beyoncé.

Chapter 15

Toni

After I wake up, I jump in the shower to wash off the remnants of my bowling night. I smell like stale beer and foot spray. I would have cleaned up last night, but I wanted to text with Sumner before going to bed. He's so different messaging than he is in person.

In person, Sumner doesn't act like he's particularly interested in me. He's nice and engaging, but there are walls up. He appears to have the same level of interest in me as he would for a stranger at the grocery store. No lingering gazes, no standing too close, no finding excuses to touch my hand. I can't help but find it a little disappointing. I asked him to act like we weren't anything special at the office, but the man should receive an Academy Award for his performance.

Conversely, I feel like I've known his texting persona my whole life. He's carefree and funny. Flirtatious too, really flirtatious.

Sumner has three sisters who outshine him when it comes to education and jobs (one is literally a brain surgeon). The poor guy has a family full of over-achievers who are apparently disappointed that he doesn't have a doctorate in something. He runs a successful business and does a lot of good in the world at the same time, which, if you ask me, should be enough for any parent to feel proud. Why the heck should he have spent years and hundreds of thousands of dollars furthering his education only to wind up in the same job he has now? *Seriously, who are these people?*

I'm crazy about Sumner's texting personality, and I cannot wait for our date so we can flirt in person and see where it leads. (Hopefully to us standing in front of a minister, saying our vows this time next year.)

After putting on my red sweater dress, I'm once again smacked in the face with the fact that I've gained a few pounds. I feel like Nicki Minaj or Kim Kardashian with my caboose on display like this, but now's not the time to be coy.

After applying all the makeup, I throw strategic beach waves in my hair. By the time I slip into my black pumps with the ankle straps, I'm ready to take over the world. A quick glance in the full-length mirror has me wishing I had been wearing this when I met Natalie the other day. There is no way she would have treated me like anything less than an equal.

I send Archie a quick text.

Me: Can you pick me up on your way into the office today? I look too good to take the subway.

Archie: If you can be out front in three minutes.

Me: I'll be there.

I snag my coat and purse and run out the door. Archie barely slows down long enough for me to get in.

"Why are you in such a hurry today?" I ask.

"Holly has a scan this morning, and we get to hear the baby's heartbeat, but first I have a couple of things to do at the office before picking her up."

"I want to hear the baby's heartbeat," I practically whine.

"I need you at the office to sign for a bunch of stuff Natalie is sending over. How about if we both go to the next one?"

"Fine, but don't forget. This baby means the world to me."

I'm pouting when Archie glances at me and says, "You look really nice today."

"Thank you." I suddenly feel smug.

"Are you trying to impress someone special?" He waggles his eyebrows. "Perhaps someone whose number I gave you recently?"

"Maybe." I unlatch my seatbelt as he pulls into the parking lot. "But I don't want to talk about it in case I jinx it."

I get out and lead the way into the building. After hanging up my coat, I make a pot of coffee and wait for Sumner to show up. I feel like a kid standing in line to see Santa Claus. Archie takes the elevator down, and it comes back up with Sumner.

"Sumner, hello! How are you today?"

He takes a step back and nearly trips over his own foot. Clearly my outfit is doing its job. "Toni, hi. You look nice today."

I look nice? No, I look radiant, gorgeous, like sex on heels, but of course I don't tell him that. "Why, thank you. I feel good today."

"Why?"

Shimmying up to him, I run a finger down the center of his dress shirt. "Because I've been texting an exciting man who makes me feel all kinds of wonderful things."

His eyebrows knit together in confusion. "That's very nice for you. I wish you all the best."

Not exactly the reaction I was expecting. "How about you? Do you have anything promising happening on the relationship front?"

He sidles past me to the coat hooks. "Not at the moment, no."

"Really?"

He stops. "There's no one special in my life right now."

"Sumner," I say. "I know I said I wanted to keep things out of the office, but don't you think this is taking it to an extreme? I mean, we're the only ones here."

He looks more confused than a nun at a rave. "I don't know what you're talking about."

A prickly heat crawls up my spine. "I'm talking about our texting relationship. I'm talking about our plans for Valentine's Day."

"What plans?"

What's this guy's deal? "You said you were going to take me out for an amazing meal."

He furrows his brow until his eyes are practically closed. "When did I say that?"

"About a week ago, remember? I said I wanted to take things slow so we should just text each other for a while …"

"I honestly don't know what you're talking about, Toni. Whomever you're texting, he isn't me."

Holy mother of corndog hell. "Of course it's you. Archie gave me your number."

"Are you texting 212-555-1654?"

Heart. Thud. Floor. "I'm texting a 917 area code."

"That's not me."

Who in God's name have I been talking to? "You didn't tell me about getting lost at the opera? Or your nasty science teacher who was unreasonably hard on you about your uninspired papier-mâché volcano?"

"I would never have gotten lost at the opera. I've been going to the MET since I was a baby. Also, I've never in my life made a papier-mâché volcano, but I agree with whoever that teacher was. Papier-mâché is generally uninspired."

Reality sets in. I've been flirt-texting (and let's face it, falling for) some random guy who, for all I know, could be an old married man or a fourteen-year-old boy. I swallow hard, realizing he's waiting for a response. "I'm sorry for the confusion. Please forget I said anything or, you know, touched your … person. That was highly unprofessional."

He offers me what I'm sure is a polite smile when he wants to make a cuckoo hand gesture next to his temple. "Should we get started on our plans for the cruise?"

"Right, the fundraiser." Dammit. Figuring out who I love texting with is going to have to wait.

I get my laptop, a pad of paper, a couple of pens, and precede Sumner into the conference room on wobbly legs. I am humiliated. I've just told him I thought we were dating, and he clearly has absolutely no interest in me. He must think I'm totally insane or this was some ploy to get him to ask me out.

I sit, intending to get this meeting over with as quickly as possible. Then I can buy a plane ticket to Tasmania (or some other island on the other side of the planet) and never come back. I give him what I hope looks like a smile but fear is more of a constipated grimace. "Should we get started?"

"Yes, let's do that." He opens his briefcase and pulls out his laptop.

I look for signs he's wishing he could be anywhere but with the woman who just hit on him so shamelessly, but I see none. He doesn't shift in his seat, doesn't clear his throat awkwardly. He seems perfectly at ease, whereas I'm pretty sure I'm going to have to wring the sweat out of my dress when our meeting is over.

I spend the next hour forcing myself to concentrate on what he's saying when my brain is screaming at me to run out of here and find out what's going on with my love life. I feel frigging bad and *super* disappointed that Sumner is not the man I've been texting. All this time, I thought I had quite possibly found the one, but I haven't. The worst part is not knowing who I did find.

"Toni?"

I look up from my computer into his eyes. "Yes?"

"Are you all right?"

"I'm great, thanks."

"Are you sure? Because I just asked you what day we should send out the press release, and you said yes."

I wince. "Sorry, I'm a little distracted by what happened earlier."

He nods, giving me a sympathetic look that morphs into a small smile. "You know what? I just realized that if you thought you'd been texting me and agreed to go out, you might actually *want* to go out with me."

"That was the general idea." I feel more awkward than a room full of chimps trying to perform Shakespeare.

"Maybe you can tell whoever you've been texting that there's been some horrible mistake, and we can go out instead, maybe an intimate dinner for two. I know an incredible place with an amazing view."

He gives me a smile that would definitely make me

weak in the knees if I weren't in such a panic over the stranger I've been falling for. Reminding myself he's the one I've wanted all along, I clear my throat. "That would be really nice. In fact, I'd love to."

"Perfect. Our first official date will be on Valentine's Day."

"That sounds great." I should sound more excited than I do.

We wrap up the meeting quickly after that, and although I'm relieved he doesn't think I'm some weirdo who made something up to score a date, I'm also completely antsy to figure out what the heck is going on.

"Do you mind if I use the conference room for a few minutes before I leave?" he asks. "I need to make a few calls."

"Sure," I tell him, practically leaping out of my chair.

As soon as I get back to my desk, I send Archie a text.

Me: I know you're at the doctor with Holly, but this is time sensitive. Whose number did you give me when you programmed the New Guy into my phone?

Archie: Cooper's. That's who you meant, right?

Oh, no. Nononononononono … It cannot be Cooper. Anyone but him.

Me: I wanted Sumner's number.

Archie: Sumner Livingston? Why?

Me: I'm trying to change the kind of man I'm going after in hopes of finding a forever kind of love.

Archie: Cooper's different. He'll never use you for free rent. In fact, he could probably buy your apartment building without batting an eye.

Me: He's trouble. Trust me, I know. And now I've got to tell him the truth—which is that I was never interested in him. Thanks a lot.

Archie: Awkward. I'm sorry, I shouldn't have assumed.

Me: What a nightmare.

I've been texting Cooper Flint. No wonder he was so weird last week when Archie and I showed up at the construction site. He thought I was ignoring his messages from the night before. Not only have I been dreaming about him, but I really liked him. This is so, so bad.

Picking up my phone, I wonder what I can possibly say to Cooper to end things, but before I can formulate anything, the elevator opens and the man himself walks in.

What now?

Chapter 16

Cooper

"Hey, you," I say, stunned at the sight of Toni. She is unbelievably sexy in that red dress. "I see you went from farm girl to *damn girl!*" Her face falls, and I'm suddenly self-conscious about my lame joke. "Too cheesy for you? That wasn't my best material."

She holds up one finger, then folds it back in with the rest of them, looking extremely uncomfortable. "Hello."

Glancing around, I lower my voice. "Are there people here?"

"Our fundraiser is here today."

I wink and tap the side of my nose to show I get it. Adopting a professional tone, I tell her, "Archie said he'd meet me here. I'm a little early though."

"Right." Her cheeks turn bright pink. "He's going to be a while; you should probably come back."

"He texted he'll be here in fifteen, so if it's all the same to you, I'd rather wait." I search her face for a hint that she's happy to see me, but I see no sign of anything resembling joy. In fact, she seems downright agitated.

"Did he?" she asks loudly. "That's … great! I thought the ultrasound would take a lot longer."

"Guess not." I take a seat in the waiting area near her desk.

"Would you like a coffee while you wait?" Her expression is unreadable, but if I had to label it, I'd say it's almost pained.

I kind of want to say yes so I can watch her walk away but decide against it. It's really nice to sit here and look at her. Not only is she totally gorgeous, but she's sweet and funny. She's also noticeably on edge. "You okay?"

She nods and lets out an um-hmm sound, but it comes out strangled. "Great, yeah." Picking up a pen, she resumes whatever it is she's doing over there.

I bounce my leg restlessly. When she glances up, I give her what I hope is a panty-melting smile. "You do look especially pretty today."

"Toni, I'm going to run," someone says.

Sumner Livingston, the giant asshat himself—Rae's ex-fiancé. I flash back to the moment when I discovered who he really is—a cheating, lying, sack of crap—and tense all over as his eyes lock on Toni. If I'm not mistaken, he's staring at her chest. *Eyes up, pal!*

"Stay tuned, because I'm fairly certain I can get us a table at Chez Louis for Valentine's Day," he tells her, sliding his arms into his trench coat.

Toni stands quickly and interrupts him. "Sumner, this is Cooper Flint." She gestures to me. "Cooper's the contractor building the homeless villages for us. Cooper, this is Sumner Livingston, our fundraiser."

Wait. Was he just talking about plans he has with Toni on Valentine's Day? As in, a date?

Sumner stiffens when he sees me and goes a little pale, and I know he's reliving the moment when he realized I was right outside his car window, screwdriver in hand, ready to kill him. He recovers quickly. "We already know each other. How have you been, Coop?"

"Great." I give him a smile that allows me to bare my teeth like a rabid animal. We stare at each other as I try to decide if I should out him for the bastard he is. Doing so would mean having to admit to my bad behavior that night, and airing your dirty laundry in front of an important client isn't professional—even if the bastard totally deserves it.

"Glad to hear it," Sumner says finally. He pivots to Toni. "I'd better run. See you soon."

"You sure will."

Sumner hustles past me and lowers the elevator door with a quick yank before disappearing, leaving Toni and me alone. I'm relieved when the phone rings. It gives me a moment to get my thoughts together.

I pace while she talks. Sumner is the last person I thought I'd have the misfortune of running into again, but not only is he working with the foundation, he's interested in the same woman I am. And she's interested in *him*? How does that jackass manage to fool such intelligent women?

I knew what a jerk he was in high school, but I pushed those memories aside when he started dating Rae. People grow up. They usually get better as they age. Not Sumner. He is, and always has been, pond scum.

I'm downright furious. Even though Toni and I aren't actually dating, we'd made plans for Valentine's night. Even though we haven't shared as much as a hot dog in Central Park, or a kiss, we've shared pretty personal stuff via text. She came right out and told me she wasn't seeing anyone. Now she has two dates for the same night?

As soon as she hangs up, I say "You have a date with *Sumner* on Valentine's night? I thought *we* had plans."

"Yes, but——"

"I've already booked the best table at Brasserie."

"Brasserie?" She throws her hands out in front of her like she's about to do jazz hands or sing "Stop! In the Name of Love." "There's been a terrible misunderstanding."

"And what might that be?" There's so much adrenaline flowing through me, it feels like my head is going to pop off.

"I asked Archie for the new guy's phone number, and he thought I meant you." She does not look me in the eye.

What? "Are you telling me you thought you were texting Sumner all this time?"

She nods slowly. "I'm really sorry about this."

She looks sorry too, which makes me feel bad for her. But I feel a heck of a lot worse for me. I really like her. I thought we could have had something good. "Yeah, well, what can you do? If I'm not your type, I'm not your type." I want to tell her exactly who Sumner is, but then I remember why I can't.

"It's not that you're …" She doesn't finish her sentence and instead goes with, "The thing is, I promised myself to expand my search for *the one*. I haven't exactly had luck with …" She heaves a sigh. "I just … no."

Just no. Ouch.

She nibbles her bottom lip. "I enjoyed our text conversations, and I'm sure you'll find someone else." She rambles on, absently fiddling with the cuffs of her dress.

But Sumner? He's going to break her heart.

"I want to see where it goes," she practically whispers.

I can tell her where it'll go. "Sumner Livingston is not who you think he is."

Toni's eyebrows draw down. "Listen, Cooper, I know you're not usually turned down by women, so this must be hard for you to accept, but it's really happening, and trying to make Sumner look bad isn't going to win me over, so just stop, okay?"

Her words are like a direct hit to the solar plexus. "Sure. If that's what you want, I'll leave you to it."

"It *is* what I want."

There's nothing else I can say, so I let the sting of rejection render me mute.

Chapter 17

Toni

I feel lower than a worm. Cooper is sitting fewer than ten feet away, staring daggers at me. It's all I can do not to crawl under my desk and hide.

When Archie returns, it's clear he knows something is wrong. Why wouldn't he? The tension is so thick you can cut it with a knife. He shakes Cooper's hand and then glances at me. "Everything okay?" He looks afraid, as he should.

"About as good as you'd expect, being that you gave me Cooper's number instead of Sumner's." I'm not going to let him off the hook.

"About that, I owe you both a big apology," he says. "It's just, well"—he turns to Cooper—"based on some of Toni's past boyfriends, I assumed she wanted *your* number."

Cooper tilts his head and stares at me, his expression unreadable. "Apparently not."

Archie glances back and forth between us, looking more uncomfortable than I've ever seen him. "I am sorry. Cooper, let's go to my office."

I wait until the door closes behind them before exhaling. Then I get up and cross to the coffee pot. My cheeks are flushed, and my skin is prickling like it's covered in fresh bug bites. I was really looking forward to today, too. Now all I want to do is go home and crawl into bed. I wish I was still asleep. On the off chance that this is a particularly realistic nightmare, I give my arm a sharp pinch. Crap, it hurts like hell.

Back at my desk, I toy with the idea of taking the rest of the day off, but before I can carry out my plan, the elevator opens and Natalie walks out.

That's just perfect. She's the last person I want to see. I'd rather sit down to tea with Ted Bundy.

Instead of greeting her like I should, I turn to my computer screen (which is running my screensaver of a cat licking the screen) and pretend I'm busy. Lick, lick.

She comes over to my desk. "Hi there, I'm Natalie. I'm the designer on the homeless project."

Looking up at her from under my eyebrows, I say, "I know. We met last week at the Bedford Falls site."

Her expression moves rapidly from confused to surprised. "Tonya?"

"Toni."

She looks me up and down. "That was you? What happened?"

"I believe I mentioned Archie picked me up early, without notice." Not that she deserves an answer to such a nasty question.

She takes off her coat, unveiling a dress nearly as sexy as mine. "Honey, I would have thought a woman like you would know enough to keep a man waiting before leaving the house unprepared for the day."

"A woman like me? What does that mean?"

"A woman who can look this good when she puts a little effort into it." Draping her coat over her arm, she adds, "You looked fresh from a prairie zombie movie that morning."

She's not wrong, but she didn't have to say so. "Are you here to see Archie?"

"Yes. He's expecting me."

I don't bother to announce her. I point to his office. "He's in there."

She sashays in that general direction. I don't like her. She may have been nice enough to me today, but last week she was a complete cow. Who judges someone on their looks alone?

Then I realize what a hypocrite I am. I've decided Cooper isn't right for me using a set of criteria some may call shallow —his career choice, his complete cockiness, and the fact that he's far too hot to live. But in my defense, I have a load of experience backing my actions, whereas Natalie is just a bitch.

When my phone pings, my first thought is maybe it's Cooper. That's not likely, as he's in a meeting with Archie, and yet my stupid heart is hopeful.

It's Holly.

Holly: Archie told me about the mix-up. I cannot believe you've been texting the wrong man this whole time!

Me: You're not the only one who can't believe it. I'm in shock.

Holly: What are you going to do? Pretend you knew all

along who you were texting, get married to Cooper, and live happily ever after? That gets my vote.

Me: No can do. The cat's already out of the bag, and I'm afraid things are about to get wildly awkward.

Holly: Seriously?

Me: It's a long story, which I'll tell you over a bottle of vodka (for me; you can have orange juice). Now tell me about the baby.

Holly: We heard Joy's heartbeat this morning, and it was beautiful! I'm still tearing up about it.

Me: I'm coming to your next appointment no matter what.

Holly: I can't wait. I still need to go shopping. I'm tired of walking around with the button of my pants open, and at some point, they're going to fall off me. Would you be up for a day of girl talk and shopping tomorrow?

Me: Yes, please!

Holly: Sounds great. We'll pick you up at ten.

Me: See you then.

I stare at the phone, and in my mind, I'm already browsing clothing racks with her and disclosing every horrible, confusing detail of what happened. I want to rush over to her place and spend the day on her couch, telling her what a jerk Cooper is being—trying to warn me off

Sumner and all—because he's not getting his way. I have a half a mind to storm into that office and tell him off, but I won't. This is my place of employment, not a high school cafeteria.

Grrr, being an adult sucks raw eggs sometimes.

Chapter 18

Cooper

"Cooper, Natalie," Archie says before we wrap up our meeting. "We're having a fundraiser for the Bedford Falls project on February twelfth. Holly and I would love it if you could both be there."

A fundraiser that's no doubt being overseen by Sumner Livingston. I want to go about as much as I want to jump off the Chrysler Building, wearing nothing but a Speedo and a Batman cape.

"I love fundraisers!" Natalie gushes. "Is there a theme?"

"It's a Harry Potter cosplay cruise on the Hudson," Archie says.

"That's different." I don't know what else to say. It's not something I would have chosen to go to in a million years.

"It is," Archie agrees. "But Sumner, our fundraiser, assures us it will be all the rage. He already has the yacht rented and a good number of guests invited."

"Count me in!" Natalie says. "I love to play dress-up!"

"What about you, Cooper? Can I put you down as a yes?"

"Um, yeah, sure. Why not?" As much as I'm not looking forward to it, I tell myself I'll be able to keep an eye on Toni. Maybe even get her to see Sumner for who he really is.

"Archie," Natalie says. "I wanted to go over some ideas with you about how you'd like the office space to look at Bedford Falls."

I take that as my cue and stand. "I'll catch up with you both later. I have a meeting with a tile supplier."

My stomach clenches as I leave the office and head into Toni's domain, but she's not at her desk. I don't linger; I hightail it out of there.

I'm on autopilot the rest of the day, doing what I'm supposed to, but with no real interest. I'm pulling up to my house when my phone rings.

"Cooper, it's your mother," my mom says.

Adelaide Flint is a brilliant woman, so I'm sure she knows what Caller ID is. Nonetheless, she persists in announcing herself every time we talk.

"Hi, Mom." I unlock the front door of my house and step inside. "How are you?"

"I'm doing well, thank you. How's work?" she asks in her "I'm trying to be supportive even though I vehemently disapprove" voice. It's like Cruella de Vil asking after your puppies. You want to think her interest is altruistic, but common sense won't let you.

"I'm great, thanks."

"Glad to hear it." No, she's not. "I'm calling because Willa has asked us to host a family brunch this Sunday. I know it's not a lot of notice, but she's ready for us to meet Ted."

"You haven't met him yet?"

"No. Why, have you?" She sounds borderline defensive.

"Nope. I assumed Willa would have brought him by to meet you and Dad by now."

Ignoring my jab, she clears her throat. "Brunch is at eleven. Can you make it?"

I'm not too sure she wants me to say yes, but since I love my sister (even though she can be an obnoxious know-it-all), I answer, "Sure. Can I bring anything?"

"Just yourself. I'm having it catered." Now she'll make her customary excuse for not being more domestic (as if I've ever cared). "I'd cook myself, but my patient roster is packed this week, and there's not enough time for me to prepare."

"I'm sure you're swamped." I go into the kitchen and flip on the lights.

"Always. I imagine you're busy, so I won't keep you."

"I'm not busy at all. I just got home." That's me being passive aggressive. She hates small talk almost as much as she despises my choice of career. Telling her I have time to chat will make her uncomfortable.

"Well, you're probably in need of a shower."

"Not really." I crouch to untie my work boots. "I spent the day doing paperwork, so I'm not as disgusting and sweaty as I usually am."

"Oh, well, I have about a dozen more calls to make."

If I really wanted to make her crazy, I'd talk about my new project, but I don't have the energy for the lecture that would likely ensue. "Okay, Mom, see you Sunday."

"Excellent," she says, then quickly follows that with, "Are you planning to bring anyone? I'm not trying to pry, but it's always best to give an accurate headcount to the caterers. We don't want to run out of crepes."

God forbid. "Nope, just me," I tell her, gut churning as thoughts of Toni pop into my mind.

After I hang up, I set my phone on the counter and stare at it. I'm fighting the temptation to scroll through my entire "relationship" with her. That would be a huge mistake, as it could lead to me either calling her to tell her off or confiding the truth about Sumner so I can convince her to dump him and give me a try. I'm not sure which would be worse.

The thought of her with that bastard has me completely torn up. He'll hurt her, I know he will, but she won't believe a word I say. She's already drunk his evil Kool-Aid.

I get a bottle of Stella from the fridge and twist the cap off while looking through the shelves for something to eat. All I have are ingredients, and I'm in no mood to cook. I decide to treat myself to a big juicy burger and fries.

Another evening of eating fast food in front of the TV. Alone. Yay.

"There you are!" Willa says, stepping aside to let me into our parents' massive Tudor-style home. She gives me a quick hug. "Thanks for dressing up."

"I thought I looked okay," I tell her, looking down at my dark jeans and light blue button-up shirt.

"You're fine," she says, "but you could have rethought the jeans."

"Should I go home and change?" I'm filled with excitement at the thought of leaving right now and not coming back.

"It's too late for that," she says as a short, skinny guy in chinos and a crisp, white dress shirt joins us.

He puts his left arm around her waist and holds out his right one to me. "Ted Lassiter."

My eyes flick down to his hand on my sister's waist, and my jaw tightens (which is ridiculous, as Willa is an adult, and they're already living together). There's just something about him I don't like. "Cooper."

"Oh!" he says, letting go of my sister. A smile spreads across his face. "Baby brother Cooper, the *working man*. Willa's told me so much about you."

"Has she?" I shrug off my coat. Why did he feel it necessary to point out that I'm a working man? Isn't he also a working man? Isn't every man with a job? I fight off the temptation to say something rude when a woman in a caterer's uniform takes my jacket and hangs it in the closet. "I'm sure she's said only good things about me."

"*Some* of it's been good," he says with a smirk.

This guy is a douchebag. "As the black sheep of the family, there's only so much success expected of me."

"Hey." Willa tilts her head in that condescending way of hers. "You could definitely make it as a lawyer."

I'm about to offer her a sarcastic thank you, but Ted cuts in with, "Or you could make it *with* a lawyer." She smacks him on his stomach, which immediately causes Ted to go into hurt puppy mode. "What? You said you wanted to set him up with Diane. I was trying to give you a smooth segue."

"Oh, sorry, babe." She gives him a lingering kiss. "Of course you were." When their disgusting display of PDA is finally over, she lets go of Ted and links arms with me. "Let's go find you a drink while I tell you about this terrific new lawyer at the firm."

We walk up the four steps from the enormous foyer into the expansive living room while I tune out my sister's description of the woman I *just have to meet*. A bar stands proudly in the far corner, where my parents only stock the best of the best.

Stepping up to the gleaming marble top, a man in uniform asks, "Mimosa?"

"Got anything stronger?" *Like pure grain alcohol?*

"I've been instructed to serve only champagne." He looks chagrined as I eye the bottles of Macallan behind him.

"Super. Hold the orange juice."

I wish I'd brought a fake date so I could avoid the conversation my sister is intent on having with me. While Howard—he's wearing a name tag—pours my drink, my mind wanders to Toni, and I briefly allow myself to wonder what she would make of my family. I'm guessing she'd hate it here as much as I do. I imagine her squeezing my hand to let me know I'm not alone. After we left, she'd listen patiently while I complained about my nearest and dearest. By the time I'd completely vented my spleen, I'd have forgotten all about how belittling they are, because I'd be with the one person who sees me for who I really am. The person who loves me for me.

Only she doesn't.

"… but don't let that fool you, because underneath it all is a heart of gold," Willa says.

Oh, God. Has she been talking this whole time? I probably should have been listening. The bartender slides my drink over on a cloth cocktail napkin.

"Anyway," she says impatiently. "What do you think? Can I give her your number?"

"Give who my number?" I ask, stalling.

"*Diane.* Have you not heard a word I said?" She narrows her eyes at me.

"Oh right, her." I pick up my drink and almost drain it. "I don't think so. It never works out for me and that type of woman."

"Why not?" she demands forcefully.

"I like to pick my own dates."

"I knew you were going to say that. But Diane isn't like the women Mom tries to set you up with. Her last boyfriend was a male stripper."

I blink, not having the first clue how to respond to that. Before I can conjure a reply, Ted sidles up to the bar and orders two mimosas, then grins at me. "Diane's a great girl. Lots of fun. And she isn't picky about who she dates." He gives me a conspiratorial wink, as if that's supposed to sell me on the idea. Spoiler alert: it doesn't.

"Cooper, you made it," Dad booms while crossing the room to join us. He and I exchange a quick, distant pat-on-the-back hug. "Your mom and I made a bet on whether you'd show up or not."

"Who won?" I ask, as in which one of them has enough faith in me to know I'm a man of my word?

"Your mother, of course." He aims his index finger at the bartender to indicate he wants another drink. "Never make bets with a psychiatrist when it comes to people." Turning to Willa, he adds, "Did you tell him about that woman at your firm?"

She nods. "He says no."

He sounds shocked. "But she sounds perfect for him, and she makes an absolute killing."

"I'm doing all right for myself," I interrupt. "I don't need to marry for money."

"You can never have enough money," he says pointedly.

Mom chooses that moment to join us from the kitchen, where she has no doubt been micromanaging the catering staff. "Cooper, you came!" She sticks her hand out to Dad, "You owe me a hundred bucks."

"Hi, Mom." I give her a hug, distracting her from making my dad pay up in front of me. I don't understand how my family can be so clueless.

She gives me her traditional embrace, with one sharp squeeze, then pushes me away and looks at my sister.

Before she can replay the entire conversation, I announce, "I'm not interested in dating Willa's coworker, even though I appreciate her looking out for me." Not. "I'm fully capable of finding women on my own."

"But this one's not going to be bothered by what you do," Mom says. "Her last boyfriend was a *male escort*."

"Stripper," my sister corrects.

"Right, stripper." Looking at me over her glasses, she adds, "A contractor is a step up from that."

"Just the one step?" I ask and run my teeth along my top lip.

"Don't be so sensitive, son. Act like a man." My father claps me sharply on the shoulder.

"Phillip, what did we say about toxic masculinity?" Mom asks him.

He offers a half shrug. "That it's bad for some reason?" He looks over at Ted. "My wife thinks I'm being sexist, but the truth is, I don't want women being all sensitive either."

Ted does what any guy who's sucking up to his girl-friend's dad would do. He laughs like it's the funniest thing he's ever heard. Then he seems to realize he also needs to impress our mother, because he suddenly stops and says, "I *also* know how important it is to find a healthy way to express one's feelings."

The doorbell rings, saving Dad and Ted from my

mother's reply. They both make a break for the front door, like a couple of wusses.

"Honestly," my mom says and sighs. "You'd think your father would know better."

"Men," Willa mutters.

"Pathetic." I polish off my second drink.

Much to my delight, I hear Rae-Anne's voice coming from the foyer. Finally, my only true ally has arrived.

I start over to her to share a moment of camaraderie, but Mom claps her hands together and announces, "Now that we're all here, let's go to the dining room."

Rae-Anne and I are seated next to each other at the end of the table (which we call "the kids' end," since we're usually the only two who don't show up to these brunches with a date). Neither one of us has an opportunity to say anything as the rest of the family monopolizes the conversation. Instead of talking, we eat.

Eggs Benedict with smoked salmon, home-cut hash browns, seasoned and fried to perfection, fresh fruit, blueberry sweet rolls with a lemon glaze, and an assortment of bite-size tarts and cookies. I consider telling my sister about seeing Sumner, but I don't want to bring it up. It'll only hurt her. My need to unload what's been happening in my life is not so strong I'd upset Rae over it.

As we're finishing our meals, Rae leans in and says, "According to Weight Watchers, I just ate a week's worth of points. Mom's been shooting daggers at me every time I put something else on my plate. What does she expect me to do? Come to one of these banquets and nibble on a corner of dry toast? Not likely, Adelaide. Not bloody likely."

The rest of the table is talking about who played the best Macbeth—according to my father, it's Peter O'Toole, but our mother isn't having it. She's an Ian McKellen fan. They'll be locked in this debate for a good five minutes, so I use the opportunity to tell Rae about Diane and how her history of slumming makes me a perfect fit for her.

"They said that?" she whispers, gesturing to the sweet rolls.

"Essentially." I reach for the platter and hold it in front of her so she can pick the best one. "The good news is Mom thinks my career is a step up from being a stripper. Dad also made sure to let me know she's loaded. You know, in case I'm as broke as they think I am."

"They always know exactly what to say to make their kids feel better. Mom called me three times this week to ask how my new weight-loss program was going." She rolls her eyes. "Under the guise of caring, of course."

"Speaking of caring, I need your help with something."

"Shoot." She licks icing off the tip of her finger.

"I need a costume for a work thing I have to go to. I was wondering if you could meet me at the store and help me pick one out."

She sits back and grins. "Who's the woman?"

"There's no woman." I sound defensive enough to alert her that there's most definitely a woman.

"Where did you not meet this woman you're trying so hard to impress that you've asked for your sister's advice?"

Dropping my shoulders, I tell her, "I thought there could have been something with a woman at the foundation, but it turns out she's interested in somebody else."

"In that case I better help you look your best so you can win her away from this lesser man." If she only knew. She lifts her phone off the table and opens her calendar. "I have time on Saturday morning at ten, but I'm only free for an hour."

Happy I don't have to do this on my own, I tell her, "An hour should be more than enough."

"Good, 'cause that's all you're getting."

Chapter 19

Toni

Holly sent me a text in the middle of the night, canceling our shopping plans. Her heartburn was so bad, she was having a hard time getting to sleep. She predicted she would be spending the whole day in bed. Note to self: consider adoption. My friend is making impending motherhood look super hard.

With a whole Saturday ahead of me, I have no idea what to do. If I don't stay busy, I'll sit around and obsess over the whole Sumner/Cooper debacle. Which I would probably have done anyway.

While I'm trying to decide if I should clean the bathroom or the kitchen first, my phone pings.

Sumner: Hello, Toni. How are you this morning?

Me: Great! How are you?

Sumner: Better, now that I'm chatting with you.

That's sweet. I think it's time to get to know Sumner better.

Me: I read an article about fun questions people just getting to know each other could ask. It's a twenty questions kind of thing. Want to play?

Sumner: I guess.

Me: Okay, question: If your family had a motto, what would it be?

Sumner: Never invest your own money.

Huh. I'm not sure what that means. Maybe it's a rich person motto?

Sumner: What about you?

I think about the answer I gave to Cooper, and for some reason I don't feel as comfortable sharing it with Sumner.

Me: In for a penny, in for a pound. When my family makes a decision, they put themselves entirely into it.

Sumner: That's admirable, as long as they're known for making good decisions.

I don't suppose now would be the time to mention the year Mom decided to raise minks to turn into a coat. Due to space, she could only get two at a time. When it came time to euthanize them, she was too attached to Pinky and the Brain and couldn't do it. Being that she'd need a minimum of thirty-five minks to make a coat, she decided to donate them to a local school. Good decisions are kind of hit-or-miss in my family.

Me: What's your all-time favorite song?
Sumner: "Music of the Night" from Phantom of the Opera.

Me: That is not what I was expecting.

Sumner: What were you expecting?

Me: I don't know, maybe something by Arcade Fire that reminds you of your college days.

Sumner: I did love "Reflektor" back in my pub crawl phase.

I wait for him to ask me the same question, but instead he writes: What's your next question?

Me: What's your favorite board game from when you were a kid?

Sumner: Sorry! But between you and me, I was never sorry.

Me: Ha! Okay, favorite television show?

Sumner: Succession.

Me: What would you like to know about me?

Sumner: I don't know. Let me think for a minute.

Sumner: …

Sumner: …

Sumner: What Disney character do you want to be?

Me: Um, you mean like a Disney princess? I'd have to say Merida from Brave. I like that she's so tough.

Sumner: Good answer. What's something you don't want to ask but you really want to know?

Me: Ooh, juicy question.

Sumner: I thought so.

Before I can change my mind, I ask: How do you and Cooper know each other?

Sumner: …

Sumner: …

Me: I'm only asking because I have a feeling there's a story there.

Sumner: There's a story all right. The guy's a psycho. I dated his sister briefly. It ended the night he slashed my tires.

Cooper slashed his tires? I stare at the words, finding it hard to reconcile the Cooper I know with this information.

Me: What the hell???

Sumner: He doesn't like anyone touching his sisters. We were in the car at the time. He happened to walk up on a moment that wasn't exactly PG13.

My heart pounds, and I can't help wondering if this is something Archie needs to know. If Cooper is unstable, it could create a problem for the foundation. He doesn't seem like the type to resort to something so … primal, but maybe I don't know him at all.

Sumner: I wasn't going to say anything, because it's unprofessional of me to speak badly of him, but I care about you, and I want you to know who you're dealing with.

Me: It's wow, shocking.

Sumner: It shocked the hell out of me at the time, that's for sure.

Me: Did you press charges?

Sumner: I didn't want to humiliate his sister and the rest of the family. I made a quiet exit.

Me: Under the circumstance, I'd say that was the kindest thing you could do.

Sumner: I thought so.

$\sim$

I can't get Sumner's story out of my mind. I'm furious on his behalf, as I imagine what it would be like to be inside a car while some raging maniac slashes your tires. He and Cooper's sister must have been terrified.

That's the kind of thing my ex, Joey, would have done. Total caveman move.

Thank God I didn't let myself get mixed up with Cooper and discovered the mix-up when I did. It goes to show that changing my ways was the right thing to do.

Chapter 20

Cooper

"Thanks for meeting me, Rae." Based on her red cheeks and nose, she's been standing in front of Ruth's Costume Emporium for a while.

"No problem," Rae-Anne says with a deadpan expression. "It's not like I work seventy-two hours a week or anything."

"I wouldn't have asked if it wasn't important." I open the door and gesture for her to go ahead. Warm, stale air greets us, along with what I'm pretty sure is the soundtrack from *Gladiator*. Lots of dramatic effect. "You're the only one in the family who knows anything about Harry Potter, so it was either you or calling Aunt Helen to see if one of the twins could help me out." The twins are creepy sixteen-year-old girls who whisper to each other all the time in some weird made-up language they share. Either that, or they stare into each other's eyes, then nod as if they're having a conversation in their shared brain. As a rule, we don't talk about them. We also avoid them whenever possible.

Rae convulses in horror at having to talk to the twins about anything. "I've got forty-five minutes before my Pilates class, so let's get to it."

"Don't worry, I have no intention of spending a second longer here than I have to."

"Ahem." The voice behind me causes me to jump.

I see possibly the shortest woman in Queens. She's dressed like Tinker Bell, complete with a bright yellow wig and green dress; she's clearly offended by what I said. Giving her a sheepish grin, I say, "Hi. I'm looking for a costume for—"

"Let me guess: a Harry Potter cosplay dinner cruise?"

I tilt my head in surprise. "Yes."

"Your future cruise-mates have been my only clients this week. Well, except for the usual furries." She gives me the once-over, then does the same to Rae-Anne.

"I thought I got here in plenty of time. The cruise isn't for another two weeks."

"Because everyone wants to be who they want to be. The only way to ensure that is to pick your outfit early."

I can't imagine that degree of devotion to a cosplay event.

Tinker Bell spins on her little green slippers and starts toward the back of the shop. "I think I still have a slutty Hermione costume left, but I'm afraid there's not much available in men's sizes. I can't get you two into a couples' costume. If you wanted to go as a matching pair, you should have come in at least a week ago."

"We're not a couple," Rae tells her as we follow Tink. "He's my brother. I'm here to make sure he doesn't look like a total ass. It's his first date with the woman of his dreams."

"No, it's not." We pass the *Star Wars* aisle. "It's a work function."

"Where you will see the woman of your dreams," she reminds me.

I say to Tinker Bell, "It's business, not romance."

Tink stops and turns to Rae. "I'm not buying it. Are you buying it?"

Grinning down at her, Rae says, "Nope. He definitely wants to play hide the wand with someone."

Now that my sister and the shop girl have bonded, the two of them giggle away while we pass the trampy vampire aisle and finally arrive in Harry Potter hell. Tink wasn't kidding. It's been picked over to the point where only a few costumes hang among a bunch of empty rods. No matter; I'll grab glasses and a tie, paint a lightning bolt on my forehead, and say I'm Harry.

"In your size I've only got Dumbledore or Mad-Eye Moody," Tink tells me.

"Mad-Eye Moody?"

The shop girl points to my other option, which is a long medium-gray robe with a strange hat topped with a ball and tassel.

"I'm not wearing that," I say. "It's got lace on the hem. I'll go as that mad guy."

Tinker Bell gets up on her tiptoes and plucks a long brown coat off a hanger. "Try this on while I fetch the rest of it. We have to keep the eyes in back, or people steal them."

She flits off and I slip on the coat and look at myself in the mirror. "Not bad. At least it's not covered in lace."

"Yes, but I'm not sure you're getting the full effect." She picks up a tall staff capped with a skull and hands it to me.

Okay! This is pretty manly. I pretend I'm casting a spell with it.

"Here's your wig and the glass eye," Tink, who has snuck up on me again, says.

"Wig?" I ask, staring at her hand.

"Mad-Eye's a total ginger," Rae tells me.

"Um, maybe not," I say, second-guessing the entire plan. I should forget about this and cancel. Maybe move to Tibet to live among the monks for a few years. That lifestyle sounds so much less complicated than what I've got going on right now.

"Try it on," Tink says. "It's the only way you'll know if you like it."

I duck my head and allow her to put on the weird glass eye and adjust my wig. When I show my sister, I'm assaulted with a blinding flash.

"Got it," she says, staring at her phone screen.

"Do not send that to anyone," I tell her in a menacing brother tone.

"Too late. Willa and Lily are likely killing themselves laughing already." She lets out a loud burst of laughter before adding, "You really do look hilarious."

"I'm so glad I asked you to come with me." My head is already hot and itchy, and the eye patch is heavy and uncomfortable. I move to the mirror and bump into a display of Quidditch brooms. I have zero peripheral vision on that side. "Do I have to wear the eye patch?"

"It's the whole point of the costume," Tink says.

"It may not be the safest choice on a boat, though," Rae says, glancing at me, then laughing some more.

Flipping up the eye patch, I look around for something cooler to wear. "What if I get a cape from the vampire section and one of the brooms? That ought to be good enough, no?"

"A vampire cape?" Rae gasps. "First of all, witches and wizards wear robes, not capes, and second, you do not want to show up out of costume for this kind of thing."

Tink nods. "She's right. If it's a work thing, you don't want to look like you're just throwing it together."

Why am I doing this again? Oh, yeah, so I can see Toni and hopefully catch her witnessing Sumner at his finest. Which I can't do if I'm in an eye patch, bumping into everything.

"All right, let's try the Dumbledore costume." I hand the eye patch and wig back to Tinker Bell.

"I'll go get the beard," she says excitedly.

I remove the jacket and stare longingly at the empty "Gryffindor Robes" shelf.

"Tell me about this woman?" Rae asks.

"I already told you, she's interested in somebody else. There's no point in telling you anything because nothing is going to happen between us."

"I guess there's no point in my staying then," she says. "If I go now, I can grab a quick espresso on my way to the Pilates studio."

"You can't leave me," I tell her, panicked.

"Then out with it," she says, folding her arms.

"Fine. Her name is Toni. I thought she liked me, and we had been texting for a while, but it turns out she thought she was texting a different guy at the office, which is bizarre because he's pretty much my complete opposite."

She tucks her lips between her teeth, trying not to laugh.

"What?" My irritation level is at a nine.

"Nothing." She spins around to look at miniature sorting hats.

"Something's obviously funny."

"I was thinking of all the times you went on and on

about us girls wanting what we couldn't have." There's a twinkle in her eye that says she'll be calling Willa and Lily as soon as she leaves so they can laugh at their idiot younger brother.

"What does that have to do with anything?"

"It seems like that's where you are right now. You're only going on this cruise to try to win over this woman, even though you tell me you can't have her. I've never seen you like this, all bothered over someone who isn't throwing herself at your feet." She's definitely enjoying this.

"Nobody throws themselves at my feet," I say and purse my lips.

"Angelina Webber?"

"Oh, for …" I shake my head in exasperation. "That was senior year in high school, and she was clinically insane."

"Lovesick is more like it," Rae teases. "Like the entire cheerleading squad." Putting on a girly tone, she adds, "Is Cooper your brother? He's *soooo* dreamy. Does he have a girlfriend?"

"That happens to every guy on every high school football team in America. I've been shot down plenty of times since then."

"But not like this," she says, taking careful aim and hitting her target with pinpoint accuracy. "You like this one, and it's killing you that she doesn't like you back."

"I'll get over it. Where's Tinker Bell? I don't have all day."

"She's right here," Tink says, giving me another jump scare. She really should add bells to those slippers. She thrusts a long gray beard and wig at me. "Here you go, Albus."

Three minutes later, I gaze at myself in the mirror while Rae shakes with amusement. I wonder how in the hell I let things go this far. I'm going on a cosplay cruise to stop the woman I want from being hurt by Sumner Livingston.

Sighing, I mutter, "This is my life now."

Rae nods. "I'm so happy I got to see it."

Chapter 21

Toni

I told Archie I'd meet him at the job site today to get an update on Bedford Falls and toss some ideas back and forth. I appreciate how much he values my opinion and am really looking forward to jumping into this project. The only downside is that I will almost certainly run into Cooper, and I'd rather lick the pavement than have another painful scene like we had at the office the other day. I feel horrible for leading him on, but now that I know he's a tire-slashing thug, I'm anxious to put some distance between us.

I decide to fortify myself en route with Mr. Bagel. I'll pick up some to take with me, too. That way I can eat another one when I get to the warehouse. It's a good thing I'm wearing leggings and an oversized sweater; I can let my stomach pooch out with no one the wiser. Carbs are my love language, my comfort language, my coping mechanism.

When I leave my apartment building, the blustery wind greets me like a smack to the face. Pulling my scarf across my mouth, I keep my head down and rush to my destination. I'm still focused on the pavement when I open the door to Mr. Bagel. For this reason, I don't realize I'm about to run into someone until I'm knocked back.

Strong hands reach out to steady me, then I hear, "Toni, is that you?"

"Sumner, hi." I look up at him. "Fancy meeting you here." He's slick looking in his dark suit with a cashmere overcoat and wingtips.

"Archie turned me on to this place. I've become something of an addict." He holds up a small brown bag.

"You didn't come here when you were a kid?" Mr. Bagel is a New York City fixture.

"Um, no."

"But you grew up around here, didn't you?"

"Forest Hills." Before I can question how it's possible he's never been to Mr. Bagel, he says, "I can't get enough of these things. My trainer is going to have complaints."

"You have a trainer?"

"Gotta stay in shape for the ladies." Sumner gives me a slow wink.

"Well, it shows," I announce boldly.

"You're looking lovely today." His smile makes my stomach flutter.

I'm wearing leggings, riding boots, and the biggest turtleneck sweater in my closet. "I was in the mood to be extra cozy today."

"You look like one of those women in a commercial for fancy pumpkin-spiced coffees. All you need is a book in your hand and a golden retriever."

I laugh. "And a fancy coffee."

"That, too. Do they serve them here? Maybe I could get you one."

"I'm pretty sure they only have plain coffee."

"How about letting me buy you a bagel, and we sit down and eat together?"

This sounds suspiciously like a date, which is not what we're supposed to be doing at this stage of the game. "As much as I'd love to, I'm meeting Archie at the job site. I stopped in for a little sustenance."

"Come on, one bagel as colleagues. I won't flirt with you, I promise."

I glance at my watch. I have time. And if I leave now, I'll get to the site ahead of Archie, which means potentially being alone with Cooper. "Sure, why not?"

After ordering, we sit at a small table near the front window. The heat is blowing on us from an overhead vent, but my left side is freezing from a draft along the floor. I tuck the bag carrying a box of assorted bagels off to the side, then place my everything feast with extra cream cheese, lox, and capers in front of me.

Sumner takes a plain bagel out of the bag, and we dig in. Neither of us says anything as we enjoy the first few bites.

Finally, Sumner groans. "Mmm … This is worth all the extra push-ups I'll have to do later."

I chuckle and wipe my mouth. "Or you could do like I do and start wearing bigger clothes."

He gives me a quick once-over. "Whatever you're doing, keep it up. You're the full package."

My face turns hot with embarrassment and maybe a little something else. Could it be desire? "I thought you said no flirting."

"Right, sorry." He holds his hands up in surrender.

"You're making the 'let's take it slow' thing kind of hard though. But when you're ready to seal the deal, I'll take my time."

Once upon a time, a promise like that might have gotten my motor running, but not anymore. My expression must convey my thoughts because he hastens to say, "I'm sorry, that sounded much better in my head. I was trying to let you know how much I like you, but it came off as creepy."

"It kind of did." I wipe my mouth with a napkin.

"Do you think you can find it in your heart to give me another chance?"

Who doesn't say the wrong thing from time to time? If people wrote me off every time I did that, I'd have no friends. "Of course."

He gives me a big smile. "You won't regret it, Toni."

I hope not.

The rest of our conversation goes well. We discuss a wide variety of things, from the best place for pizza—a huge topic of debate among New Yorkers—and our favorite things to do in Central Park. Mine is eating hot dogs while sitting on a bench by the fountain. His is horse-back riding, which he promises we'll do together someday.

After we've finished eating, I glance at the time and say, "I should get going."

"How about I give you a lift? That way we can keep getting to know each other."

"That would be great." I've never owned a car. The truth is, I don't even know how to drive. My dad is a firm believer that New York City is no place to put a kid behind the wheel.

"I assure you, the pleasure is all mine," he says, jingling his keys.

Turns out Sumner drives a black Porsche with red leather interior. The inside is roomier than it looks, but our shoulders pretty much touch the entire twenty-minute ride to the job site. I try hard not to be impressed by the heated, soft leather seats or by his ability to maneuver through traffic so effortlessly. But darn it, this ride is a huge step up from Joey's twenty-year-old pickup with the nearly non-existent shocks and a glove box that wouldn't stay closed.

I'm careful to keep the conversation about business. We mainly talk about the Valentine's weekend cruise until he throws me this curveball: "What are you doing tonight?"

"A long bath and probably *The Office* reruns."

"Might I be able to persuade you to come with me to Valentino's for dinner?" Giving me a delicious smile, he says, "They're catering our fundraiser, and I have to go for a tasting. I'd like to get your opinion on the menu."

"Oh, um, it's just that …" *It sounds like a date.*

"I haven't given you any notice, but it has to be tonight." He turns off the road and pulls up in front of the office trailer. "I leave tomorrow for Philadelphia, where I'm doing an event for the American National Cattle-Women. I'll be gone a week."

"American National CattleWomen?" I can't help laughing. "What are they doing in Philadelphia?"

"They took a vote on where to have their convention, and the Liberty Bell won out over Hawaii, if you can believe it."

"I can't. I'd take palm trees and beaches over Phil-adelphia in the winter any day of the week." I add a theatrical shiver to emphasize my point.

"Yes, well, you're obviously not an American National CattleWoman." I giggle. "What about Valentino's tonight?"

"I don't know. It sort of sounds like a date."

After he parks, he adds, "Work only, promise. I could use your help. How am I to choose between oysters and calamari without assistance?"

How indeed? Gathering my purse and box of bagels, I say, "I guess that would be okay. What time?"

"The reservation is at seven, but the restaurant is in Manhattan. Why don't I pick you up at six?"

I give him my address and reach for the door handle. I'm about to open it when Sumner says, "Don't move." He hops out and rushes around to the passenger side, then opens the door with a flourish. "Milady." He holds out a hand to me.

Chuckling, I place my fingers in his. He pulls me harder than is strictly necessary, and I practically fly into his arms. My breath hitches as I gaze up at him.

We're definitely sharing a moment when a slamming sound makes me jump. Cooper is coming down the steps to his office and stops dead in his tracks long enough for Sumner to say, "I'm looking forward to tonight."

"Me, too."

Cooper shoots us both a look of death before storming off in the direction of the warehouse.

"Uh-oh," Sumner mutters. "He's not related to the Hulk, is he?"

"Not that I know of." Cooper did look like he was on the verge of coming unglued, and I can suddenly picture him vandalizing a car.

"Thank God. These tires cost a small fortune," he smirks. "I better run. Have a wonderful day, Toni."

"Thanks for the ride. And the bagel." He pulls out of the parking lot, and I try to decide whether to wait for Archie in the office with that nice Yuma or go into the warehouse, where I'll be alone with Cooper. There's an angel on my shoulder telling me to go the trailer, but the devil wants to put an end to all this craziness, and she seems to be in charge at the moment.

Chapter 22

Cooper

To say I'm angry enough to spit bullets would be an understatement. When Toni was texting with me, the rule was that there would be no dating for three weeks. Then she shows up at the job this morning in Sumner's car? What are the chances they just bumped into each other this morning? The thought of them spending the night together turns my stomach, but it looks like that's what happened.

I pick up a sledgehammer and use my frustration to demo the interior wall I had planned to leave for my crew. I'll be a sweaty mess for my meeting with Archie, but I couldn't care less. Each time my hammer connects with brick, a tiny bit of anger is extinguished. When I'm done, I see Toni staring in my direction.

"What did that wall do to you?" she asks, sounding apprehensive.

"If you're going to be in here, you'll need a hardhat

and safety glasses." I point to the cubby by the door. "And you might want to stay back."

Pulling my safety goggles back in place, I go to the next wall slated for demolition and slam the hammer into it so hard, my whole body practically vibrates. I hit it again and again, until my brow is covered in sweat and my arms are shaking from the effort. I pause to catch my breath. Toni is sitting at the far end of the building at a worktable. She's moved plans aside and has set up a bagel station. That's just great. Here I am trying to hate her, and she's being thoughtful.

Sliding my goggles off, I walk over and pick up a bagel, then slather it in cream cheese and salmon. As I shove it into my mouth, she says, "I brought bagels for everyone."

"Looks that way," I say with a full mouth.

"You're welcome," she snaps and crosses one long, black-clad leg over the other.

I should have thanked her, but I'm pretty sure the less I say to her, the better. But then I can't help myself. "It looks like things are going well between you and Sumner." I say his name like he's Adolf Hitler.

"Mm-hmm."

What kind of answer is that? "No more taking things slow, huh?"

She pushes her chair back so abruptly, it scrapes the concrete floor, making a nails-on-a-chalkboard screech. Standing, she raises her voice. "Why exactly would that be any of your business?"

"It's not," I say casually. "I'm trying to figure out whether I can trust you or not. We have to work together, and so far I'm disappointed to discover you're not a woman of your word."

"Not a ..." she sputters. "It was a misunderstanding,

Cooper, and as soon as I found out about it, I told you what happened."

"That's not what I'm talking about." I take a big bite of the bagel. Damn, that's a good bagel. "I'm talking about you lying to me."

"I lied? Are you kidding? I *never* lied to you."

I make her wait for an answer while I chew, swallow, and wipe my mouth with a napkin. "Sure you did. You told me the foundation has a strict rule against employee dating, but Archie told me differently."

She turns red and averts her eyes.

I move toward her until I'm practically standing on her feet. "You also told me there would be no actual dates until we'd been texting for three weeks. Based on what I just saw, it seems like that was a lie, too."

She lifts her chin and startles at how close I am. "I'm not sure what you think you saw, but again, how is it any of your business?"

"I saw you getting out of that asshole's car, and I heard him tell you he'd pick you up again tonight for more of … whatever you two are doing."

"What we're doing is none of your concern." She glares at me. "And calling a colleague names is pretty immature."

I am so conflicted, I can't find the words I need. Here's a woman I really like, and she's dating a guy I know isn't close to good enough for her. But she doesn't want to hear the truth. Taking a deep breath, I inhale the faint spicy fragrance of her perfume. I should be angry, but what I want to do is pull Toni into my arms and hold her close.

She stands. "You're acting like an ass."

"Says the woman who just said name-calling is imma-ture." I'm pretty sure I'm smirking.

"You *are* being immature." She crosses her arms.

"Throwing your sledgehammer around like you're two and it's your binky."

She's not wrong.

We stare at each other, both of us breathing heavily. I can't decide if I want to keep fighting with her or kiss her senseless.

Archie opens the door and heads our way. "Hello, you two. Sorry I'm late."

Toni and I simultaneously back away from each other. While I feel like an idiot for my childish behavior, Toni clears her throat, and in a surprisingly calm voice—as though we weren't just in the middle of a ridiculous argument—says, "I brought bagels."

"Thanks, but I already ate."

"My guys should be here in about twenty minutes," I tell Archie. "It's going to get noisy after that, so anything you need to discuss, you should do it now." I don't even look at her.

Archie takes off his gloves. "In that case, maybe you can give us a quick tour of what's been going on."

For the next fifteen minutes, I fight to stay focused on the conversation. I want to know what Sumner told Toni about me. There's no way he shared the truth about our history—not about why I no longer speak to him, anyway. She probably thinks I'm some raging lunatic who needs to attend anger management classes every week.

She jots down notes for Archie. He says something that makes her laugh, and I find myself wishing we could go back to the beginning and start over. I have no idea what I'd do differently, but I'd make damn sure not to end up where we are now.

Chapter 23

Toni

"Valentino's?" Holly asks. "That sounds suspiciously like a date."

I have her on speakerphone while I rush around the bathroom in search of my favorite lipstick, Addictive Rouge. I finished giving her the lowdown on running into Sumner at Mr. Bagel and how he gave me a ride to the job site, skipping over what happened with Cooper. No good can come from talking about him with my fiercely loyal bestie, who also happens to be married to Cooper's and my boss. What if she insists on firing him? As tempting as that sounds, it would be bad for the project.

Ah, found it! I run the tube of lipstick over my lips before saying, "It's totally a work thing, with a side order of seeing what dating might be like. But it is *not* a date."

"Gotcha. Sumner seems like a good guy, and it seems you two have been hitting it off."

"He's a grownup." I blot my lips on a tissue. "It's nice to be with one for once in my life." Unlike some immature people I know. *I'm talking to you, Cooper.*

"You deserve a grownup."

"I do." I twirl so that my red dress spins out at my reflection in the mirror. "Sumner is smart, funny, responsible, and thoughtful."

"Sounds like he checks all your boxes," Holly says, then adds, "Does he? Check *all* your boxes?"

I burst out laughing. "Some boxes aren't going to get checked until I get to know him better."

"Fine, but when that happens, I'll need details."

It's a couple of minutes to six. "Perv," I joke. "He's going to be here any second though, so I'd better run."

"Have fun," Holly says in a sing-song voice. "But not too much fun."

"You look amazing," Sumner says as soon as I exit the building. He's leaning against his car and watches me walk down the steps to the sidewalk. The wind has calmed, and the sky is clear and dark, giving the stars a perfect backdrop to shine.

"You don't look so bad yourself." He's wearing a navy suit jacket with a pair of gray slacks. Every hair on his head is perfectly in place. He almost looks too good to be true.

Sumner glides toward me and holds out his hand. I let him lead me to the passenger side so he can open the door for me. This is what I've been waiting for: a gentleman.

A bouquet of pink roses is on the seat. I look at him with a *Really? For me?* face.

He nods. "Those are 'I appreciate my new work colleague' flowers, in case you thought I was trying to turn this into a date."

I pick them up, slide into the car, and touch one of the

soft, cool petals while I wait for him to get in. "They're lovely. Thank you."

"You're welcome." He starts the engine and peels away from the sidewalk. A squeal, followed by a quick burst of laughter, erupts from me. "Wait until you see the flowers you get once we're dating."

"Oh, yeah? Will they be orchids or something?"

"Or something." He quickly changes lanes to get around a slow-moving bus. "On the romcom scale, what number would you give our budding relationship? One through ten …" he prods.

"At least an eight." I love a man who can talk romcoms.

"That's solid, but I'm going to work on raising that score until we get to a solid ten."

"A ten is Bridget Jones. I'm not sure that's possible in real life."

"Let's see, shall we?" He presses down on the accelerator, and we whizz past all the other traffic. It's exhilarating if not a bit frightening.

"Right this way," the maître d', Paulo, says, and leads us through the dimly lit restaurant. I can't help but notice all the tables are for two, and the other patrons look like they're on dates.

Sumner holds my chair out for me before turning to the waiter. "We'll have a bottle of the 2010 Jaboulet Domaine de Terre Ferme Châteauneuf du Pape."

I have no idea what that is, but it sounds impressive. Before Paulo can walk away, Sumner tells him, "We're here for a catering tasting."

Paulo's expression morphs to understanding. "Ah, for your wedding?"

"This beautiful woman is not my fiancée—yet." He winks at me. "We're hosting a fundraiser for the Faith Foundation."

"Ah yes, the homeless village. Chef was telling me about it this morning. I know he has wonderful items for you to try."

"We're looking forward to being spoiled," I announce.

"I specialize in being spoiled," Sumner says. "It'd better be good."

Paulo gives us a shallow bow, then hurries to the kitchen, leaving me and my not-a-date alone. "You specialize in being spoiled, do you?"

"I was fortunate to grow up as a child of privilege. As such I accept only the best." I feel he's talking about me, and I flush at the compliment.

The rest of the evening is nothing short of wonderful. We're given dozens of sample-size dishes to taste, along with the wines that pair well with them. I start out taking notes, but by the end of the meal, I'm so buzzed, I'm not sure if I can spell my name. I slam back the remnants of my fourth wine sample. "My favorite wine was the Jabba de Hut Papa Smurf."

Sumner's cheeks are flushed, and his eyes have a glassy look, but he's nowhere near as gone as I am. I'm guessing he has a much bigger alcohol tolerance than I do. "You mean the Jaboulet Domaine de Terre Ferme Châteauneuf du Pape?" He laughs.

"I don't know. Is that what I mean?" The tip of my toe touches his under the table, and I give it a less than gentle tap. I've got no game when I'm drunk.

Our waiter arrives with the bill, and Sumner hands over his black card. "How are we going to get home?"

"I haven't even thought about it. Are you too wasted to drive?"

"Not wasted, per se, but I've definitely had more than I should." He looks at our waiter, who is putting our card through on the handheld payment device. "Will my Porsche be okay in the lot under the building for the night?"

"It should be fine, sir. We've had a number of guests leave their vehicles overnight and have never had any complaints."

"Perfect." Sumner takes his card back and stands. "Come on, work friend, let's get you home."

It takes a few minutes to get a cab, but I don't even notice the chilly night air. Good wine will do that to you. After sucking in a long, deep breath, I'm aware of a feeling of contentment I haven't felt in a long time. Maybe this is what love is. Fancy dates, flowers, a little too much wine on a Thursday night.

I'm jolted out of my reverie when he opens the cab door and steps aside to let me in. After we're settled, the cabbie asks, "Where to?"

Sumner looks at me. "Your place or mine?"

My mouth drops open, and I'm suddenly sober. "I thought I was clear when I …"

He puts his hand on my knee. "I'm just kidding. We'll get you home first, then me." He tells the cabbie, "Cross the Queensboro Bridge, and we'll go from there."

I'm not sure, but I suspect he hasn't given up on the thought of us getting out at the same destination. "Thank you," I say tentatively.

"This cab ride is going to cost an absolute fortune, but you're worth it." Sumner leans his head against the seat back.

"That's sweet of you." I'm uncomfortable that he's bringing up the cost of taking a cab.

He squeezes my knee again before lifting an arm. "Snuggle in here so I can keep you warm."

I do it, because quite frankly, the cashmere coat he's wearing is too cozy to resist. I'm also tipsy, and he's ridiculously handsome. And maybe this is something that might last.

After he puts his arm around me, I close my eyes and drift off into a lovely little nap. I don't open my eyes until the cab stops.

"There she is," he says. "Sleeping Beauty awakens."

"Sorry," I tell him, picking up my purse. "I didn't mean to doze off like that."

"I thoroughly enjoyed the feeling of you sleeping in my arms." He tells the driver to give him a minute. He opens the door and gets out, then helps me out.

As we stand on the doorstep, he says, "Should I tell him"—he gestures with his head to the cab—"to leave? I am heading off to battle in the morning."

I purse my lips. "You're going to Philadelphia to raise money for some ranchers."

"Exactly," he says with a sexy grin. "So …?" He gestures to my building, trying to charm me into sleeping with him. "Send the cabbie off to his next fare?"

"Not unless you want to sleep on the sidewalk," I answer sharply. He is practically perfect, if not for the fact that he's pushing so hard to move things along between us.

"Had to try." He offers me that Prince Charming grin of his. It softens my irritation but doesn't quite douse it.

"Good night, Sumner."

"Good night, Toni. Dream of me while I'm away," he says with a mock dramatic flourish and walks down the steps.

"You're a very bad man. You know that, right?"

"Yes, but it's only because you're so darn hard to resist." He opens the back door to the cab. "See you in a week, fair Toni."

I chuckle. "Good luck with those cattle women."

Chapter 24

Cooper

Natalie: Coop, I got a line on discount windows. My distributor is changing manufacturers, and they're clearing everything out. We need to act now though, to get them. Meet me at Anderson's in an hour?

Me: I'll be there.

I check the time, then dash over to my foreman, Tristan, to let him know I have to leave for a while. In the last week, we've managed to knock down the warehouse and get a good start on jackhammering the old cement floor. It's loud and messy, but I love every second of it, because every inch of progress we make means the village is taking shape. In a month, this site will look nothing like it does now. By the end of the summer, a new neighborhood will exist where I'm currently standing. Homes for people who need them.

I've had to tell myself frequently about how important

this work is, and it's worth whatever frustration I have to deal with regarding Toni and her stupid choice of men. While she's not now, nor ever has been, mine, I can't get my heart to accept it.

I enter the trailer, and Yuma looks up from her computer. "You're still in the overly-positive-pretending-everything's-fine phase?"

My shoulders drop. "Who's pretending? Everything *is* fine."

She does nothing to mask the *tsk*ing sound she so loves to make when she's sure she's right and I'm wrong. It's actually surprising how often that occurs. "Keep telling yourself that until it's true."

"Thanks, I will." I take a fresh T-shirt out of a desk drawer. "I have to get washed up. I'm meeting Natalie shortly. She's got a line on deeply discounted windows."

Yuma nods. "As long as that's all you're doing with her."

"Boundaries, Yuma. Boundaries." I walk past her into the tiny bathroom.

"I wanted to make sure you know she's not right for you," she says loudly when I shut the door. While changing shirts, I wonder why I hired her. She's like a nosey sister, except I pay her.

It takes longer than it should to wash my face with this beard. I should shave it off, but by the time I get home, I don't seem to have the energy. My mother would diagnose me with some sort of blue-collar, identity crisis disorder, but she would be wrong. I'm pretty sure I'm depressed, and it's sucking all the energy out of me.

～

"Cooper, there you are," Natalie says, striding across the showroom floor. "I got here a few minutes early to scope out what's left, and I have to say I'm thrilled. We might actually be able to get all the windows we need for the entire village at cost."

"At cost—those words are music to my ears."

Looping her arm through mine, she steers me to a display in back. She's showing me the windows she's interested in when we're interrupted by someone.

"Natalie, hello. It certainly didn't take you long to get here," he says.

"Yes, well, when you call to tell me there's a deal, I know to come running." She approaches him with her arms out.

After giving each other quick air kisses, Natalie introduces us. "Hans, this is Cooper Flint. He's the contractor building all those tiny homes I was telling you about. Cooper, this is Hans, the embodiment of style and class."

"Oh, I like that," Hans says, grinning broadly. "I'm going to have that printed on my next set of business cards." He looks back and forth between us for a second. "I'm sensing some sort of connection between you two."

Natalie's face turns bright pink. "No connection. We just love working together."

"Are you sure? Because I have a sixth sense about these things, and if I'm not mistaken, there is a delicious opposites attract, high-class-city-girl-meets-hunky-country-boy vibe going on here."

I should have sent Yuma to look at the windows. "We're just friends. Natalie can do a heck of a lot better than me."

"He's perfect for you, Nat," Hans says. "You should give this man a try."

"I don't have much time today, so we should probably get on with it," I say, hoping I successfully side-stepped that minefield. I do not need the complication of dating someone with whom I have a tight working relationship.

An hour later, Natalie and I leave the store, a little high off the great deal we just scored. I accompany her to her car and wait while she searches for her keys. "Archie and Holly are going to be really happy when they find out how much money you saved them today. Good job."

She grins up at me. "Now we can afford that fountain I have my eye on."

"Or they might want to put the money into the next village. Archie said something about finding their next location before the end of the month."

She finally finds her keys. "Now that we've got our windows, maybe we should talk about Hans and his whole 'love match' idea." She pauses, looking shy. "We like each other and work really well together. And, drum roll, please … we're both finally single at the same time. What do you say?"

The more she talks, the more she's got me thinking this might be a good idea. She's a beautiful woman. She's fun, smart, and driven. She's seen me at my sweaty messiest, and that doesn't seem to be an issue. "Why don't we start with dinner and see where that takes us."

"Good idea. It's important we agree that whatever happens, we need to be able to continue our mutually beneficial working relationship."

"Agreed."

"I know this great place that just opened up called The Skate Club. It's meant to look like an arcade and roller rink from the eighties, except there's no actual roller skating because they serve alcohol. They have the best burgers, possibly anywhere in the world, and if you like dancing, they have a great DJ—old school stuff that gets your heart going."

"What if dancing isn't my thing?"

"They also have pool tables and arcade games."

"That sounds fun." I could use a night off from being home alone, thinking about Toni. "Does tonight work for you?"

"It does." She sounds pleased. "Pick me up around seven?"

"Perfect. See you then."

"This place is great," I tell Natalie after we finish our dinner of burgers and fries. We head to a room at the back of the restaurant called the Fun Zone. It's massive, with dark walls and disco balls spinning above the wooden dance floor. The perimeter is lined with vintage arcade games, pinball machines, and pool tables.

"What do you want to do first?" she asks. "You indicated that dancing wasn't your bag, but how about just one?"

Though I'd much rather hit the arcade games, I say, "Sure."

"Gonna Make You Sweat" by C+C Music Factory is playing, and the dance floor is packed. Grabbing my hand, Natalie cuts a swath through the rest of the revelers. When we're right under the biggest disco ball, she uses my hand like a prop to spin around. I easily pick up the beat and pull out my best moves. Before long, I'm having a good time. We already know each other so well that everything feels pleasantly comfortable. Kind of like hanging out with an old friend, which I guess she is.

"Who taught you to dance?" she shouts over the music.

"My sister, Rae," I tell her, moving close so I can talk in her ear. "Before the homecoming dance, junior year. She said she wasn't going to let me ruin her reputation by bringing my lame moves to school."

She laughs, then rests her hands on my biceps. "She did a great job."

"I'll thank her for you."

We stay out on the dance floor through OutKast's "Hey Ya!", then Beyoncé's "Single Ladies (Put a Ring on It)" comes on next. I do my best worst impression of the video, pointing to my finger while singing the chorus. She's in stitches at my ridiculous impersonation.

I remember flirting with Toni about her being Jay-Z and me being Beyoncé in this song. I do my best to brush that thought aside, but it won't leave.

After copying the move from the video, the one where Beyoncé punches the ground to the beat, I look up to discover I've drawn a crowd of admirers. I offer them a goofy wave, only to notice the last person I thought I'd see tonight.

Toni's standing with Archie's wife, Holly. Their mouths are hanging open—à la mounted sea bass—as they stare at me.

Chapter 25

Toni

Two Hours Earlier

Holly: Any word from Sumner?

Me: Nothing since Wednesday, but he did say things were a total disaster when he got to Philly, and he doubted he'd have any time to sleep, let alone be in touch.

Holly: What do you think about that?

Me: I don't have any reason not to trust him. Giving me advanced notice that he'd be MIA shows he's thoughtful enough to think about me ahead of time so I don't feel neglected. Total grownup move.

Holly: Good point. Enough about you. Now that I'm

feeling better, I want to go out and have some fun. Archie is meeting his uncle, hoping to get a big fat donation from him for the foundation, so I pick you as my partner in crime.

Me: Oh, how about dancing?

Holly and I used to go out dancing all the time before she became Faith's guardian, but even after that, Mrs. Firestone would watch her once a month so we could get our groove on.

Holly: You know it! I also want a huge, juicy burger and salty fries.

Me: I'm already looking for my dancing shoes.

Holly: Pick you up in thirty?

Me: Squeeee!!!! Girls' night!!!!

I'm ready in under twenty minutes, so I go down to the lobby in case Holly manages to get here early. While I wait, I text Sumner again to let him know I'm thinking of him.

Me: Hey you, I wanted to check in and say hi. I hope everything is going smoother in the City of Brotherly Love. I hope you raise a billion dollars for those cattle women.

I stare at my phone, hoping to get something back. Even a quick word to hear how much he misses me.

I told Holly I'm fine not hearing from him while he's away, but the truth is, I'm bothered. I feel like if Sumner really liked me, he'd make the effort for at least a quick hello.

On the other hand, I did tell him I was okay with him not being in touch and "doing his thang," but I'm regretting that line for multiple reasons, including my use of the word thang. But what's done is done, and it's better for him to think I'm not going to be some super clingy girlfriend. No man wants that. Not even the Joeys of the world.

Archie's limo pulls up in front of my building, and I swing the lobby door open with gusto and run down the steps. I beat Gregory to the car door and open the back door myself.

"Party!" Holly and I scream at each other as I scramble to get in. I shut the door behind me, and we continue to squeal like we are still in junior high.

"How long has it been since we've done this?" I ask.

"Feels like years, doesn't it?" She opens a mini-bottle of champagne, sticks a long straw in it, and hands it to me before opening the fridge again to get herself a Pellegrino. She raises her bottle. "To going out on the town!"

"Amen, sister." I clink my bottle against hers and suck deeply from the skinny straw. Wrinkling my nose from the onslaught of bubbles, I ask, "Archie was cool with this?"

"Of course. He's a modern guy."

"He's also a wee bit on the protective side," I remind her.

"True. I think it helps that Gregory is here. He's been given strict instructions to wait outside the bar for us and not to move, even if he gets a ticket."

"You got a good one," I tell her, nodding in approval. "I have a feeling tonight is going to be a night to remember."

∽

After a double-bacon cheeseburger with guacamole, fries, and onion rings, Holly jumps to her feet. "Are you ready to work off some of this food?"

I push my chair out and stand. "You know I am!"

As we cruise to the back of The Skate Club, we hear Beyoncé sing "Single Ladies," and I feel a kinship with her younger self like I can't even express. I've waited for more than one guy to put a ring on it, but alas, either they weren't interested or they weren't worthy—likely a combination of both.

The crowd is singing along—All the single ladies! All the single ladies!—as we make our way to the floor.

Holly stops short in front of me, and I bump into her back. "Oh. My. Gawd." She points. "That's Cooper Flint."

Shock flows through me as the Long Island iced tea I drank at dinner makes my stomach turn over. "Looks like it."

"Our contractor is here, partying like it's nineteen ninety-nine!" She claps her hands together in excitement.

My heart pounds at the sight of him. Literally pounds so hard, I'm pretty sure I can't feel the beat of the music. Cooper is here and look, he's with Natalie, the woman who can't seem to remember my name.

"He's got some pretty serious moves," she says, as if I can't see that for myself. "He could be a backup dancer for Beyoncé."

"That sure would be something." A crowd forms around him and Natalie. She's laughing and trying to keep up with him, and I recall our first text conversation. Before I can tell my brain not to let my thoughts come out of my mouth, I practically shout, "This is *our* song."

"What?" Holly yells to be heard over the music.

"Nothing," I tell her when Cooper makes eye contact with me.

He stops dancing and straightens, which causes Natalie to turn in our direction to see who he's looking at. She glares at me triumphantly.

Cooper breaks our staring contest to lean down and tell her something. I'm sure it's, "Oh, look, it's that awful Toni person from work who led me on, lied to me, then dumped me."

"I wonder who he's with?" Holly says.

"Her name is Natalie. She's the designer on the Bedford Falls project."

"*That's* Natalie?" Holly sounds ticked. "Archie didn't mention how beautiful she is."

"She may be beautiful, but she's a bee-otch." *Oh great, they're coming over here.*

Cooper waves to his fans, who are crestfallen that he's not finishing the song, then guides Natalie in our direction with a hand on the small of her back. Of course, it could be on her butt for all I know. My heart squeezes at the thought.

"Hey," he says, giving me a curt nod, then smiling at Holly. "Holly, I wanted to introduce you to Natalie Palmer."

Holly holds out her hand. "Nice to meet you. Archie's really impressed with your work."

"Thanks. It's an amazing project. I'm grateful Coop got me involved." She tucks her hand under his arm like she owns him. "Did you see his dance moves?"

We nod and Holly smiles, but I just can't.

Natalie croons to me, "Would you ever have thought he could dance like that?"

"Never would have guessed." My throat is so tight it feels like I can't breathe.

"There's nothing he can't do," she says with a huge "I've got him and you don't" grin.

Well, honey, you can have him, because I don't need some tire-slashing, sledgehammer-wielding meathead in my life.

Natalie sucks up to Holly, like I knew she would. This leaves Cooper and me looking around awkwardly so as not to have to acknowledge each other's existence. I'm suddenly desperate for some space. When the next song starts, I grab Holly's hand and pull. "Come on! We have to dance." I give Natalie a "sorry, we have to run look," before announcing, "It's my favorite song of all time."

"Your favorite song is 'I Touch Myself' by the Divinyls?" Natalie asks.

Crap, is that what this is? Might as well go with it. "Yup," I answer loudly. "The best."

I pull Holly out on the floor before risking a glance at Cooper. He looks far too amused for my liking. I attempt to ignore him, but he and Natalie dance right next to us. I imagine putting a hand on her face and shoving her away.

Maybe not.

Is it suddenly ridiculously hot in here? Why the hell can Cooper dance like that? He's got the body of a male stripper and the moves of Hugh Jackman. Men like him should be banned from America, shipped off to an island where they can't cause any harm. *Is he glaring at me?*

Ignore him. Just keep dancing like nobody's watching, which is true because they're all watching Cooper and probably thinking of how amazing he'd be in bed. OMG, now *I'm* thinking about that. I have to get out of here pronto, before I forget all the good reasons for not dating him and try to steal him away from Natalie.

I tap Holly on the shoulder. "We should probably go, huh?"

"Why? We just started dancing."

"You have to be getting tired, growing a little person and all." Yeah, I'm grasping at straws.

"I'm fine. I haven't had this much fun in ages."

I smile at her. "Okay, a few more songs, but then we go home so you can rest."

She leans into me. "Are you okay? You seem really tense."

"I'm fine. I'm just not a big Natalie fan." I don't bother keeping my voice down. Let Natalie know where she stands with me.

Holly shakes her head. "That's not it. I can tell."

"No, you can't." I sound defensive and a touch petulant.

"Yeah, I can. You're upset about something."

"Can we talk about this in the car, please?"

She glances at Cooper, then nods, a knowing smile on her face. "Sure." She turns to Cooper and Natalie and yells, "We're going to run."

Natalie makes a face, and Holly points to her emerging belly. "I'm getting tired!"

"Oh, of course," Natalie says and gives her a goodbye hug.

I scowl. *You met her ten minutes ago, you ho-bag. You don't get to goodbye-hug my bestie.*

Natalie turns to me with a satisfied smile. "See you soon, Tracy!"

I lock eyes with her for a second. The energy flowing between us is enough to power the entire city for a month.

I spin on my heels and stride in the direction of the front door like a model owning the catwalk. It would have been such a great exit if I hadn't gone the wrong way. Holly grabs my sleeve to point me in the right direction, and I pray a sinkhole will open under me.

As soon as we're settled into the quiet of the backseat, Holly demands, "Spill it."

"Spill what?"

"You promised you'd tell me when we got into the car."

I sigh. "I was hoping you'd forget that."

"Talk."

"Cooper and I had an argument the other day at the warehouse. No big deal." I sink into the plush seat and kick off my heels.

"And …?"

"And we pretty much hate each other now and probably always will, but only because he's a total egomaniac who can't seem to wrap his head around me choosing Sumner over him."

"You know what feels a lot like hate?"

"Loathing?"

She shakes her head vehemently. "Love."

"Lust, maybe. I've learned the hard way that lust is not enough of a foundation for a solid relationship."

"No, but it's not a bad place to start. Look at me and Archie. We had a bunch of stuff to overcome. If we weren't as attracted to each other as we are, we might not have bothered."

"Cooper is nothing like Archie. Now if you don't mind, I'm done talking about the man. There is no way that he and I will ever be anything more to each other than what we are now." Annoyed-with-each-other work colleagues.

Holly scoots over and rests her head on my shoulder. "If you say so. I love you like a sister and only want the best for you."

Me too, but the best for me isn't Cooper Flint.

Chapter 26

Cooper

"Thanks for a wonderful evening," Natalie says.

We're standing at the front door of her building after dancing the night away.

"I had a great time," I tell her truthfully. I'd needed to vent some of my stress, and what better way than to channel my inner Beyoncé? Or Jay-Z? They played him too.

She positions herself so she's directly in front of me in the "I'm totally cool with you kissing me" stance. I smile at her but inside I'm torn up. Seeing Toni tonight was the last thing I needed. I was doing my level best to forget about her, and I thought it was starting to work. Then, boom! There she was.

"Are you glad you took Hans's advice and went out with me?" she asks, trailing a finger down my chest. "Because I'm sure glad we did."

"I … um … yes." *Way to sell it, Cooper.*

She rises on tiptoes and whispers, "I'm glad."

Angling her head, she lowers her eyelids and closes the distance between us. I give her a gentle kiss, and my gut twists while a tiny voice in the back of my head tells me I'm kissing the wrong woman. Except the right woman is off kissing someone else.

Ignoring my conscience, I wrap my arms around her and deepen the kiss. There's a beautiful woman in my arms who deserves to have all my attention.

She lets out a little moan as her hands roam across my chest. Crap, I know what comes next. An invitation inside. Nope, nope, nope. I pull back and let go of her abruptly.

"What is it?" She looks shocked.

Running one hand through my hair, I sigh. "Believe me, it's not you. You're amazing."

Her eyes narrow. "But …"

"My life is complicated right now." Talk about the understatement of the century.

Raising one eyebrow, she says, "Complicated how? Are you seeing someone?"

"Not really. There was a woman, and I thought things were headed in the right direction, but she changed her mind. And, well, it's—"

"Complicated. I understand. You don't get to our age and still be single without complications." She leans over until she's fully pressed up against me. "But that doesn't mean we can't have fun together, does it?"

"I … uh, think it does." I'm not one of those guys who's happy to sleep around when there's someone else taking up real estate in his brain.

She sticks her lower lip out in an exaggerated pout. "That's too bad."

"I wish things were different, Nat. You're a great girl, and you'll make some lucky man really happy one day."

"I could make you really happy. Give me five minutes, and I'll prove it to you."

I hold her in place and take a step back, then let her go. "I don't want to lose your friendship."

"I already have a lot of friends, Coop. What I don't have are friends with benefits."

"That's not my thing." How much clearer can I be?

After a long pause, she says, "Fine, but if things don't work out with you and this mystery lady, remember that I had the best time with you and would love to go out again." She tilts her head. "A lot of guys would have come inside anyway, knowing we didn't have a future."

"You deserve better than some lothario playing you like that. You're smart, talented, and a good person."

"Don't forget I've got style, too," she says with a little grin.

"You've got style for days, and when the right man comes along, I want to meet him and make sure I approve."

"Okay, *Dad*."

I chuckle. "We okay?"

She nods. "For now. Just remember we could be more than okay if you change your mind."

"I'll remember." But I'm one hundred percent sure Natalie is not the woman for me. "Tell you what, I'll scope out the men on the cruise and let you know if I meet anyone I think could be a contender."

"I suppose I can't complain about that."

"See you Saturday?" I walk down the steps.

"See you then, and thanks again for tonight. I had a great time."

She goes inside and goes down a short corridor to the elevator. I wait until she gets on, then return to my truck.

On the way home, I decide I need to tell Toni about

Sumner. Even if she doesn't believe me, I can't sit back and be quiet. I also need to tell her how I feel about her.

I've fallen for Toni Cappelli, and there's no point in denying that anymore. I suspect she feels the same way about me, but for some reason, she doesn't want to give me a chance. I need to change her mind.

Chapter 27

Toni

I haven't run into Cooper since that night at The Skate Club. I've barely heard from Sumner, either. He got back from Philly six days ago, and the only thing he's texted is that he's so busy getting ready for the Harry Potter cruise that he probably won't be in touch before the event. What. In. The. Hell?

How busy can he be? It's not like he's doing any of the grunt work. There's staff for that. I wonder if not sleeping with him the night we went to Valentino's was a deal breaker.

Whatever. I'm not going to let it bother me. I'm going to enjoy this cruise, if for no other reason than I want to have a fun night out since Cooper ruined my last one. This time, I won't let his presence bother me.

There's a knock on the door and then Faith calls, "Aunt Toni, can I come in?"

I'm over at Holly and Archie's house getting ready.

"You bet, squirt." She comes in wearing a Gryffindor cape and a sorting hat. "You look great."

"I do," she says and strides to the bed in the guest room. "I look so good, you'd think I'd be invited to come along tonight, wouldn't you?"

"I can see why you might think so, but you'd be bored stiff. This is an adult affair. Lots of talking and sipping drinks."

"Are you going to be bored?"

"I hope not." I tighten the sash on my robe. "But I'm an adult, so I tend to find adult functions fun." I sit at the vanity and apply my makeup. I'm going as Ginny Weasley, so there isn't much to do.

"I'm a future grownup," she says. "I don't think this is fair."

"I'm sure you and Mrs. Firestone will have a fun night."

She humphs and grumbles. "Maybe, but shouldn't the person the foundation is named after be at the party? I'm the Faith of the Faith Foundation."

"I totally get it, kiddo, but not having you there will add a real sense of mystery to the whole affair."

Shrugging, she says, "I suppose."

"How does your mom look?"

"Fine."

"How about Arch ... your dad?"

"Fine."

"How would you like a great big booger sandwich?"

"Fi ... Oh, ha ha, you're so funny."

Who knew a kindergartener could have such a finely honed sense of sarcasm? She lies flat on the bed and heaves a huge sigh. Poor little monkey.

"How about I promise to take you on our own special

adventure one day this week? Would that make this easier for you?"

"Where would we go?" Her arms are crossed like I'd better make this good.

I pin my hair on top of my head to prepare for the long ginger wig I bought. "We could take the boat out to the Statue of Liberty."

"Would we have hot chocolate and pizza?"

I remember how I could once be bought with such meager offerings. Who am I kidding? I still can be. "Absolutely!"

Faith moves to the edge of the bed and then hops down. "Fine, but I might need Red Vines, too."

"Even if you don't, I will," I tell her seriously.

There's another knock on the door, and Holly says, "Can I come in?"

Faith runs to the door and opens it but blocks her. "It occurred to me that you're taking Joy on this cruise and not me. I think you're playing favorites."

Holly laughs. "Your sister isn't going to have any fun, I promise you. She may even hate being on the boat so much that she gets nauseated."

"Then you shouldn't go. I'd hate for her to get sick."

"Faith, honey," Holly says, "I will take you on all sorts of exciting adventures in life, but there are going to be some things we can't do together. Go help Dad figure out how to put on his tie. He's having trouble with it."

"I don't know how to put on a boy tie."

"It's a clip-on."

Faith puts her hands on her hips. "He can't figure that out?" On her way out the door, she grumbles, "What would you people do without me?"

After she's gone, Holly says, "I can't imagine my life without that girl. Now that I'm pregnant and so emotional,

I cry all the time at the thought that my sister never got to know her at this age." She hiccups.

"I'm not sure how I know this, but I know that Joy is watching over you both and knows exactly what's going on. She'd be so proud of you, Holls." I hand her a tissue. "Stop crying or your makeup is going to need to be redone."

She crosses to the mirror and looks at her reflection. "Are you excited about tonight?"

"Yes."

"How about Sumner. Is he excited?"

I walk into the closet. "I wouldn't know. I haven't talked to him since he's been back."

"What's going on?" She follows me in and sits on a stool tucked into the corner.

I shrug. "He texted to say he's been tied up getting ready for tonight."

The look on her face is comical. "What's he doing, painting the boat?"

So it isn't only me who thinks that excuse is total BS. "I was wondering the same thing, but I've never hosted a party of this magnitude." The biggest do I ever threw was my sweet sixteen party, where we all dressed like flappers and mobsters. Sans the alcohol, of course, as my mother declared it a Prohibition event.

She kicks her legs out. "I'm looking forward to seeing the two of you together."

"Uh-huh." I'm not that excited to see Sumner. I feel more than a little neglected, and that's never been my favorite emotion.

She holds out her hands. "Help me up, will you? It's getting harder and harder to do the smallest things."

I pull her to her feet. "I should be ready in another

twenty minutes. You'd better go get your Hermione Granger on."

"I'm sure a knocked-up Hermione will be the belle of the ball," she jokes.

"It will be controversial, given that Archie is going as Harry Potter." I tell her in mock anger, "You're poaching my man. Harry and Ginny wind up together in real life."

"In real life, huh?" She laughs. "I'll let you dance with Harry once and then it's hands off, Miss Weasley." She walks out and pauses. "What is Sumner going as?"

"Lucius Malfoy, which I hope isn't a red flag, to be honest."

"On account of who would want to be dressed as a baddie?" Holly asks.

"Exactly."

Holly doesn't try to reassure me, which I take a sign that it could be a red flag. Hmm…they're adding up, aren't they?

After a moment, she asks, "I wonder what Cooper will be wearing?"

I can tell by the way she tried to casually float the question, that she's trying to steer me back in his direction. "I don't care if he's dressed as the sorting hat."

I can tell she doesn't believe me. "Fine, but I've got twenty on Natalie showing up as Bellatrix Lestrange."

"I might as well hand you the money right now." Natalie would make the perfect sexy, evil wildcard.

"Are you jealous?"

"Pish, no. Why would I be?" But I can't help wondering if I am. I remind myself that Cooper is a thug and a vandal.

Damn you, Sumner. I shouldn't be thinking about Cooper, and I wouldn't be if you'd bothered to return a text or two.

Chapter 28

Cooper

Tonight is the night. My chance to find Toni and tell her the truth about Sumner. I may also be planning to lay my heart at her feet, but we'll have to see how things go. For the moment I remain optimistic—a happenstance partially due to the fact that I'm dressed like an omniscient wizard and partially due to my inability to accept I don't have a chance winning over the woman of my dreams.

There's a chill in the air I barely feel as I jog down the pier. This heavy robe, wig, and long beard are heating me up like I'm sunbathing on the equator. I suspect the urgency that's coursing through my veins has something to do with my elevated temperature as well.

I should have just told Toni about how Sumner and I know each other, but she was so adamant that it would be sour grapes on my part that I kept quiet. My mistake has allowed Sumner the opportunity to spin whatever web of lies he wanted. This has worked in his favor, as he's with her and I'm not.

A Harry Potter movie soundtrack plays loudly over the speakers as I start up the gangplank leading to a truly impressive yacht. I knew there would be over two hundred guests, but I hadn't imagined such an imposing ship. The outside of it is lit up with plain white lights which contrast beautifully with a dark purple glow emanating from inside.

"Ah, Dumbledore! There you are," Voldemort says as I climb aboard. His costume is complete, with the horrific noseless mask and the sickeningly long and pointy, light purple fingernails. "I am the Dark Lord, here to welcome you to a very magical evening."

I squint at the man under the mask, but I have no clue who he is. "Sumner?"

He shakes his head. "My name is Milton. I'm head of the Eastern Seaboard Harry Potter Cosplay Society. I've been hired by the foundation to give the guests an authentic experience."

"Gotcha." I peer around, looking for Toni, though I'd never admit it. "Nice to meet you, Milton."

"You may refer to me as the Dark Lord."

Um, yeah. Let me get right on that, weirdo. I go through the open doors ahead. An enormous dining room has been painstakingly decorated to resemble the dining hall at Hogwarts, complete with lit electric candles dangling from the ceiling. As much as I hate to say it, Sumner knows how to do his job.

I glide past eight Harrys, a whack of Rons, and at least four Professor McGonagalls—most of whom have their wands out, showing off their wrist-flicking talents—carefully studying faces on the chance that Toni's costume renders her unrecognizable.

Winding my way toward the bar, I finally spot her.

Instead of making a beeline over to Toni, I worm my way to the front of the crowd in search of liquid courage. After catching the bartender's eye, I hold up two fingers. "Double scotch on the rocks."

With a plethora of enthusiasm, he announces, "One double beetle berry whiskey coming up!"

I'd eat beetle berries—whatever those are—if they could take some of the edge off my anxiety.

A woman next to me bumps me on the shoulder and in the most irritatingly wispy voice says, "You're a Muggle, aren't you?" She adds, "Don't worry, I won't tell anyone. I'm very observant and happened to notice you don't look comfortable in the magical realm."

"Good catch."

"I'm Luna. Luna Lovegood," she answers in that sing-song way of the character in the movies.

"Coop—Dumbledore."

She gives me a nod of approval. "Better. Are you one of the guests, or are you with the foundation?"

"I'm the contractor for the foundation."

"So nice of them to invite staff. You usually don't see that at this type of thing. Mostly it's people with deep pockets."

I can tell she's stopping herself just short of saying "like me," but there's no way I'm going to inquire about what has brought her here tonight. I don't give a crap about the opinions of these people, and I'm more than a little annoyed to be categorized as staff, but in a few minutes, this yacht is going to set sail, and I'll be stuck with them for the next three hours, so I'd better not get my dander up this early.

When the bartender hands me my drink, I reach into my robe for a twenty and slide it over to him. Then I move away, leaving Luna behind.

When I'm making my way through the hall, I hear, "Cooper, is that you?" Natalie is examining me closely, trying to see me beneath my costume.

I smile at the sight of a familiar face and then notice her boobs are out in full force. She's wearing a tight black leather bodice that leaves very little to the imagination. Her lipstick is blood red, and she's sporting a wild, long, curly black wig. "Wow, you really went all out."

She laughs and runs her fingers up my lacy sleeve. "So did you. Very authentic."

"Dumbledore was one of the last costumes left at the shop."

"I got my Bellatrix Lestrange online." She's smiling like a cat who's been given a bowl of cream. "I have a feeling it will come in handy."

"Do you go to a lot of Harry Potter events?" I didn't peg Nat for a magic geek.

Lowering her lashes slowly, she says, "You don't have to go to an event to play dress-up."

Uh-oh, Natalie is flirting again, which is awkward after our last encounter. My elbow gets bumped, and I have to catch myself before tossing my drink.

"Be careful of this one, my friend. She follows the Dark Lord." Creepy Luna appears to be following me.

"That's okay, she's a friend of mine." I angle my body as a hint that I don't want to talk to her. *I mean, I am staff, after all.*

Luna insinuates herself between me and Natalie and gives Nat what can only be described as the evil eye. "I see. Well, good luck to you then." She spins away, leaving us alone.

"Do you know any of the guests?" Natalie asks.

"I'm guessing it's a bunch of people with more money

than they know what to do with, some of whom seem to take their borrowed personas a little too seriously." We share a quick chuckle, then I do another visual sweep for Toni.

"Are you looking for eligible men for me?" Natalie purrs. "Or are you looking for that woman who's complicating your life?"

"I think you know the answer to that question, but I'll keep an eye out for you, too."

"It's Toni, isn't it?"

"How did you—?"

"I mentally replayed our date to see when I lost you and realized it was when she showed up."

"I'm sorry about that." I'm a heel for going out with Natalie when I really didn't want to, but at least I didn't let things progress into truly uncomfortable territory.

"Don't worry about it. You're a good guy, Coop." She discreetly points at a man in his fifties, who's dressed as Sirius Black. "What about him? Could you see us together?"

"Too old. If he's single, he has at least two ex-wives."

"Ooh, you might be good at this." She playfully nudges my shoulder. "I should bring you along as my love advisor from now on."

"When you have three sisters, you learn to spot the duds quickly."

It's at that exact moment I spot the biggest dud of them all—Sumner Livingston, costumed as Lucius Malfoy. My jaw tightens in response to how perfectly his costume suits him.

Sumner is talking to one of the servers in what can only be described as a highly flirtatious manner. His hand is on her hip, and his face is so close to hers you'd think he was about to perform CPR. I'm half-tempted to pull out my phone and record this exchange for Toni, but I don't get the chance. He spots me and joins us.

His gaze lands on Natalie's cleavage, then moves slowly up to her face. "Hello there, I'm Sumner. I'm the brains behind tonight's fundraiser. If you need anything at all, come find me, okay?"

Natalie grins at him, seemingly charmed. Clearing my throat noisily to break the mood, I say, "Sumner."

He looks at me in surprise. "I didn't recognize you in that ridiculous beard and wig." He turns his attention back to Natalie. "I hope you're not with this guy. You can do so much better."

"I could use another drink, Sumner." I shove my empty glass at him.

With his gaze still locked on to Natalie, he says, "Get it yourself."

"I thought I was to let you know if I needed anything. Isn't that what you just said?"

He laughs. "I was talking to the lovely Bellatrix, not you."

I'm tempted to pick him up and throw him overboard, but I glimpse Toni out of the corner of my eye. She looks wholesome and lovely as Ginny Weasley, not to mention drop-dead sexy, which is something the movie Ginny never was.

Toni's looking around, probably for numbnuts here. I smile at Natalie. "I'll catch you in a bit." I point to Sumner. "Trust me. He's not the one."

Chapter 29

Toni

I notice Sumner within seconds of arriving in the dining room. He's hard to miss with that nearly white blond wig he's sporting. I blink hard when I see he's talking to Natalie and Cooper. If I'm not mistaken, Sumner's staring down Natalie's nonexistent top. Once again, I wonder why he hasn't bothered calling since he got back from Philly. Is there someone else?

Squaring my shoulders, I decide that two can play at this game. While I won't be openly gawking at anyone's breasts, I can most assuredly be charming and attentive to the male guests.

Holly taps me on the shoulder and points across the room. "There he is."

"I see that, but you know what? I think I'm going to play it cool. I'll let him come to me instead of rushing over to talk to him."

"That's my girl," she says with a nod of approval. "We are the chased, not the chasers."

Archie laughs and pulls his wife into his arms. "I'm glad you let me catch you."

"Me too," she practically purrs.

God, they're cute together.

Archie glances at his watch. "Time to get the evening started. I'm going to nudge Sumner and have him give the captain the high sign." He weaves his way through the crowd, leaving me and Holly to people watch.

She leans into me. "I don't see Cooper and Natalie as a couple, do you?"

Cooper is no longer stationary. He's walking toward us. My heart beats like a jackhammer, which confuses the heck out of me. Why does he have this effect on me?

"I'm sure they'll have adorable babies," I say with an edge. "Do you want to get some fresh air?"

Holly narrows her eyes. "I thought you said it was freezing outside."

"I changed my mind. Let's see if the stars are out." Cooper is closing in.

Before I can make my escape, Archie calls, "Holly, come meet the Bilkingtons."

"Duty calls," she says. "Sorry."

Forcing myself not to reach out for her to stay, I look around for someone to strike up a conversation with. There's a guy near me dressed like Sirius Black. "Great costume," I tell him.

He gives me the smug, self-satisfied smile of the very rich. "You, too." Holding out his hand, he says, "Derrick Cox."

"Toni Cappelli." We shake.

"I was hoping there'd be beautiful women here tonight, and so far, I'm not disappointed."

Cooper's almost reached me. "Are you here with your wife?"

Derrick grins. "Smooth. I like that. I'm free as of last Tuesday, when my divorce was finalized."

Cooper arrives in time to hear that and snorts out a laugh. I stiffen and refuse to look at him. "That's, well, what can I say …?" I tell Derrick. "Congratulations? Or maybe that's the wrong response. Maybe you're upset."

"Meh, divorces get easier as you go."

"You don't say?" *Are there no decent men left on the planet?*

"True story. My first one took a while to get over. Nearly three months. Number two was an entire weekend of moping. But this one? I've finally gotten my sea legs." He laughs like he's the funniest man alive.

Cooper takes me by the elbow. "Excuse us, Sirius, my colleague and I need to have an urgent chat."

Derrick looks annoyed, but instead of asking me to fill out an application for wife number four, he says, "Whatever, pal. I need a refill of my drink anyway."

I glare at Cooper. "Shouldn't you be over there with your date and all her tatas?" There are only two, but they're practically pushed up under her chin, making them look like a boob army.

"We're not here together."

"I thought you two were an item."

"It was only one date."

I raise my eyebrows and purse my lips in a way that says I'm not buying what he's selling. "Oh? I thought she was the one."

"Not even close." He steps forward until the top of my head is practically tucked under his chin and leans down so the warm air from his lips caresses my earlobe. "There's something I need to tell you."

Chills form in the tips of my toes before shooting

through my body like an electric storm. I instinctively reach out to grab hold of his arms. It's either that or fall to the floor as my knees give out.

A loud screeching fills the air. Sumner's voice booms over the system. "Is this thing on?" He taps the microphone. "Testing, testing. Can everyone hear me?"

They can probably hear him on Mars.

"Welcome to the first ever Faith Foundation fundraiser. On behalf of Archie and Holly Harrington, the creators of the foundation, I'd like to welcome you to a magical evening on the Hudson. The captain has informed me we're about to set sail, which means we'll be having dinner soon."

"A magical evening?" Cooper snorts. "Not with you here, butt munch."

I watch Sumner smile at the room. *Is it me, or does he look like some cheesy game show host?*

He continues, "There is a silent auction in the room adjacent to this one, so please make your way over there at some point this evening to bid on our wonderful donations. All proceeds will go to building housing for the homeless, so bid high."

"I need to talk to you," Cooper whispers in my ear.

I lightly shove him. "No, thanks."

"Toni, it's important."

"I can't imagine you have anything to say to me, but even if you did, now is not the time or place."

Sumner is urging Holly and Archie to the stage. They walk up to a round of applause, and Archie takes the mic. "Welcome, everyone, and thank you so much for coming this evening. When I first met my wife, Holly, she opened my eyes to a lot of things, including the plight of those who aren't as fortunate as we are." He pulls Holly close and drops a kiss on her forehead. "She made me realize I could be doing something far more important with my life than making more money than I will ever need. That is how the Faith Foundation was born. Our mission is to create villages for those experiencing homelessness so they can have a safe place to live while working toward a fresh start. We'll provide our guests with health care, skills, and training, not to mention all the tools they need to get back on their feet again."

Applause breaks out, and Archie grins at Holly, who looks a little green. He seems to notice and whispers something to her. She shakes her head and nods to the microphone. If I had to guess, he's asking if she's okay, and her gestures are telling him she's fine and get on with it.

He does. "We hope you'll agree this is a worthwhile cause and you'll donate generously this evening so we can make a real difference in the lives of those in need." More applause.

Sumner takes control of the mic again and goes over tonight's menu, which brings to mind our "non-date" at Valentino's. I remember how hopeful I was that he would be important in my life, but that was before he totally ghosted me.

He catches me staring at him, and without missing a beat, throws me a wink and a smile. I respond with a terse nod as he goes over the rules of the yacht. Not only are we not allowed to jump or throw anyone overboard (laughter from the audience), but he points out that the bedrooms on the upper deck are strictly off limits. Archie suddenly grabs Holly's hand and makes a beeline for the exit.

"Uh-oh," I mutter and rush after them. Not only do I want to help my friend, but I need to get away from Cooper.

Holly and Archie are on the stairs to the private quarters. "You okay?" I ask, following them up.

"I'm queasy," she says, her pallor almost identical to that girl in *The Exorcist* right before she blows. "Yachting might have been pushing it."

Archie turns to me. "Please tell her we should get the captain to let us off at the next pier so I can get her home."

"No way," Holly says. "This fundraiser is too important for us to skip out on. I only need a few minutes to lie down, and I'll be fine. You go and mingle. Toni will keep me company."

Sighing, Archie looks at me pleadingly. I assure him, "She's right. You get back to the guests. I'll get her settled in one of the staterooms."

Fifteen minutes later, Holly's fast asleep under a luxuriously soft velvet duvet. I tiptoe out in hopes of finding food to bring back. The best way to deal with this night is to stay sequestered with my bestie.

When I get to the dimly lit hallway, I bump into Sumner.

"I've been looking for you," he says.

"Really?" I sound as cold as the water we're traveling on.

"Please don't tell me you're upset that I was too busy to call. I didn't take you for the clingy type."

"I don't understand how you could have been so busy that you couldn't find a moment to send a quick hello. Come on, Sumner. Even with all you had to do, you had a free thirty seconds at some point."

He gives me what I'm sure he thinks is a charming smile. "You're right, I could have. But the truth is, I didn't want you to think I was too desperate."

"Desperate?"

"I made my feelings about you very clear, and you were less than forthcoming in sharing yours."

"Because I didn't jump into bed with you on our first date, which wasn't even a date?" Of all the nerve. "I don't play games, Sumner, and I get the distinct impression that's what's going on here."

He touches my cheek. "I can see why you might think that. I normally don't screw up this badly with women I want to be with, but with you——"

"Please don't tell me I'm special."

He glances at my lips. "I like you more than any woman I've ever met." I search his eyes for the truth, badly wanting to believe him, but a nagging part of me is telling me to run. He lowers his lips to mine. "Let me show you how I feel about you."

He grazes my lips with his before planting a trail of light kisses down my neck. "We can go to one of the bedrooms. Have you ever done it on a yacht? It's glorious."

I back up, only to find myself pinned against the wall. "I'm not going to sleep with you after you've ghosted me for almost two weeks. What part about my wanting to take my next relationship slowly don't you get?"

He presses against me. "I thought absence made the heart grow fonder."

"Not this time, buddy. In fact, I don't want to see you anymore." I try to slide along the wall to get away from him. "You aren't the gentleman I mistook you for."

"Oh, come on," he says, planting a hand on either side of me. "Nobody's buying this whole born-again virgin act. We both know you're only doing that to make yourself more alluring and guess what? It worked." He grinds his body against mine.

Ew! "Get off me!" I push him as hard as I can, but he doesn't budge.

"Come on, Toni," he says, leaning down so his lips brush against my neck. "You know you want this."

I'm about to knee him in the part of his body that he thinks with when a flurry of gray blows past. There's a loud smacking sound, then a thump. I look down to see Sumner laid out on the wooden deck at my feet.

"She said no." Dumbledore stands over him like some kind of wizard vigilante, his long beard blowing in the wind.

Sumner's wig sits at a strange angle on his head as he scrambles to his feet. He trips on his black velvet robe, loses his balance, then rights himself using a life preserver hanging off the rail. As soon as he gets up, he throws a wild punch that connects with Cooper's beard, just clipping his chin. Then all hell breaks loose. I press my body flat against the wall and start to sidle away while the two of them wrestle like a couple of juvenile delinquents from the Dark Ages. Cooper pins Sumner to the deck while Sumner grabs his long wig and tries to choke him with it. Cooper rips the long hair off and tosses it aside, then winds up to punch Sumner again.

"Stop it!" I shout.

Cooper holds his right hand back behind his shoulder, ready to let go, but my words must have gotten through to him because he just glares at Sumner. He gets up and dusts off his robe, then says, "You're not worth it."

Sumner, who suddenly looks a lot less terrified than he did a second ago, staggers to his feet. "What's the matter, Cooper?" Sumner asks through gritted teeth. "Can't stand that she wants me, not you? It hurts, doesn't it?"

"Not as much as this will," Cooper answers and socks him in the face, knocking his blond wig off his head and over the side of the yacht into the icy waters below.

Sumner's mouth drops open. "That wig was over a hundred dollars!"

"You're lucky that's the only thing that's overboard right now," Cooper mutters, giving him a menacing glare.

"Enough, both of you!" I scream.

It isn't until I hear a deafening whistle blown next to me and a crew mate yelling, "Knock it off, the pair of you!" that they finally pull away from each other. They're heaving and sweating and wiping blood off their faces. Cooper's lip is split, and Sumner's nose is gushing blood.

"Idiots," I mutter. I turn to the crew mate. "Thank you for stopping them."

She glares at me. "This part of the yacht is strictly off limits."

"I know that, but I was helping my pregnant boss—the one who's paying for this whole evening."

That seems to irritate her further. "There's someone else up here?"

"Holly Harrington," I say, emphasis on the Harrington.

"I don't care who she is. We have rules in place for a reason. The event was to take place on the main deck only, meaning we don't have staff up here, which means no guests up here. No exceptions."

"Would you rather she vomits all over the deck so you have to clean it up?"

"The rules exist for a reason, ma'am. Now if you'll follow me, we need to see the captain."

"You knuckleheads are going to get us kicked off this boat," I growl at Cooper and Sumner. I follow them into the navigation room, where Archie is already talking with the captain.

Archie demands, "What in the world is going on here?"

"It's not my fault," Sumner whines. "He's the one who started it!"

"Oh, please," Cooper says, sneering. "I was only up there to check on Toni and make sure you didn't try anything—which you did."

"God forbid anyone else have sex when you're not getting any," Sumner hisses.

"That's not what this is about, and you know it." Cooper is shooting daggers with his eyes. "We both know what you're after, and we both know once you got it, you'd drop her."

"Enough," I yell. "The pair of you sound like a couple of four-year-olds. Actually, no, I've met four-year-olds who are more mature." I glare at Sumner. "We're done. Over. Lose my number if you know what's good for you."

"Toni …" he pleads.

"You know what else? Tonight is the last night you'll be working with the Faith Foundation. You're fired."

"You can't fire me," Sumner yells, turning red. "You're not my boss."

"But I am," Archie interjects. "And if Toni says you're fired, then you're fired."

Go, Archie!

"What about him?" Sumner asks, pointing at Cooper. "Shouldn't he lose his job for attacking me?"

"He's none of your business," Archie says and turns to the captain. "Will you please dock at the next pier and let Mr. Livingston off?"

The captain shakes his head. "I'm only allowed to do that in the case of a medical emergency. I can make sure he stays below until we return to our slip though."

"This is ludicrous," Sumner sputters. "I didn't do anything. I was attacked!"

"You were trying to force yourself on me," I spit out. "No means no, loser." I storm out into the cool night air, wondering how this night took such a ridiculous turn.

"Toni," Cooper calls after me. "Please let me explain."

I shake my head violently. "I appreciate your stepping in with Sumner – really I do. But honestly, you really need to deal with your anger issues. Nothing you say will make the least bit of difference."

Cooper sighs. "Just hear me out."

Even if I was tempted to listen to his excuse, I'm finished with men who have bad tempers and can't commit. I'm over guys who don't believe me when I say no. I think I'm done with dating. It might be time to get a dozen or so cats and call it quits on men altogether.

Chapter 30

Cooper

The party was a bust. So much for declaring myself to Toni. I'll be lucky if she ever speaks to me again. At least she didn't fire me. I've gotta give the lady credit; she gives as good as she gets.

After putting my key into the lock of my front door, I stop short of turning it. I'm tired of coming home alone. I'm tired of feeling like I'm never good enough for my parents or the women who want to go out with me. I finally found someone who liked me as I am—or so I thought— and then boom, nothing.

Dread washes over me. Holy crap, I'm Bridget Jones. I curse my sisters for making me watch their favorite romcom with them so many times. They told me it was so I'd know how to treat women when I got older, but the only thing I've successfully recreated from that movie is the fight scene between Hugh Grant and Colin Firth.

As pissed-off as I am at Sumner for putting his hands on Toni, I'm equally angry at myself for acting like a bone-head. There are easier ways to intervene than turning into a psycho. All I did was confirm Toni's belief that I'm the poster child for anger management issues.

I head straight to the shower, de-robing, de-bearding, and de-wigging as I go. After turning the water as hot as I can stand it, I climb in and wash off the horror of this night. Thirty minutes later, the spray cools, and it's time to get out and face my troubles head-on.

As I step out into the cold bathroom air, a lightbulb turns on in my head. Toni may not want to listen to me, but I'd bet my last dollar she'll read something if I write it down. Wrapping a towel around my waist, I go to the kitchen in search of my phone, then text her before I can change my mind.

> Me: I know you don't want to talk to me or hear me out, but I'm hoping you'll read this. I don't know what Sumner told you about our history, but I'm almost 100% positive it's not the truth.

Before I finish, her words from earlier this evening come back to me. She made it crystal clear she doesn't want to hear from me. Any attempt I make at this point would be crossing a line defined by her, one I'm meant to stay on the other side of. I delete the text and stare at my phone for a full minute, trying to decide what to do. If I can't make things right with her, I at least have to try to make them right with Archie. This project is too important to me.

> Me: Archie, I want to apologize for the scene this

evening. It was extremely unprofessional of me, and I
would really appreciate it if we could sit down and have
a chat sometime this week.

I take my phone to the bedroom and keep my ears
open for a response while I finish drying off. Then I crawl
into bed as a wave of exhaustion takes over. I have one of
those dreamless sleeps, like I've been put under sedation.
It's exactly what I needed.

It's nearly eleven in the morning by the time I wake up,
and I feel hung over. It's not an alcohol hangover, more of
an emotional one. First thing I do is look at my phone.

Archie: We're good, but if you still want to talk, I won't
be able to do it until Thursday at four. My office.

Me: I'll see you then. Thanks.

The next few days are a blur. Between wrapping up the
McMillan house and pushing forward on the Bedford Falls
project, I fill practically every moment. I'm grateful for the
distraction my work provides because it keeps me from
thinking about Toni too much. She's still there in my brain,
popping up at the most surprising times. Like this morning.
I had a bagel for breakfast, and there she was, smiling and
moaning while eating her everything nosh piled high with
all the fixings. It was a positively erotic image.

I've been going to work every day before seven and
haven't made it home before nine any night this week.
Thank God it's finally Thursday. I probably checked my
watch forty times, waiting for three thirty to arrive so I
could leave for Archie's office (and hopefully see Toni).

I even took special pains to get ready last night. We're talking a clean shave and making sure to have clean clothes to change into so I don't show up dirty from the job site. It's my version of Bridget showing up to work in a see-through top.

My heart pounds like I'm at a heavy metal concert as soon as I step on the elevator to take me to the third floor of the Faith Foundation building. As I step out of the elevator, I see her sitting at her desk, looking gorgeous in a pink fuzzy sweater.

"Hey," I say, startling her.

"What are you doing here?"

She doesn't sound happy to see me. Taking off my coat, I throw it over my arm. "I have a meeting with Archie."

"He didn't say anything to me about it." She pushes her chair back and abruptly stands. "I was just leaving." She picks up her purse and coat and walks past me.

I watch her until she gets on the elevator, but I don't say anything. My heart is totally breaking. After the doors close, I go to Archie's office. He holds up a finger and says, "Give me one second to finish this."

I sit across from him, feeling awkward. He said we're good, but I'm still embarrassed by my behavior. When Archie looks up from his computer, I say, "Thanks for agreeing to meet with me. I really appreciate it."

He sits back. "I've been thinking a lot about the other night, and I do think we have something to discuss."

Uh-oh, what's that supposed to mean? "About that whole thing with Sumner …" This is it; I'm going to get fired. I quickly explain, "That was a specific and unusual situation. It might seem like I'm some rage-a-holic who goes off on people for nothing, but I've known Sumner for a long time. He isn't the good guy he pretends to be."

"I gathered that. As far as I'm concerned, you did the right thing."

"I probably didn't need to beat the guy up."

"If someone had been doing that to Holly, I would've done much worse."

"But Holly is your wife, and Toni is someone who doesn't even want to talk to me, so it's a little different."

He shrugs. "Is it? We don't know how pushy Sumner would've gotten with her. I don't even want to think about that. I'm glad you came along when you did."

I nod, grateful he can see my side of things.

"But I doubt you came here to talk about Sumner." He raises a hand to stop me from answering right away. "I don't normally stick my nose into my employees' personal lives, but Toni is not only my assistant and right-hand woman, she's also my wife's best friend. And she's been completely miserable lately. I owe her a lot, and if there's anything I can do to make her life better, I'm going to do it."

I'm glad Toni has someone like Archie to watch out for her, especially as she won't allow me to do it. "I think Toni and I would be perfect for each other. For a long time, I was pretty sure she felt the same way I do, but she's made it more than clear that's not the case, and I have to respect that." I pause before adding, "Even if I do think there's some reason holding her back that I don't know about."

Archie steeples his fingers. "Look, Cooper, I'm good at reading people, and I could tell when I met you that you're one of the good guys. As Toni's friend, I want to make sure she ends up with the right man. I think it's high time we take things into our own hands."

My entire body surges with excitement. "What did you have in mind?"

"If there's anything I've learned from watching a hundred romantic comedies with Holly, it's that sometimes you need to get the hero and heroine alone together for a long period of time so they can sort things out. And I have just the way to do it."

Chapter 31

Toni

After hightailing it out of the office—so I don't have to talk to Cooper—I take a taxi over to Holly's. Deciding not to go back to work today, I stop off at Ferrantelli's and pick up comfort food.

The good news about my decision to give up men is that I'm no longer worried about getting fat. Last night I threw away all the old pants that don't fit anymore. Gone are the days when I hold on to them, only to deprive myself so I can wear them again. I am liberated! This, of course, means extra cannoli.

When I get to Holly's, I let myself in. She's in the living room, surrounded by boxes. Looking up at me with an overwhelmed expression, she says, "I did some maternity shopping online."

"I thought we were going to make a day of it soon." I heft the bags on top of the entry table before shutting the front door.

"We'd have to wait until all this nausea passes, and by then I'd have to pull the curtains down to fashion something that fits."

"Holly von Trapp," I tease. "I'm going to take the food into the kitchen. You want anything?"

She rips open another box. "I want *all* the things, but let me try on some of this stuff first, so I don't get it covered in sauce or grease. You know, in case I have to send some of it back."

After getting a look at the dress she's holding, I tell her, "I am almost certain my grandma had a sofa set in that pattern."

"What was I thinking when I ordered this?" She shoves the dress back into the box.

"It probably looked cute on the model who had a stylist, makeup artists, lighting directors, and photographers. You can't trust them as far as you can throw them." I schlep the food down the hall to the kitchen, where Mrs. Firestone is opening cabinets. "I brought food, Mrs. F. No need to cook tonight."

"Thank you, Toni." She pulls down a stack of dishes and puts them on the counter. "I couldn't decide what to make. I was thinking casserole, but then I considered meatloaf."

"I brought Italian."

"My favorite." She opens bags to see what's inside. "I'll go ahead and eat now." While she fills her plate, I grab the container with calamari and head back into the living room. Holly looks like she's about to cry.

"What's wrong?" I plop down on the couch and put my feet up on the coffee table.

"I'm going to look huge in this stuff." Her eyes actually tear up.

"I hate to point out the obvious, Holls, but you're

cooking a person in there. You're only going to get bigger."

She lifts her pant legs to show me her ankles. "I'm not quite four months along, and my ankles are already getting fat." She pulls herself up on the couch to sit next to me.

"Your ankles are perfect." A pregnant Holly turns out to be a dramatic Holly.

"Just wait until it's your turn."

"About that …" I swallow the most heavenly bit of fried octopus dipped in garlic aioli. "I might not have kids."

"Where did that come from?" She sounds genuinely panicked.

"Didn't I tell you? After the Harry Potter cruise, I came to a decision. I'm officially giving up men forever." I wipe my mouth on a paper towel and smile.

"What do you mean, you are giving up on men? Why would you do that?"

I pull a plush throw off the back of the sofa and drape it over me. "I'm sick to death of dating guys who only have one thing on their minds. I'm also sick of dating liars and cheaters and men who can't keep a job."

She looks like she's about to cry again. "What about getting married and having babies?"

"I might hit Tinder and see if I can find myself a nice girl. We could register for a turkey baster so we can expand our family."

"What?"

I laugh. "Why not? Fluid sexuality is a thing. There might be a whole new world out there for me."

"Are you serious?"

Poor Holly, I'm really rocking her world with this conversation. "No, I'm not serious, but I am staying single for a nice long time. I have dating PTSD or something."

She puts her feet up on my lap. "I can't believe Sumner

turned out to be such a turd. He didn't give off those vibes at all."

"That's the scariest part. Neither of us saw it. Either our radar is broken or guys are devolving in a way that we can no longer detect it." What a terrifying thought.

"My radar might have broken when I got married. But you're always good about sensing a loser when you see one coming."

"And then I promptly hook up with them." I shovel more calamari in my mouth.

"What about Cooper?"

"What about him?"

She grabs the aluminum container from me. "You two were really getting along when you were texting. Maybe you can go out for real and see where things go."

It's getting dark, so I turn on the side table lamp. "Cooper, the man who beats up other men?"

"Sumner had it coming."

"He may have," I concede. "But that's not the only bad thing Cooper did. He also slashed Sumner's tires once. Apparently they have some history."

"How do you know that?"

"Sumner told me." I stick my hand back in the calamari.

"And you believe him?"

She might have a point. "Well, I did. He had no reason to lie to me at the time. He knew I was interested in dating him."

She shakes her head. "Men are like toddlers. They always want what they can't have, and when they get what they want, they never trust it."

"Even Archie?"

"Well, no, not him, but he's the exception that proves the rule."

"In that case, I really am screwed. You might have gotten the last decent man out there."

She picks up a remote and turns on the TV. "You know what you need, don't you?"

"Doris Day?" I ask with a grin.

"Yup. I think *That Touch of Mink* is exactly what the doctor ordered."

"Yum, Cary Grant. If anyone can re-inspire my love of the opposite sex, it's him." Worst case scenario, I'll be setting myself up for great dreams tonight.

We kick back and watch one of our all-time favorite classic romcoms. We're at the scene where Doris, aka Cathy Timberlake, is breaking out in a rash in the hotel suite at the thought of Cary, aka Phillip Shane, joining her. Faith walks through the front door and says, "I'm done with boys."

"Smart girl," I murmur. Louder, I ask, "Booger eater?"

"I wish!" She drops her backpack and joins us. "Jordan Farnsworth told me he wanted to marry me some day."

"And?" I prod.

"He smells like boiled hotdogs."

"I thought you liked hotdogs," Holly says.

"I like to eat them, but I don't think people should go around smelling like them." Her face scrunches in distaste. She looks at the TV. "Uh-oh."

"What, uh-oh?" Holly pushes a strand of her daughter's hair behind her ear.

"You're watching Doris Day. That means one of you" —her eyes shift to me—"is having man problems."

"Guilty," I say. "But it's not so much problems as a determination not to date them anymore."

"You're gonna be a lesbian, like your sister?" Faith nods like she thinks that might be a good idea.

"Probably not," I tell her. "But I'm definitely on a man

break. Your mom thinks all I need is a couple of hours with Cary Grant, and I'll change my mind."

Faith shrugs. "What is it that old movie star you like says? 'Que sera, sera?' Whatever will be, will be, Aunt Toni. Sometimes you have to have a little Faith." She points to herself and laughs. "Get it? Have a little Faith?" Now she's doubled over.

"There's Italian in the kitchen, funny girl," I say. "Don't give up your day job."

Faith leaves and the front door opens again. This time it's Archie. He takes his coat off and lays it on a chair in the entryway before coming over to give Holly a kiss. He looks at me. "You took off early, huh?"

"Yup. I hope that was okay." I should have told him that I wasn't coming back, but I didn't want to hang out any longer than I had to.

"It's fine, but I need you to do a favor for me."

"Shoot." Please let it have nothing to do with Cooper.

"I have to drive up to New Hampshire and pick up a sign I had special ordered for the Bedford Falls project. I was hoping you'd come with me."

Confused, I ask, "Why don't they just ship it?"

"Because while I'm there, I have to meet with the director of the Bureau of Homeless and Housing Services about a village they'd like us to build there. Since my partner in crime is out of commission, I need my right hand with me for a meeting of that magnitude."

Nodding, I say, "I can see that. I *am* indispensable. When do we leave?"

"Next week. Tuesday. Does that work?"

"Yup." I look at Archie, and for the briefest of moments, wonder if there isn't a nice guy like him out there somewhere for me. "Thanks again for letting me fire Sumner. I promise I won't make a habit of doing that."

"You have my permission to fire anyone who tries to take liberties with you that are not welcome."

"I appreciate that, but now we need to find another fundraiser."

"The city is full of them. We'll find someone better than Sumner in no time." He looks at the empty food container and asks, "Was that calamari?"

"There's another in the kitchen," I tell him.

As he leaves the room, he says, "Back to your movie. Whatever man crisis you're having, Toni, Cary will fix you right up."

I throw my paper towel at the back of his head. If only love were as easy as it is in romcoms.

But just because everything always works out for Doris Day and Julia Roberts does not mean I am fated to be so lucky. More's the pity.

Chapter 32

Cooper

Rae-Anne: What are you doing tonight? I'm having the worst week ever, and I could use some face time with my little brother (so I'll feel better about my life).

Me: Thanks (read that with a heavy dose of sarcasm). When and where?

Rae-Anne: Your place at six. You supply the pizza.

Me: And what are you bringing? The whine?

Rae-Anne: Dad joke already, Coop?

Me: See you in a bit.

I finish stacking logs by the hearth so I can keep the fire going. One of the many reasons I fell in love with my house—even though it's way too big for one person—is the massive stone fireplace in the family room.

The doorbell rings and before I answer it, I hear two female voices outside. That can only mean one thing. I swing the door open and confirm my suspicion. "Hey, Willa. I didn't know I invited you."

"Surprise!" my middle sister says as she and Rae come through the door at the same time. My sisters are alpha women who are used to getting their way. It doesn't occur to either of them to wait while the other precedes, which is how they get stuck.

Grumbling, pushing, and tussling ensue until they finally burst into my entryway. When they're inside, I poke my head out, then come back in.

"What are you doing?" Rae asks.

"Checking to see if you brought any women I *just had to meet*."

"Oh, Chicken Coop," Willa says, invoking my least favorite nickname. "You're not still sore about me trying to help you find love, are you?"

"It's not so much you wanting to help me find love as it is the incredibly low standards you set for me." I lead them into the kitchen/great room, and they plunk themselves down on stools at the island.

"I was trying to set you up with a successful lawyer," Willa says. "That sounds like high standards to me."

Hmph, she would see it that way, wouldn't she? I sigh, taking a beat before I snap at her. While my sisters have their faults, and sometimes they even tow the family line, in the end they have always been there for me, even Willa in her own mostly-awful way. I don't bother to argue with her. If I know one thing, it's this: I never win an argument with my sisters. It doesn't matter if I say the sky is blue, and they say it's green. They win.

I grab a bottle of red off the counter, take out the corkscrew, and get to work opening the wine. "Tell us about this horrible week you're having, Rae."

"I've actually had a great week," she says.

"I thought you needed brotherly support and came over to unload on me."

She shakes her head. "More like Willa and I thought you could use a little intervention."

"What?" *What?*

Willa nods. "Rae sent screenshots of your sad little texts this week about the woman who won't give you a chance."

Glaring at Rae, I get two glasses out of the cupboard and fill them both. "So you're here under false pretenses. Nice."

"We thought so," Willa says. "Oh, wait! I told Lily I'd patch her in on Zoom. One sec."

My shoulders drop, and I give Rae a dirty look. "Why don't you just tell the entire world about my problems?"

"Come on," Rae says, sniffing her wine. "We're family. We're supposed to help each other."

Turning to the fridge, I grab a beer. "Not by ambushing each other. This is ridiculous."

"COOPER!!" Lily's voice takes over the room. Willa has propped up her phone so we can all see her. She waves excitedly, then pulls a face. "You were right, Rae. He *does* look awful."

Rae nods. "Poor little Coop. All sad about a woman."

"You know what you should do, Cooper?" Lily says. "Come stay with me in San Diego for a while. There are so many nice, single girls here and they'd definitely be more your type. They're all so laidback."

"I'm pretty busy with work," I tell her grumpily.

"Ah yes, your little homeless shelter project. How is that going?" Willa asks.

"It's not that little." I take a long pull on my beer.

Lily says, "We have homeless people in San Diego, too. I bet they'd love for you to come here and build them houses."

"I'll keep that in mind."

The doorbell rings again, this time saving me from my sisters for a few seconds. "Pizza's here." I temporarily consider walking out and not coming back until morning.

When I return, Rae is searching my cupboards for plates and Willa's opening drawers to find the cutlery. "Just make yourselves at home." I place the pizza boxes on the counter. Glancing at the phone screen, I say, "Can you believe these two?"

"So rude, right?" Lily says. Of the three of my sisters, Lily is the most laid back.

"I feel bad about us eating in front of you," I tell her.

She holds up an individual-sized pepperoni pizza. "Don't! It's a cross-country pizza party. Let's discuss that awful scruff you have going on, because I think it may be the reason the love of your life isn't interested."

"It's not the beard. She thinks I'm a violent thug."

"What?" That loud screech comes from all three of them in unison.

"A thug? Not likely!" Lily says at the same time Rae says, "She clearly doesn't know you then."

Willa says, "You have been known to have a temper. Dare I mention Sumner Livingston?"

"You had to bring *that* up?" Rae yells.

"He was right to do what he did," Lily interjects. "It's a good thing Cooper was there, because if it had been me, I would have killed the son of a bitch."

I open the top box and feel the heat off the veggie pizza Rae always insists we order. "I think the tire slashing thing is what Toni based her low opinion of me on. That and the fact that I punched Sumner in the face during our work cruise."

"Excuse me?" Rae says, freezing with a slice halfway to her mouth.

"Turns out numbnuts has—*had*—a job working for the same foundation as me." I pull out a slice of pizza and take a bite, letting the gooey deliciousness soothe my nerves while they absorb that bit of information.

"Are you kidding?" Willa asks.

"I wish. Turns out he preemptively told Toni about that tire thing, and that was enough of a red flag for her." I look over at Rae, who's got her poker face in place, which means she's upset. "I'm sorry, Rae. I didn't want to tell you."

She shrugs, then takes a large gulp of wine. "I'm only sorry he's causing you grief. We would all be better off if he'd disappear forever."

I give her a little half grin. "I'm all for hiring a hit."

Her eyes light up with amusement. "How is it that you beat him up? Good job, by the way."

I go back to the beginning and spend the next forty-five minutes telling them everything, from our early texting relationship all the way to how she can't stand to be in the same room with me.

They interrupt, gasp, get angry, and hypothesize a hundred different ways I could win Toni back. By the time we're done eating, I'm full of pizza and drained of emotion. As we're tidying the remnants of our feast, I declare, "Now that I think about it, this is all your fault."

"What?" This comes from all three at once.

"You made me watch *Bridget Jones's Diary* so many times, you turned me into her."

"We did not," Lily says. "You don't even smoke."

"Or talk too much," Rae adds.

"You're also not accident-prone." Willa plucks one lonely olive out of the box and pops it in her mouth.

"That may be true, but I have a habit of falling for the wrong woman at every turn."

"If anything, you're Mark Darcy in this scenario, not Bridget," Rae tells me authoritatively.

"Agreed, you're Mark," Lily adds. "You're the one who's been *laboring under a false pretense*. Is that the line?"

"No, I think that's Toni. She's the one who thinks she knows who I am but doesn't."

"You might be right," Rae says. "You're Bridget—"

Lily cuts her off. "What you need is for someone to tell her what really happened so she'll realize you're the hero."

"Maybe, but I still slashed Sumner's tires and beat him up."

"What are you going to do about it?" Willa demands. "You can't just give up."

"I do have one last Hail Mary planned. Her boss came up with it. She's supposed to go to New Hampshire for a couple of days to scope out new sites for the next village. Archie is going to back out at the last second so I can go with her instead."

Silence fills the space, and I know immediately what's going to happen.

"That's a terrible idea!" Lily shouts as Willa says, "She's going to be pissed."

I offer Rae a hopeful look, to no avail.

"They're right, Coop. She's going to feel ambushed."

"Remember how mad you were just because we planned an intervention tonight?"

"I wasn't really mad. Just annoyed."

"Uh-huh," Rae says. "All we're saying is that women hate feeling like they've lost control of a situation. By tricking her like this, you might lose any chance of winning her back."

"Or it might be the only chance I have," I retaliate.

"There's only one thing to do," Willa says.

Lily yells, "We need to watch *Bridget Jones's Diary* again!"

"Oh, no," I tell them. "I'm through taking advice from old romcoms. This time around, I'm going to do it on my own."

"God help you," all three sisters say at the same time.

It's nice to know they have so much confidence in me.

Chapter 33

Toni

Two days and nights with Archie isn't exactly my idea of the perfect New Hampshire getaway, but I'm not complaining. I'm thrilled to be getting out of Dodge for a while. I've been thrown through the mother of all loops ever since finding out what a loser Sumner is. The bitter truth of that whole fiasco is that I no longer trust my judgment in men.

In another dimension, my doppelgänger is getting ready for a romantic getaway with the man of her dreams while I'm packing my Dr. Who fleece onesie with the built-in feet so I can stay warm.

I tried and failed to get Joey to take me to New Hampshire for a long weekend, because he never saw the point. His idea of a getaway was binging *Monster Truckers*, *Ice Road Truckers*, or his all-time favorite, *Mother Truckers*. How did I ever convince myself that he was the man of my dreams?

I'm filling my overnight bag with the bare essentials—

toothbrush, hairbrush, flannel shirt, jeans, and the over-sized wool sweater my dad let me steal from him—when my phone pings with an incoming message.

Archie: Hey, I've gotten tied up. Is there any chance you can meet me at the office?

Me: I can wait here until you're done.

Archie: …

Archie: …

Me: Archie? Are you there?

Archie: Yeah, sorry. I need you at the office before we leave. I'm expecting new plans from the architect, and you need to sign for them.

Me: Okay, but can we stop by my place to pick up my stuff on the way out of town?

Archie: You'd better bring it with you. I don't want to risk getting caught in traffic.

Me: I'll be in by eleven.

Archie: Can you make it ten?

Me: I guess.

I try not to be irritated by the change in plans. Starting the Faith Foundation has come with a learning curve, and

Archie is doing a bang-up job of immersing himself in his new vocation.

Glancing at the clock, I realize I have to walk out the door in fifteen minutes if I'm going to get to the office on time. There goes my Mr. Bagel run. I scurry around and finish getting everything together before rushing out the door.

It's a dreary day. The ground is depressingly dirty, and the sky is thick with clouds nearly bursting with unfallen snow. It makes me feel claustrophobic, like I'm in a short jar and someone has screwed the lid on. I need this getaway.

Archie isn't at the office when I get there, so I let myself in, flip on the lights, and get a pot of coffee started. When I exit the kitchen, I discover I'm not alone.

"What are you doing here?" I demand none too kindly.

Cooper looks like an ad for a Hallmark movie—jeans, hiking boots, parka, scruffy beard … My whole body reacts to him like I've stuck my finger into a live electrical outlet. Jolt, sizzle, burn.

"Archie asked me to meet him here."

"Why?"

He shrugs. "I guess he'll tell us when he gets here."

I sit at my desk and open an online Scrabble game. The droid turns my opening play of "Quiz"—forty-four points, thank you very much—into quizzically, hitting the triple point box and nearly doubling my first play. This better not be an omen of the way the rest of my day will go.

The elevator opens, and Archie appears. "Hey, you guys. Thanks so much for meeting me here." He seems harried and more than a bit disheveled.

"You okay?" I ask.

"I will be, but I have bad news."

My blood runs ice cold, and I worry something has happened to Holly or the baby.

As though reading my mind, Archie says, "There's a supply chain issue with getting all the lumber needed for the job."

"Isn't that Cooper's problem? He *is* the contractor after all." I don't dare look at him while I say that.

Archie answers, "It's a problem for all of us, because if we don't get the lumber shipment on time, we won't open on time, and there are a lot of people relying on us." He takes off his camel hair coat. "I have a meeting with a friend who thinks he can pull some strings for us, but that means I won't be able to go to New Hampshire with you."

"So we'll reschedule. No biggie."

"We can't," he says. "We have several stops to make to scout locations for the next homeless village, and one of the properties is going up for auction over the weekend. I'd like to see if it's right for us before we lose our chance at it."

I'm confused. "How are you going to do that if you can't go?"

"I hope to be able to get there tomorrow."

"We'll leave tomorrow then." Why couldn't he have told me this on the phone?

"*You* leave today," he says. "*I'll* join you tomorrow."

"How am I leaving today? I don't have a driver's license." I glance at Cooper and then it all comes together in my pea brain. Nonononononono.

Archie says, "I want Cooper there to help choose the next location. Since he was going to meet us there tomorrow anyway, he offered to take you up today so you could pick up the sign. I'll meet you both at the lodge in the morning."

"Why can't we just pick up the sign tomorrow?" I demand. I do not want to go anywhere with Cooper Flint.

"The artist is going away. If we don't pick up the sign today, we won't be able to get it for two more weeks, which will mean another trip to New Hampshire." Archie is stern and seems moderately overwhelmed.

I want to point out that the artist can ship the sign then, but I don't get a chance because he adds, "Toni, please just go. I thought this all through, and the only way everything works is for you and Cooper to leave today."

I can hardly stand here and tell him no. Not only would that be unprofessional, but he's working hard, and I need to do my part.

"Fine." *Not fine, but what can I do?*

"Thank you." Archie shoots me two thumbs up and goes toward his office. "Have a safe trip. Call if you need anything." Then he's gone.

The air around me is suddenly a vacuum, and I struggle to catch my breath.

Cooper picks up my overnight bag. "You ready?"

I force a nod, then, like I'm trudging through a four-foot snowdrift, I move in his direction.

I'm going to one of the most romantic places in America with Cooper.

Holy. Crap.

Chapter 34

Cooper

Dammit. My sisters were right. This was a terrible idea. Toni looks like she'd rather ride with a truckload of rabid dogs to New Hampshire than go with me.

Picking up her purse, she faces me with an expression resembling that of someone smelling toxic waste. "I'm all set."

We leave together like we're on our way to a joint execution. Neither one of us is at ease.

I open the passenger door for her, then put her bag in the backseat with mine. As soon as we're both settled, I ask, "Have you had breakfast?"

"I brought an energy bar with me. Do you want to split it?" Her tone suggests she wants to do no such thing.

"I thought we'd hit a fast-food place after we get out of the city. You up for an egg sandwich or bagel?" I pull out into traffic.

She turns so she's looking out the passenger window

instead of at me. "No bagels outside the city will be as good as Mr. Bagel, but a breakfast sandwich sounds good."

We drive in silence for a couple of minutes, and I get anxious. There's no way she doesn't know this is a setup. It was all I could do not to cringe openly when Archie explained why she and I had to take this trip together. I wrack my brain to think of something to say but only manage to come up with, "Are you warm enough? I can turn on your seat warmer if you'd like."

"No, thanks."

Her response is so deadpan, I decide to leave all further conversation up to her. She takes out her phone and gives it her full attention. So much for idle chitchat.

Thirty silent minutes later, I pull into a Starbucks drive-thru. "What would you like?"

Without scanning the menu, she answers, "I'll take a tall mocha with an extra shot and a bacon gouda sandwich."

I order her meal and get myself a venti Pike's Place and the same sandwich as her, then pull up to the payment window. She reaches for her purse. "I got it."

"I don't think so." She pulls out her wallet and hands me a ten.

The young guy at the window says, "That'll be $18.72."

Ignoring Toni's cash, I hand him my Visa. "Don't worry, I'm not going to get the wrong idea and assume we are on some kind of fast-food breakfast date. I'll write it off as a business expense."

"Fine."

Aaaaaaaand we appear to be done talking again.

I pull back out on the road while Toni searches in the white paper bag for my breakfast sandwich. My stomach growls as soon as the savory scent hits my nose. She pulls it halfway out of the bag, tucking the wrapper underneath, then holds it up to me.

"Thank you," I tell her and take it.

She gives me a short nod. We're acting like we're an old married couple after a big fight. The thought of it both amuses and tortures me.

My first bite of the warm, toasted sandwich makes me wish I'd ordered two of them. It's so good, I almost forget how badly I'm striking out in my attempt to win Toni over again. I savor every bite of the salty, cheesy goodness, like it's going to be the best part of my day. Which it very well may be.

I wait until Toni's finished to address the elephant in the truck. "Look, we're going to be stuck together for the next four-and-a-half hours. There's no reason it has to be awkward."

"There's a very good reason," she says firmly. "I know what's going on here, Cooper. You and Archie cooked up this little plan so you could get me alone and try to ..." She lets out a huff and folds her arms.

"Explain to you what you refused to let me explain?" I demand.

"I can think of no explanation that makes your behavior acceptable." She gives me her full attention. "Forcing me to be alone with you so you can try convincing me you're not who I know you are isn't going to work. I learned my lessons the hard way, and I will not be with someone who has a bad temper."

"I'm not that guy."

"Yes, you are. You slashed Sumner's tires and then you beat him up. There's a tiny part of me that's grateful you hit him, but I think I've mentioned before that there are more civilized ways to handle that situation."

I release a loud sigh, full of resignation. I know when

I'm beat. "Maybe this wasn't the best idea, but I only agreed to this because I believe you might be the one for me."

"You can make that judgment after a few days of texting?"

"Texting is very personal. People say things via messenger it takes months to screw up their courage to say in person."

"Such as?"

"I told you about my weird family dynamics and that my parents aren't particularly happy with my career choice. That's not something I tell people I don't have feelings for."

"I can't help if you're an over-sharer." Her words are mean, but she sounds uncertain. There is a flicker of hope.

"You told me about Joey and how you realized he wasn't right for you. You talked about your close friendship with Holly and Faith, and you even intimated you thought I was pretty special."

"I didn't know who you were when I said those things."

"You knew exactly who I was." I'm more forceful than I should be, but I'm fighting for my life. "I was and am the same man who opened up to you and shared some pretty private stuff. I'm the man who made you laugh and worried about you getting home safely when you were out late, who was happy to take things as slowly as you wanted to because I was sure this was the start of something long term, and I wanted to do everything right."

When she finally speaks, she says, "Regardless of any bond you think we formed, I've asked you to leave me alone and yet here we are. The worst part is, you roped *my boss* into helping you. Archie is going to get an earful when he shows up tomorrow." She sighs and faces away from me.

I don't want to rat Archie out and tell her this was all his idea. She already hates me, so there's no point in sharing the blame. "Let's drop it. From this point on, this is a work trip and nothing else."

"Good."

I'm sitting two feet away from the woman I'm pretty sure I'm falling in love with—foul mood aside—only she can't stand the sight of me. That thought is like a knife in my gut. I think back to my sisters' advice and wonder WWBJD? (*What would Bridget Jones do?*)

I turn on one of my playlists. Vintage Pearl Jam blasts from the speakers, and I lower the volume. "Is this okay?"

"I like Pearl Jam," she says, sounding like a robot.

At least we agree on that. As Eddie croons about how love went bad and turned his world black, Toni finds the recliner button on her seat and pushes it until she's as close to horizontal as she can get. Then she closes her eyes, and before long her breathing steadies to the point where I'm sure she's sleeping.

I replay our entire conversation in my head, searching for an "in" I haven't thought of yet. But the only way to prove I'm listening to her and care about her feelings is to do exactly what she's asked me to do—leave her alone. I wish I'd never let Archie talk me into going on this trip. All it's going to do is make it clear I've completely ruined my chances with Toni.

I drive for two more hours before turning off the highway and onto a tree-lined country road. The snow-covered forest makes it look like something out of Narnia.

Toni wakes up as soon as I pull into the artist's driveway and raises her seat so it's upright. "Where are we?"

"We're picking up the sign."

"How long was I out?" she asks, hand in her purse.

"A few hours. You must have needed it."

She takes out a package of gum and sticks a piece in her mouth, then offers me one. I accept gladly, hoping this is a tiny sign that things might be starting to thaw between us. The thought of spending two days together with the tension we endured this morning is nearly unbearable.

I follow the long winding driveway until a small Cape Cod-style house comes into view. The yard is filled with wood carvings, some that would barely reach my shinbone and others that would probably tower over me. There's a workshop about a hundred yards from the house, and I stop in front of it.

Cold, crisp air wallops me when I get out of the truck, and I briefly wonder what the temp is. I lift the back door, then position the third-row seats so they're flat, making it easier to slide the sign in. The only sound is the crunching of our boots on the freshly-fallen snow as we make our way to the shop door.

I knock and open the door, and the sound of classical music spills into the yard. Stepping aside, I gesture for Toni to enter first.

A woman in overalls stands with her back to us, her long gray hair swept up in a bun. She's bent over a work-bench, and a whirring sound competes with Mozart.

"Hello!" Toni calls. "We're looking for Freida."

The woman straightens and turns with a bright smile. "You found her. You must be here to pick up the Bedford Falls sign."

"We are," Toni says and steps forward to shake her hand. She trips on a wood plank and almost takes a header into a table full of chainsaws and tools. I grab her just in time.

She turns in my arms and looks up. "Thanks."

I look at her mouth, remember how things are between

us, and let go of her. "No problem."

"That was a close one," Freida says to Toni. "Good thing you've got this gorgeous hunk of man to keep you out of trouble." She sizes me up. "You might be able to carry the sign by yourself. Come with me."

Toni follows Freida, who leads us to the back of the shop. "You two aren't planning to drive all the way back to New York today, are you?"

"No. We're heading to Manchester for the night," I tell her.

"Good. There's a storm moving in that'll put even the best drivers in a ditch." She points to the sign, which is propped against the wall. It's an amazing piece of artwork, with various swirls and adornments etched into the design. Bedford Falls Village has been carved in the center.

"You do beautiful work," I tell Freida.

"I don't think of it as work. It's more an extension of who I am."

"Which is probably why it's so exceptional," Toni says.

Freida covers the sign in a mover's blanket, and I help her wrap it with bungie cords, then I pick it up and start for the door.

She looks over her shoulder. "Just look at you two. Not only are you obviously in love, but you're starting a family together, and doing so much good in the world. We need more young people like you."

I stop in my tracks, at a loss for words.

Toni says, "Oh, we're not Holly and Archie. I work for them. Well, we both do. I do more than him. He's the builder on the project, so technically he doesn't work for anyone. They're his clients though."

Freida stares, a slow smile spreading across her face. "You're not a couple?"

"Not even close," Toni says. "Colleagues."

"For now," she says with a knowing look.

"Forever," I tell her. I tilt my head toward Toni. "She doesn't like me."

"I think she does," Freida says. "I'm a little bit psychic and I definitely think there's something more going on here."

Toni's mouth drops open.

I say, "Thanks for everything. We'd better get going."

"You're welcome," she says and winks. "You two kids have fun now."

"We're on a business trip," Toni says.

"I'm sure you are," Freida says, sounding like she doesn't believe us.

It takes us another hour to get to the lodge Archie booked for us. Sixty minutes of uncomfortable silence.

The storm Freida was talking about moved in, and the snow is coming down so fast, it's difficult to see while we are driving. The lodge, when it comes into view, is a stunning building with floor-to-ceiling windows looking out on snow-covered fir trees. It's on the shore of a large frozen lake, and a few couples are out skating on it despite the storm.

I'm suddenly full of renewed optimism. This is the perfect place to start over with Toni if she'll give me a chance.

I park in the lot under a giant fir tree and hop out of the truck to get our bags from the backseat. Toni doesn't wait for me to open her door. She jumps out and crunches through the snow to the lobby.

We're greeted with warm air and a crackling fire in a fireplace big enough for six people to stand in. Toni stops short, then sarcastically mutters, "Well, this is just perfect."

"What is?"

Rolling her eyes, she says, "We're staying at what is

quite possibly the most romantic place on the planet."

"It sure looks that way." High five, Archie.

She snatches her overnight bag from my hand and storms to the front desk. I saunter up behind her as she's introducing herself to the clerk. "Toni Cappelli. I'm with the Faith Foundation."

The clerk types on his computer. "I'm sorry, I don't have your name on my list."

"Try Cooper Flint," I suggest.

The man smiles at me, then taps on his keyboard again. "Yes, here we are. Cooper Flint. Two adjoining lake view rooms for a two-night stay."

I feel Toni's glare on my right. "Adjoining rooms? Why?"

The clerk looks at her nervously. "Would you prefer the Honeymoon Suite? It has a sitting room, two full baths, and a private hot tub on the balcony."

"This is a work trip," Toni says curtly.

"Oh, I'm very sorry." He takes two keycards off the shelf behind him. "I assumed you were a couple having a fight and thought maybe the upgrade would help."

Toni narrows his eyes at him. "Why would you assume that?"

"Because you approached the front desk without him, and you've been glaring at him the entire time."

"Is it not possible for a man and a woman to travel together in this stupid state without people assuming they're on their honeymoon?" Toni demands. "We're colleagues, okay? That's it. There's no heat between us, no future for us. Nothing. We are two people who happen to work together."

The clerk looks chagrined as he hands the keycards to me and says, "I hope you enjoy your stay."

"Me, too," I tell him. "Me, too."

Chapter 35

Toni

I have a sneaking suspicion that Cooper is thoroughly enjoying that everyone seems to think we're a couple. Lucky for him, he doesn't say anything, or I'd likely bite his head off.

This inn is totally charming, and I'm sure I'd love staying here with anyone but him. When we reach our rooms, he asks, "Which one do you want?"

"I don't really care. Just hand me a key." He does so.

Turning my back on him, I insert my card into the scanner. When I hear the faint click, I push the door open and go inside, glad to finally be away from him.

When I catch sight of my lodging for the next two nights, the tension of the day drains right out of me. A king-size bed covered in a red and white flannel duvet calls to me. I drop my bag and purse by the closet, kick off my boots, and jump into the bed.

A couple of landscapes hang on the pine walls, and a

plush brown carpet covers most of the wood floors. An overstuffed chair next to the fireplace makes me glad I brought my Kindle, because after I'm on that bed, I'm spending the evening there.

I stretch out for a couple of minutes and notice an array of remotes on the nightstand. Picking up the one that isn't for the television, I tap the ON button. The electric fireplace flickers to life. I watch the flames dance around, making a mental note that if I ever do get married, I'm coming here for my honeymoon.

It's getting dark already, and it's only five o'clock. I search the nightstand drawer for a room service menu, but I can't find one. Picking up the telephone, I call down to the front desk. "Hi, this is Toni Cappelli in room twelve."

"This is William. How may I help you?" He checked us in.

"Could you send someone up with a room service menu? I'm going to eat in tonight."

"I'm sorry, Ms. Cappelli. We don't have room service, but the dining room opens at six for dinner service."

"No room service?" I sound panicky. What kind of inn worth its salt doesn't have room service?

"I'm sorry, ma'am, but there are only twenty rooms, and we don't have the staff to provide outside dining."

Crap. "Do I need a reservation?"

"No. We currently have a wedding party staying with us, and there are only a few rooms that won't be at the rehearsal dinner in the ballroom."

"How late do you serve?" I'll either get there when they open or ten minutes before they close, in hopes of avoiding Cooper.

"We're open from six to seven thirty."

"You serve dinner for an hour and a half?" That's absurd.

"Our guests generally like to retire early." William sounds uncomfortable.

I just bet they do. I hang up and wonder if I should order carry out from a nearby restaurant. A quick internet search shows there is no food delivery within five miles of here.

I pick up the phone again. "Ms. Cappelli," William says. "How may I help you?"

"How is it that there are no restaurants that deliver to the inn? I thought Manchester was a sizable town."

"We're not in Manchester," he says. "We're fifteen miles south of there."

I thank him (even though I definitely don't mean it) and hang up. How in the world am I going to ensure I don't run into Cooper if I don't eat in my room?

I take a quick bath to wash off the road and plan to be the first person in the dining room for dinner. Wearing fresh jeans and a sweater, I return to the lobby, purse slung over one shoulder.

There's no one at the front desk, but I spot a sign for the Maple Room and follow the arrow down a hall until it dead-ends at the restaurant. I'm immediately charmed by its cozy appeal. The room isn't big, but there are tea lights on every table, and a fire is raging in the fireplace. Classical music is playing, and the smell of what I already know will be delicious food makes me temporarily forget my troubles.

William greets me. "Ms. Cappelli, welcome."

"I thought you worked at the front desk?"

He bows slightly. "I'm the front desk clerk, the maître d', and the muffin man."

"The muffin man?" I laugh.

"I bake the muffins first thing in the morning." He winks. "Tomorrow is your lucky day—blueberry streusel."

"You don't also happen to own the place, do you?"

"Guilty as charged." He smiles charmingly. "My wife and I bought the inn shortly after we got married twenty years ago. We raised our children here."

This is a Hallmark movie. "That's lovely. Could I get a table near the fire?"

"Of course. Will Mr. Flint be joining you?"

I shake my head, like I'm trying to dislodge an earwig. "Just me, thanks."

After I'm seated, William places a handwritten menu in front of me. "May I bring you something to drink? A glass of champagne or wine?"

"Do you have anything more potent?"

"I can do a martini, a gin and tonic, or a margarita," he says proudly.

"I'll go with the G&T."

"I'll be back shortly with your cocktail and to take your order." He walks away to the music of Nat King Cole. Most people my age probably wouldn't even know who that is, but my grandmother was a hardcore fan, and she made sure my sister and I knew every song he ever sang.

Leaning back, I close my eyes and let his hit "L-O-V-E" wash over me. What I wouldn't give for the man of my dreams to sing this to me one day—meaning every word, of course.

Somewhere in the distance, I hear William talking to another guest. When the guest answers, my cheeks flush. Cooper's here. My ears perk up when he says, "I don't think that's a good idea."

"Very good, Mr. Flint," William answers. "How about this table over here?"

I open one eye to see where Cooper is being seated. It's the table next to mine, and he's about to sit down so he's facing me.

Opening the other eye, I practically gasp at the sight of

him clean shaven and dressed for dinner. He's wearing pressed khakis and a light green button-down shirt that perfectly matches the color of his eyes. In his left hand, he has a thick hardcover novel—something I've never seen any of my exes holding. I catch myself before letting a thread of drool escape my mouth.

We give each other terse nods, then he peruses the menu, humming along to the song. *He knows who Nat King Cole is?*

He decides what he wants quickly, closes the menu, and looks around for William. Not to be outdone, I choose the grilled salmon with rice pilaf and the house salad. As I close my menu and look up, it is clear to me that this entire meal is going to be lousy with awkward eye contact. "This is ridiculous," I tell Cooper.

"I agree."

"I was hoping if I came down early enough, we'd miss each other so we could avoid"—I point back and forth between us—"all this."

"I promise I won't bother you."

There's a sadness in his eyes that nearly kills me. He opens the book and reads while I gaze at him freely. Cooper Flint is a mystery. One minute, he's a gentleman through and through, and the next, well, he's attacking a wall with a sledgehammer or using excessive force on a Malfoy. He has me so confused, I don't know what to think. He's been nothing but good to me the entire time I've known him, barring this ill-advised trip.

Maybe I'm the villain here. I've pushed him so far away, he's never going to make a move on me. My heart pounds as I contemplate my next move. "Cooper, would you like to join me for dinner?"

He offers me a small smile and shuts his book. "That sounds nice."

When he gets up and comes toward me, I'm once again taken by how breathtakingly handsome he is. He pulls out the chair across from me and sits as William arrives with our drinks.

"Look who's decided to join each other for dinner," he says excitedly.

After we thank him, he takes our orders and leaves. Cooper sips his beer, then leans back. "When I was a kid, my parents took us to New Hampshire in the winter to go skiing. I love it here."

"I've never been before. This has always been somewhere I've wanted to see but never got the chance. My parents are more beach people than skiers." The truth is, we never had the money to go somewhere like this. It was day trips to Jones Beach for us.

"The beach is great, too," he says.

"Where did you ski?" I don't know anything about skiing or New Hampshire.

"My parents have a place on Loon Mountain. Sometimes we spend Thanksgiving there."

"Not Christmas?"

"No way would my parents skip town at a time when all of their friends are having Christmas parties. They're very social creatures."

"Did you get that from them?"

He tilts his head. "I enjoy being social, just not with *their* type of people."

I have a sip of my drink, which loosens my resolve a little. "And what type is that?"

"Well-heeled, highly-educated people who use parties as a chance to show off their knowledge."

"Ah." I nod my head knowingly. "Those aren't my people either."

"They have a way of making a person feel less than, don't they?" he asks, gazing at the fire.

"That's been my general experience." I trace the lip of my glass with one fingertip. "But you're not like that."

"I hope not. As much as I love my parents, I'm really nothing like them."

"Does that have something to do with them wanting you to go back to college?"

"They value different things than I do." He smiles at me sadly. "For instance, if my parents were here right now, they'd insist the chef make them something that isn't on the menu."

"I've never understood that. I generally accept that the items on the menu are the things the kitchen specializes in."

He nods. "You'd think. But my parents like to strive for the best of everything, even if it's getting the best meal at a restaurant."

"They sound competitive."

"I think they like to distract themselves from the truth, which is that they don't like each other very much."

Ouch. "That's too bad." I don't know what else to say.

"How about your parents?" he wants to know. "What would they do if they were eating here right now?"

A giggle escapes me, and I hurry to wash it down with more gin. "Dad would demand to know when the fish was caught, who caught it, and why it's so expensive when it's been caught locally. Mom would be casually walking around the dining room, looking for artificial sweetener packets to stuff in her purse."

Cooper's eyes are wide with amusement. "Really?"

"Really." Then I say the most outlandish thing ever. "Can you imagine what it would be like if both sets of parents were here at the same time?" *You know, like at our wedding?* Thank God I didn't add that last bit. Note to self: Cooper is not the man for you.

"I predict there would be a lot of drinking. What was your family motto again? 'That escalated quickly?'"

"Yup." I laugh.

"I'm guessing that meal would live up to it."

"Now I kind of want to force them to spend an evening together so we can sit back and watch." I feel the heat of a blush on my cheeks. The gin must be loosening my tongue.

William is back shortly with our salads and a basket of warm rolls. "Did you make these too?" I ask him. Cooper looks surprised that I'm asking the waiter if he baked the bread, so I explain, "William is the muffin man."

Cooper clears his throat like that's a euphemism for something else.

I can't be trusted to talk anymore. "William and his wife own the inn. He's making blueberry streusel muffins for breakfast tomorrow."

"Ah, that explains it. Those are my favorite," Cooper tells him.

We spend the next half hour enjoying our meal with enough small talk that I actually enjoy myself. By the time we're finished, and our drinks are gone, I have a warm feeling inside, which is at war with the alarm bells going off in my head. When William clears our dishes and offers us dessert, we both say no—I don't know about Cooper, but I'm stuffed. After he tells us he'll put the meals on our respective room tabs, we start for the lobby together.

There's something intimate about being next to Cooper in a place like this—a place made for romance. The dimly lit hall, the plush carpeting, the two of us in the elevator going up to our floor. In a different life, we'd be holding hands and going back to the same room.

We reach my door first. I'm grateful he doesn't linger.

He saunters toward his door, calling over his shoulder, "Good night, Toni. Sleep tight."

"You, too."

Oh, man. I should not have let him join me for dinner. I should have pleaded a headache, gone to my room, and retrieved stray peanuts from the bottom of my purse. But I did stay, and I had a really nice time.

I'm more confused than I've ever been. How am I going to fall asleep, knowing Cooper is on the other side of my bedroom wall?

Chapter 36

Cooper

My alarm goes off far too early, given the lack of sleep I had last night. Knowing that Toni was one adjoining door away resulted in a lot of tossing and turning. When I finally force myself out of bed, I open the curtains and take in the view. It must have stormed all night, because there's at least three feet of snow on the ground. Even the trees look weighed down.

After showering, I quickly get dressed, hoping to catch Toni in the restaurant again. Even though last night's dinner didn't start out well, we'd definitely made progress by the end. I smile, thinking about us laughing together.

I hope we retain some of that easiness today, but there's a good chance we'll be back to business-only this morning.

As I tuck my keycard into my wallet, I make a promise to accept however she treats me.

When I get down to the restaurant, Toni is sitting at

"our" table, talking on the phone. Even though she gives me a small wave, nothing else tells me what to expect. I sit down in time to hear her say, "Of course you shouldn't make the trip. Not on these roads." There's a long pause. "We'll manage just fine. I'm sure Cooper knows what to look for at the prospective sites." She says goodbye and sets her phone down on the table. "Archie's not coming."

"Ah," I answer, guilt nagging at me; I knew he was not joining us today.

"He claims it's because of the weather, but I can't help wondering if this was the plan all along. Was it?"

I pick up the small carafe on the table and top up her coffee, then pour myself a cup. "If I say yes, do we go back to you being mad at me all day?"

Pursing her lips, she breathes out of her nose loudly. "I think I've tortured you enough already."

"That's a relief," I tell her with a half grin. "I assure you I have no intention of trying to change the way things are between us. I just hate the tension."

There's a flicker of disappointment in her eyes, but she recovers quickly. Picking up her coffee, she nods. "I didn't particularly like it either."

William arrives with a basket of blueberry muffins and sets them down in front of us. "That storm was worse than we were anticipating. I hope you don't have to go far today."

"Just into Manchester," I tell him.

"Give yourselves at least an hour to get there. It's nearly a whiteout."

After he leaves, something occurs to me. "We're probably not going to be able to properly assess potential project sites with all this snow covering everything."

Her shoulders drop. "I didn't think of that. Should we

go back to the city when the meeting at the housing services office is over?"

I rub the back of my neck. "It's probably best to stay put for another night. I'd hate to be stranded on the road."

"Another night it is," she says.

Another night of torture for me.

After a slow, treacherous drive, we pull up to the Bureau of Homelessness and Housing Services building a few minutes late for the meeting with the director. When we get inside, the director greets us. He's an older man who seems more like somebody's grandpa than the head of a governmental department. He's dressed in jeans and a plaid shirt, not unlike mine. When we start to apologize for being late, he waves it off.

"On these roads, I'm surprised you made it at all." He holds out a hand to Toni. "Wes Parker."

"Toni Cappelli," she says. "This is Cooper Flint. He's the contractor overseeing the construction on our first village." She's clearly making sure there are no more misunderstandings regarding the nature of our relationship.

I shake his hand. "Nice to meet you."

We settle around a conference table in his large office. I'm careful to sit as far away from her as possible so as not to give her the impression I'm still holding out hope for us. We spend the next forty-five minutes discussing what his department's initiatives are and the challenges of finding a suitable building site for this type of project. Wes shares the frustration of people not wanting shelters in their neighborhoods. While he understands their concerns, shuffling homeless people out of town means they won't have access to the services and jobs they need to get back on their feet.

The issues between me and Toni are irrelevant. There are much bigger problems in the world. After almost an hour of talking about the number of people in need in the area, and what the foundation can do to help, it occurs to me how nice it is to be able to work with her on this. We have a shared goal, which is all that matters.

I may not like it if we're only destined for friendship, but I can accept it. She is an extraordinary woman, and I'll take whatever part of her she's willing to share.

It's nearly lunchtime when we're interrupted by a knock on the office door. A middle-aged woman pokes her head in. "Wes, the storm is getting worse. I thought I should mention it so you have time to get home before you're stuck in town."

He glances out the window and thanks her for letting him know. Turning to us, he says, "I live about ten miles out. The last time we had a storm like this, I stayed until quitting time and wound up sleeping here. I had a crick in my neck for a solid week."

"In that case, we should let you go." Toni shuts her notebook and shoves it in her purse.

Wes walks us to the main entrance as we prepare to leave. "I'll get in touch with Archie soon. I look forward to working with you. Together, I'm pretty sure we can change our little corner of the world."

I glance outside and see that my truck has at least four inches of snow on it. Turning to Toni, I say, "You wait here. I'm going to brush the snow off the truck."

She nods, looking worried. Hustling out into the biting wind, I start the SUV to let it warm up and then open the trunk. I grab the broom I keep on hand for sweeping up at job sites and spend the next few minutes brushing the snow off the windows and hood. As I finish up, I motion for Toni to come out.

She shuffles through the deepening snow and hops in. "That went well."

"Wes seems like a reasonable guy, and his heart is definitely in the right place." I turn the windshield wipers on high and squint to see past the barrage of snowflakes coming at us.

"Yikes, it's really coming down."

"I have to stop for gas, and after that, we'll take it turtle-slow back to the lodge."

She nods, looking concerned.

"We're in the perfect vehicle for this, and I have a lot of experience driving in snow." What I really want to do is hold her hand. "There's nothing to worry about, okay?"

"Okay," she says with a small smile.

We crawl along the nearly-deserted streets in search of a gas station. The tires catch a patch of ice, and the vehicle starts to slide sideways, but I manage to straighten it out. "Don't be scared."

"I'm good."

She's gripping the seat so tightly, her knuckles are white. "It's okay to admit it if you are. I'm a little nervous myself." A Shell station appears down the street. Slowing down even more, I make a left turn, pull up to the nearest pump, and shut off the engine.

Toni lets out a breath of relief. "Okay, I'm scared."

I look into her eyes, hoping she'll hear what I'm about to say as more than a statement about the weather. "You can trust me. I promise I'll always take care of you."

Chapter 37

Toni

Cooper gets out of the truck before I can conjure a response. While he's gassing up the truck, I go inside in search of snacks. If we're going to be here another night, I want to have a bag of chips on hand in case of an emergency. I don't stop there though. I fill a basket like I'm a nine-year-old on a road trip with her family. Along with the chips, I add several pretty postcards, a couple of refrigerator magnets, a pair of sunglasses, taffy, a liter of diet soda, two bags of microwave popcorn, and a container of mints.

When I approach the counter, Cooper's suddenly at my shoulder. "What, no chocolate?" He tosses several candy bars in the basket before taking it from me. "I'll add it to the gas."

"That's okay, I can pay for my stuff."

He shakes his gorgeous head. "Think of it as a booby prize for being stuck with me for another night." He unloads everything and tells the clerk, "Pump eight is mine, as well."

After everything is paid for and bagged, he asks, "Do you want to get coffee while we're here?"

I shake my head. "I'd rather have a cup of hot chocolate when we get back to the lodge."

I try to take the bag from him, but he refuses. "I'll hand it over when we're back at the truck." When we get there, he opens the passenger door for me, then hands me the stuff and the keys. "Turn the car on and get warm. I forgot something inside."

I put the key in the ignition and turn it, and Cooper's phone rings. Caller ID shows it's Yuma from his office. Normally I wouldn't answer someone else's phone, but as this is a business trip, and it's his office calling, I make an exception.

"Hey, Yuma, it's Toni. Cooper will be back in a minute."

"Oh, hey!" She sounds surprised. "I'm glad you picked up. I've been dying to know if he told you yet, and you know men, you can't get the whole story from them."

"We've talked about lots of things, so I'm not sure I know what you're referring to."

"I'm talking about what really happened between him and Sumner Livingston. I told him he should have told you, but he said you didn't want to hear it."

"The truth about Sumner?" My voice cracks.

"Ya know, about him and Coop's sister, Rae-Anne?" She pauses as if waiting for a response from me, and when she doesn't get one, she says, "Oh! He didn't tell you yet, did he?"

I sway a little in my seat, forcing myself to take a deep breath. "The only thing I know is what I heard from Sumner."

"Then you clearly don't know what really happened, because that douche is a total liar."

I laugh. "Among other things. What happened, Yuma?"

There's dead air for a few seconds. "It's not my place to say."

"Right." To say I'm disappointed is an understatement.

"But that doesn't mean I'm not going to tell you." She laughs. "Rae and Sumner used to be engaged."

"Why wouldn't Sumner have told me that?"

"Because he's a disgusting pig," Yuma says. "He snuck out of their engagement party with the maid *during* the party."

"Did she need a ride home or something?" Not that I could imagine Sumner doing something that nice for someone.

"She needed a ride, all right," Yuma answers. "Right there in front of the house. Coop pulled up in time to see the whole thing."

My stomach bottoms out like I just turned upside down on a rickety wooden roller coaster. "And that's when he slashed Sumner's tires."

"Yup. I would have done more. Coop felt horrible about losing control, but he couldn't stand seeing someone two-time his sister, at her engagement party, no less."

I'm such a fool. Cooper tried to tell me the truth multiple times, but I wouldn't listen. I was so determined to believe Sumner over him, and why? Because I was scared. Holy crap, I've made a mess of things.

"Toni, you still there?"

I clear my throat. "I am. Thank you for telling me this. I really appreciate it."

"You bet. Cooper is an insanely honorable man, so

when you said you didn't want to know, he was willing to respect that, even if it meant you wouldn't give him a chance." She pauses, then adds, "But lucky for both of you, I don't let myself worry about other people's boundaries."

"You did the right thing. Do you want me to have him call you back?"

"That won't be necessary. I was only calling to see how things were going. Sounds like they might be okay now though." She snickers.

"Thanks to you." Cooper exits the gas station. "He's coming back. Bye, Yuma. You're the best."

"Damn straight, I am."

Cooper Flint is not the man I thought he was. Well, that's not strictly true. He's exactly the man I thought he was when we started texting each other, except for his name. Had I let Holly set me up with him, like she wanted to, there would have never been this misunderstanding between the two of us.

I have to accept responsibility, but I don't know exactly how to go about doing that though. I think about what I would have done if I'd caught Archie cheating on Holly, and I might have gone for someone's throat instead of their tires.

Cooper opens the driver's door and gets in, then hands me a lottery ticket.

"What's this for?"

"I always get a lottery ticket when I'm out of state. If I win, it gives me an excuse to come back."

"Did you get one for yourself, too?"

He pulls another one out of his coat pocket. "Even if we can't scout locations on this trip, we might still be able to make it worth our while."

"Cooper …" I don't finish. I need time to think

because if I say what I think I'm going to say to him, there will be no going back.

"What?"

Inhale. Exhale. "Would you like to have dinner with me tonight?"

"Sure," he says, putting the truck in gear. "I know a great place."

The rest of the drive, we're lost in our own thoughts, and there's none of that horrible tension between us. It's actually quite pleasant. I don't know what Cooper is thinking, but I'm busy plotting how best to apologize to him for my horrible behavior.

I like this man, and I'm going to do everything in my power to get him to forgive me. I only hope it's not too late for us.

Chapter 38

Cooper

I spend the rest of the afternoon answering emails and poring over spreadsheets to distract me from speculating on what's happening with Toni and me. There's been a shift between us that's filling me with hope I'm afraid to fully feel. But there was something in her voice when she asked me to have dinner with her tonight that tells me this evening might be the start of something new.

I shut my computer off just before five thirty to shower and get ready. At 5:55, I get a text from her. *Meet me in the sitting room at six.*

My heart pounds as the elevator opens on the main floor. I ask William where the sitting room is, and he leads the way.

I open the door. Toni is sitting on one of two over-stuffed brown leather armchairs that are angled in front of the fireplace. A side table between the chairs holds a bottle of wine, two glasses, and a candle. Toni is in that red dress

I've seen her in once before. She totally takes my breath away.

She offers me a tentative smile. "I convinced William to let us eat here. I hope that's okay."

Nodding, I sit in the other chair. She pours us each a glass of wine, then takes a deep breath. "You look nice tonight."

"So do you." We sip the wine.

"I've been thinking a lot about what you said about being scared. The truth is that when we met, I *was* afraid of you." She glances at the candle on the table, then back at me. "I was afraid of how you made me feel and what would happen if you weren't the man I thought you were."

"I kind of figured that out when you dumped me for Sumner."

"I'm embarrassed about that. You are far and away the bigger man. The better man. I just didn't trust myself."

"What makes you say that? Up until yesterday, you didn't want anything to do with me." I'm not trying to push her away, but I want her to be sure about what I think she's trying to say.

"I was so drawn to you. Like, ridiculously attracted to you, which was hugely problematic, because before I met you, I decided my gut instincts were not to be trusted. After my last relationship broke up, I was determined to date with my head and not my libido."

"That's why you started with a texting relationship. You wanted to get to know me first to make sure there was something more substantial than physical attraction?"

She sighs loudly. "I bet that sounds crazy to you."

"I've had my share of dating disasters, Toni. I understand the need to try something new."

"It was going so well, too, don't you think?" She sounds so hopeful.

"Yes."

"All I've ever wanted since I was a young girl was to get married to someone who loves me as much as my dad loves my mom and then to build a life together. But every time I let someone in, they let me down."

"How so?" I'm sure I can guess some of it, but I want to hear her say it so she realizes I'm nothing like those guys who were stupid enough to let her go.

She takes another fortifying sip of wine. "I've been stolen from, had my credit ruined, and I've been used for free room and board. I thought my last boyfriend, Joey, was going to be *my last boyfriend*. I was sure we were going to get married and have a couple of kids, but then he kept getting fired and acted like it was my fault or something. He was almost resentful of me being gainfully employed."

"Hence the need for dating someone you wouldn't normally," I conclude.

She nods. "I told myself to find someone responsible and stable."

"I'm responsible and stable."

She lowers her eyes. "You're also insanely hot."

That's always nice to hear.

"I was so fixated on getting it right this time that I completely messed everything up. I was terrified you were another bad boy, out to score and use me as an emotional punching bag before stealing my toaster and leaving."

"But I'm not that guy." I fight the urge to touch her hair, her cheek, her hand … any part of her. "I already have a toaster. It even handles four slices at once." I hold up four fingers to emphasize how cool that is.

Her pupils are so big, they make her eyes look black. "I'm so sorry, Cooper. I'm sorry I wouldn't listen to you. I'm sorry I wouldn't give you a chance. I was unfair to you. You deserve better than that."

I glance up at the ceiling. "Agreed."

Grinning, she says, "That whole stupid thing with Sumner … Yuma told me what really happened."

Trust Yuma to stick her nose in and fix things. "When did you talk to her?"

"When you were inside the gas station. I only answered your phone because I thought she might have information regarding our trip." The grin fades. "If it were Holly being cheated on, and me in your shoes, I wouldn't have stopped at slashing Sumner's tires."

"That's good to know." I hope I never do anything to make Toni that mad at me.

"I see you, Cooper Flint. I see who you really are. You're one of the last of the good guys. You're honorable, kind, and thoughtful, and … and you're everything I've been waiting for all this time, only I was too stupid to know it."

I want to believe her. God, do I ever. "Are you sure, Toni? Because I don't want to start down this road with you if you're going to change your mind."

"I have never been so sure of anything in my whole life. I was downright awful to you, but it was only because I was at war with myself over you." Tears fill her eyes, making them shine like stars in the night sky. "If you could see it in your heart to give me another chance, I promise I won't get scared again. I won't push you away. Cooper Flint, will you please give me another chance?"

I can't resist anymore. I stand and hold out my hands to her. She lights up and swipes away the tears that slide down her cheeks.

"On one condition," I tell her.

"Anything."

"Promise to tell me if you start to feel scared again. I can't fix things if I don't know what's wrong." I pull her up onto her feet and into my arms, cup her cheeks in my hands, and lower my mouth to hers.

Right before our lips touch, she whispers, "I promise, Cooper."

And finally, after all the confusion and heartache and longing, I'm kissing her, and she's kissing me back. It's a kiss that says I want it all, I want her forever. Our mouths move together urgently until nothing else matters but this moment with her. I pull her closer, and we stay like this, touching and kissing, completely forgetting where we are.

When she finally pulls away, we rest our foreheads together, panting. "We're going to take this slowly, Toni."

Disappointment crosses her face, then she nods. "But not too slow, right?"

"Turtle-slow," I tell her with a huge smile. "I'm going to romance you properly, Toni Cappelli. I'm going to show you how a man should treat a woman he wants to spend the rest of his life with, and when we finally do this, it's going to be perfect."

Her eyes fill with tears again. "Did you just say you might want to spend the rest of your life with me?"

"I think I did. But I won't push you, because when I settle down, it's going to be forever. I'm a one-woman man."

"We're not going back to texting only, are we?"

I laugh, then shake my head. "Hell, no."

Then she's back in my arms, where she belongs.

Epilogue

Toni

There's nothing as delicious as when the temperature cools down after a blistering hot summer in the city. I tie a cardigan around my shoulders in case this breeze continues, then pick up my purse and rush out the door.

Archie's limo is out front. I climb inside. Joy is fast asleep in her car seat, swaddled in the pink blanket I knitted for her christening. Holly looks beautiful, if tired, and Faith looks like the proudest big sister who ever lived.

"Archie's meeting us there," Holly says. "He and Cooper are fussing at the site like a couple of old British ladies preparing for a visit from the queen."

I laugh. "They've worked hard on this project. We all have. I can't believe we were breaking ground on Bedford Falls only seven months ago and now we're on our way to the opening."

"I can't believe you guys think the time has flown by.

This has felt like the longest year of my life," Faith grumbles.

"Really?" I ruffle the back of her hair. "How so?"

"Well …" She lifts one finger. "It hasn't been easy waiting for Joy to get here." Another finger is raised. "Then there was kindergarten. That's a year I'm glad to see the end of." Finger three goes up. "Finally there were those booger-eating boys. The good news is, I hear the boys in first grade are more mature."

"That *is* good news." I love this kid like nobody's business.

"Aunt Toni?"

"What is it, squirt?"

"Do you think Cooper is your one true love?"

Prickles of heat infuse my nervous system. We've been practically inseparable since we went to New Hampshire last February. While we were determined to take things slowly, once I knew he was the one for me, I knew it with every ounce of my being.

Cooper tried to force me into a phone calls-only relationship for two weeks to prove he respected my wishes, but that only lasted five days. I physically couldn't go any longer without kissing him.

I smile at Faith. "I do think he's my one true love. I sure as heck waited long enough to find him."

"I think he's great," she says. "You should probably marry him and have a cousin for me and Joy to play with."

"I should, should I?" I think so, too, but it's only been seven months.

"The more the merrier, that's what Mom says."

"I do say that," Holly tells me with a wink.

When we pull off the road to the entrance that leads to Bedford Falls, I can hardly believe how amazing everything looks. Forty tiny homes line either side of Main Street.

Each one has a window box and a small patch of grass. The residents will take turns keeping the grounds mowed. There are trees. They'll also learn how to run the small grocery in the office building.

As soon as we get out of the limo, a slew of reporters stops us to take pictures. We smile and wave but don't stop to talk. We're meeting Archie and Cooper inside. Walking around a wide red ribbon stretched between two trees for the cutting ceremony, I knock on the door to the office building.

Natalie opens it. "Welcome!" She steps back to let us in. Natalie and I have called a truce. She no longer calls me every name but my own, and I no longer want to rip her hair out at the roots.

Archie waves from across the room. "Toni, there's a problem in number seven. Can you run over and check it out before we let the press through?"

Why in the world would *I* check it out? What does he expect me to do, plunge a toilet or fix a leaking sink? "What's wrong with it?"

"Someone said there are no flowers in the window box." He gestures at a nearby table. "Grab a couple of those and place them inside. You don't have to plant them or anything."

"You want me to do it?" Natalie asks.

"That's okay. Thanks for asking though." I grab three pots of mums and trot to number seven, marveling at how beautiful everything looks. The houses are perfect miniatures of my dream home.

When I get to my destination, I see the window box is full. Did Archie get the number wrong? A quick glance around tells me all the window boxes are full. That's when I hear Nat King Cole's voice crooning from inside the tiny house. He's singing "L-O-V-E."

I tentatively knock on the door. No one is supposed to move in until Monday.

Cooper answers the door with a rose between his teeth. He takes the mums from me, sets them on a nearby table, then hands the rose to me and bows. "Milady."

"What are you doing here?"

He pulls me into a passionate kiss.

I'm dizzy with all sorts of lustful thoughts by the time he lets me go. "They're about to cut the ribbon on this place without us."

"Believe me, they'll wait."

"For what?"

"For this," he says and drops to one knee. "Toni Cappelli, today is a new start for all the people moving into these homes, and I want it to be a new start for us, too. I love you more than I ever thought it was possible to love someone. These last seven months have been the best of my entire life, and it's all because of you."

Tears prick my eyes. *This is really happening.*

"There's only one thing I can think of that would make my life better than it is right now." He pulls a robin's-egg-blue box out of his jacket pocket and sets it on my open palm. "And that would be if you agree to become my wife."

"I'm ... I ... It's ... Uh ..." I sound like a bumbling fool.

"I knew at the lodge in New Hampshire that I wanted to make you my wife." He opens the box. "Will you marry me?"

Inside is the most exquisite emerald-shaped diamond with smaller baguettes on either side. I wouldn't care if it was the pull tab off a can of beer. "I would love nothing more than to be your wife, Cooper. Yes, I will marry you, and I will love you until I'm old and gray and both of my hips need replacing."

"Do bad hips run in your family?" He stands and slides the ring on my finger.

"Not so much as fat ones. The ladies in my gene pool seem to spread after giving birth." I might not have needed to be so forthcoming about that.

He smiles at me wickedly. "It's a good thing I like a little junk in the trunk." He pulls me into his arms and holds on so tightly, I can barely breathe. But when the man of your dreams is holding you close, it's worth it.

I've been holding my breath for Cooper Flint my entire adult life, and now that I've found him, I can finally breathe easily.

"We're going to live happily ever after, aren't we?" I say.

He grins and kisses me again. "We sure are."

Coming Soon: No Ordinary Hate

No Ordinary Hate
Love is a Gamble Mom-Com Series, Book 1

Life in Hollywood is easy to hate...

According to Hollywood insiders, Harper and Brett Kennedy have the perfect family life—an image that has been carefully cultivated by an army of PR experts at Galaxy Studios. The truth is, their relationship has been on the rocks since Brett cheated when Harper was pregnant with their youngest child. Four years later, he's still cheating, but this time with the nanny.

When the tabloids find out, a media frenzy ensues, all but making Harper and her kids prisoners in their Pacific Palisades mansion. Needing time out of the spotlight to regroup, Harper rents a cabin in the last place the press or anyone else would ever think to look for her—Gamble, Alaska.

There, she finds peace, solitude, and Digger McKenzie. Will the gruff lodge owner, who goes out of his way to make Harper feel like she doesn't belong, realize he's about to miss out on his one chance at happiness? Will Harper's kids adjust to small-town life and heal from the chaos of their parents' separation? Will Harper learn how to shoot a bear?

Find out in the deliciously funny and dishy first install-ment of the Love is a Gamble Mom-Com Series.

Chapter 1

Harper

You know how you can have a nightmare so vibrantly bizarre that you're one hundred percent certain there really *is* an axe murderer standing next to your bed, about to serve you pigs in a blanket before he kills you? That's how I feel right now, except in reverse. I'm currently trying to convince myself that what I'm witnessing is nothing more than a horrific dream.

Standing in the doorway of my Mediterranean-style living room—lovingly decorated in earth tones, with pops of orange and rust reminiscent of the Tuscan sunset—I'm watching my husband bone the nanny. I realize *bone* is a word that lacks class, but believe me, there is nothing classy about what's occurring over the back of my cocoa-colored leather sofa. A couch I must now burn. Possibly while they're still on it.

I should be devastated and rocked to my core, but sadly, this is not the first or even the second time I've caught my husband in a compromising position.

"Oh. My. GOD. Right there!" Justine yells.

Brett responds with, "You're so tight I can barely hold back!"

I'm about to insert myself into the conversation with something along the lines of, "*You* give birth to two children who inherited your giant head and see if you bounce back to normal." Instead, I glance outside to make sure my kids are safe in the backyard. Thankfully, they are.

"Oh, yeah, Brett, you're so… sooooo…."

"Scummy? Deplorable? Cliché?" I suggest loudly.

Brett jumps off Justine and scrambles to pull up his

pants. Unfortunately for him, there's no blood left in his brain, which obviously messes with his equilibrium. He staggers around for a few moments before falling, his ass making a slapping sound against the terra cotta tiles. I think of all the wonderful sounds I could make hitting him with an assortment of art pieces around the room.

Justine mumbles, "Oh, Mrs. Kennedy, I'm so sorry. I was just… I mean… I was choking… and Mr. Kennedy was giving me the Heimlich maneuver."

"He needed his pants down for that?"

She opens her mouth, then closes it.

That's right. Shut it. "Justine, you're fired," I say with a super-human calm I do not feel. "Get out now, and don't bother to pack your bags. I'll have your things delivered to the agency."

"Please don't tell them," she begs, pulling up her underwear. Which look suspiciously like my underwear—Agent Provocateur, Taisia. At nearly $700 a pair, I'm pretty sure they aren't in my nanny's budget. "They won't find me another position if they know that—"

"You needed my husband to give you the Heimlich maneuver with his penis?" This girl is about six eggs short of a dozen.

Brett gets to his feet and announces, "It isn't what you think, Harper."

I'm pretty sure it's *exactly* what I think. My movie star husband has a major problem keeping it in his pants. In the past, he's assured me he was seeking professional help for his lack of impulse control, but I don't even care anymore.

Every time he's promised it's the last time, he has moved one step closer to being permanently expelled from my life. I've tried to forgive him for the sake of our children, but now that he's brought his philandering into our home—my safety zone—it's the last straw.

"You can go with her, Brett. You no longer live here."

"You can't kick me out of my own house!" He's hopping around on one foot while he attempts to tug his pants up. "I paid for this house."

My spirit shoots out of my body and hovers somewhere around the ceiling. I'm seriously experiencing a *Twilight Zone* moment here. "I had a hit television show for six years, Brett. I assure you a good deal of *my* money has gone into this house as well."

"But what about the kids?" It's a question that hits so close to the cavity of my heart that I feel an almost electric shock of pain course through me.

"Do you mean the two innocent children currently playing in the yard? The ones who could easily have walked to watch as you dogged the nanny?" I'm pulling out *all* the unsavory terms now.

"I knew they weren't going to come in," he says, sounding surprisingly offended for someone still sporting a chubby.

"Because kids are so predictable?"

"Because I told them if they got an hour of fresh air, I'd buy them hoverboards."

In lieu of launching myself at his neck, which, let's face it, is just begging to be snapped, I let out a long, disgusted sigh. "Sounds like an absolutely fool-proof—and highly premeditated—plan. Not to mention, stellar parenting there, Brett. Now get the hell out before I bludgeon you to death with my Emmy."

"You're being really unfair. I have an addiction and you know it." My husband's eyes narrow as though *I'm* in the wrong.

"*Oh, please*, that's about as plausible as every celebrity

who's ended up in the hospital for 'exhaustion.'" I do air quotes for good measure, then glance at my Emmy again. My fingers itch at the sight of the heavy statue. If I don't get out of here now, I'm going to have some impulse control issues of my own.

Turning around and walking out of the room, I lay some truth on myself—my lying sack of crap husband isn't worth one night in prison for misdemeanor battery, let alone several years for murder.

I somehow manage to make my way through the enormous white kitchen, stopping at the french doors that lead to the backyard. I take a long, deep breath and realize the nightmare is just getting started. It could be months, if not years, before any kind of normalcy comes back to my life. But right now, I just have to get through the next few hours until my kids go to bed so I can eat an entire box of truffles and process what just happened.

Putting on my best "everything is wonderful" smile, I open the door and call out, "Hey, munchkins!"

My sweet four-year-old, Lily, spots me first and shouts, "You're home!" Then she runs at me like I'm a quarterback with the ball and she's a three-hundred-pound front lineman. "I missed you! What did you eat for lunch? Did you bring me a double-chocolate chunk cookie? Did you know it's impossible to lick your own elbow? Did you know Charlie likes to eat his own poop?" Charlie is the neighbor's black lab and Lily is known for her machine-gun fire ability to shoot out questions. She rarely waits for the answers.

My son Liam, on the other hand, is the quiet type. At eight years of age, he reminds me of a tiny grandpa, with his love of socks in sandals and his collection of WWII memorabilia. He also prides himself on being far more grown-up than his "way younger" sister. "Hi, Mom. How was lunch?"

"Great, buddy. Auntie Kay said to give you each a big squeeze from her, but I know how much you don't like big squeezes, so I'm just telling you instead."

"Thanks," Liam says with a serious nod. "I appreciate you respecting my boundaries. I know a lot of moms aren't comfortable doing that."

I chuckle while ruffling the back of his blond hair. "I thought maybe you and your sister might be in the mood for some ice cream."

"From the freezer or the Purple Cow?" he asks, like it will make any difference. Liam will eat *any* frozen sweet-ened milk product put in front of him any time of day in any kind of weather. I'm pretty sure he'd suck on frozen milk cubes if I made them for him.

"The Purple Cow, of course," I say, as though any other option would be insane. "I don't think I can get through the rest of the day without one of their root beer floats."

"Ooh! Let's see if Daddy can come! And Justine!" Lily says, her blue eyes sparkling with

love for the man who has just humiliated me for the last time.

"You know what?" I ask, somehow managing to keep my tone light. "Let's make it just the three of us. Your father has to get back to the studio and Justine also has some stuff going on this afternoon. But you've got me for the rest of the day."

For longer, actually. Now that the nanny has been fired, I'm going to have to cut back on my commitments. I can't stomach the idea of another person moving into my home. Especially at the same time the whole world finds out Brett and I are separating.

We'll have to get our PR people together to come up with some benign blanket statement that says, "While we love and respect each other and will always remain great friends, we've simply grown apart." That's about as honest as the exhaustion crap they try to sell people.

If Brett and I didn't have kids, I would have pulled out my camera and filmed him banging Justine, then sold it to TMZ to pay for the divorce lawyer. I have no desire to protect Brett's image for his fans. As far as I'm concerned, they should know the truth about the man they worship—that he's a cheating lothario. But I will walk the walk and safeguard his sorry hide for the sake of my kids. Liam and Lily should *not* have to hear the sordid details of their parents' split.

"Come on, guys, what do you say we hoof it?" I ask with a bright grin that could not be more forced.

"*All* the way to the Purple Cow?" Lily asks. "That's a far way, Mommy. Can we drive instead?"

"We'll make it, baby," I say, tearing up a bit. "We. Will. Make. It." Of course, I'm not talking about ice cream.

Liam narrows his eyes at me like he suspects something is wrong. "Come on, Lil, it's not that far."

I kneel down next to my little girl, who is the spitting image of me at that age, then I pull both of my kids into a group hug. "I love you so much," I tell them. "You're my world, you know that?"

"Um, Mom, boundaries. You're squeezing too tight and my guts are going to pop out if you don't let go."

I release them with a quick apology, then stare at my two perfect humans. I wish more than anything I could stop time for them right here on this perfect early-summer day. As much pain as I'm in right now, my kids are still blissfully unaware of what's coming. A soft breeze ruffles their still-baby-fine hair; the sun reflects against their white highlights reminding me of fairy children from a storybook.

"Come here." I motion to them, unable to resist the temptation to pull them back into my arms. I'm going to do everything I can to make this the best afternoon of their little lives because, far too soon, their entire world is going to come crashing down.

Chapter 2

Digger

"Did you enjoy the trip?" I ask, reaching up to help Mrs. Baker down from the float plane. The middle-aged woman, decked out in what I'm guessing is a tennis outfit, says, "I suppose.

I'm just really disappointed we didn't come face-to-face with a grizzly bear. The lady on the phone said we'd see one."

"That would be Moira, my sister, who should not be making promises I can't keep."

Narrowing her eyes, Mrs. Baker says, "I don't care who she was. We *paid* for an interaction with a grizzly bear."

"Tell you what, I'll have her give you a free supper at the diner tonight as an apology." Moira not only takes reservations for our family's lodge, cabin rentals, and flight-seeing tours, she also owns the only diner in Gamble, Alaska, population two hundred forty-six (technically two hundred forty-seven, but everyone considers the Dickerson twins one person. Mainly because it's never occurred to anyone to count them twice).

Moira is known for telling a few tall tales to get people excited about our excursions. It's great for drumming up business, but not so good when her tales don't come true.

"Rita, it's not Digger's fault there weren't any grizzlies around," her husband tells her as he forgoes my assistance and hops onto the dock on his own. "I, for one, had a terrific time. I've never seen salmon that size before. Ooooh-wee! I can't wait to show the boys at the golf club these pictures."

"Glad you had fun, sir," I tell him as I lock the passenger door of the Cessna 360.

Clearly not ready to let the matter go, Mrs. Baker makes a loud *tsk*ing sound. "We came all the way from Coral Gables because we were guaranteed a grizzly encounter. We spent three hours up in that plane, and then two hours at that stream without even seeing *one*. Not even from the air. I'd like to speak to your manager."

Nuts. Moira and I take turns being the manager, depending on who's complaining about what, but since Mrs. Baker is going to complain about my sister, I should be the one on the receiving end of the complaint. "Let's head up to the lodge," I say evasively. With any luck, Grandpa Joe will be there. He's used to pretending to be the boss.

We stroll up the windy wide pebbled path from the shore of Whistler Lake to the large one- story log cabin that houses the reception desk, the guest rooms, and our small restaurant (which serves the best plate of bacon and eggs in Alaska, thanks to me). I'm not only the pilot, I'm also the chef, the handyman, the accountant, and the part-time dentist (but only when my nephew needs a hand pulling out a tooth).

With only ten rooms in the lodge and three secluded cabins, it's usually not hard to stay on top of everything. When I'm out on a tour, we send our guests over to Moira's to eat.

"What time of day is it anyway?" Mr. Baker asks.

The sun stays high in the sky so long in June, it's easy to lose track of time. "Four fifteen," I tell him. Now he's going to say something about how it looks like early morning.

"Gosh, it might as well be breakfast time. I absolutely love Alaska," he gushes. "Rita, we should move here. Think of how much we could do in a day!"

"While it might be fine in the summer, come winter, it's twenty-four hours of night. What are
you going to do then?" she asks her husband.

With a waggle of his overgrown greying eyebrows, he says, "Stay in bed." Mrs. Baker looks like she's just sipped from a glass of spoiled milk. "I don't think so."

Here we go... another miserable couple proving that marriage is the worst idea anyone has ever had. I've always been anti-commitment and, lucky for me, I see enough unhappy couples to stay true to my beliefs.

As we come around the corner, Brewster, my dark grey Great Dane, lifts his head from his bed on the covered porch. As soon as he sees me, he scrambles to get up, clumsily makes his way down the steps, then bounds toward us with his tongue hanging out to the left.

Mrs. Baker shrieks, "Sweet Jesus, save me, I'm going to get eaten alive!"

I hold up one hand to Brewster and he stops running. I point down and he drops into a sitting position on the grass. "Wait there," I tell him.

He does as he's told, even though his hind end is in a full wag of excitement. "That's Brewster. He's big, but he wouldn't hurt a fly holding a shotgun."

Mr. Baker shakes his head at wife's histrionics. "For God's sake, Rita. It's a dog. He's not going to kill you."

"I see that *now*, Rodney," she bristles. "But from back there, I thought it was ... something else."

"A bear, perhaps?" her husband says.

"Oh, shut up," she snaps before storming off toward the lodge.

"Maybe it's a good thing we didn't have that grizzly encounter," I murmur when she's out of earshot.

Mr. Baker starts laughing while I pat my leg to release Brewster. I wait while he trots up to me and butts his head into my thigh—which is his version of a high-five—then he walks stride- for-stride next to me as we make our way to the porch.

The smell of freshly baked buns hits my nose, reminding me it's almost time to fire up the grill. Grandpa Joe is the baker. He whips up bread, cakes, and cookies that would make you think he was trained in Paris, France. But he wasn't. Everything he learned was here at the Whistler Lake Lodge.

Mr. Baker and I jog up the ten wooden steps to the double front doors, and I open the one on the right for him. Once he goes in, I follow behind, looking around to see what Mrs. Baker is up to. Oh dear, she's trailing behind Grandpa Joe complaining about not seeing a bear.

I overhear my grandfather tell her, "I bet if you slept out on the front porch tonight you'd have yourself a grizzly encounter. Want me to make up the hammock for you?"

"You can't be serious." She sounds totally appalled.

"I'm just trying to figure out how badly you want to see a bear," he says with his lopsided grin. "How 'bout a glass of whiskey? You look like you could use one."

"I really could," she replies. "I was almost knocked over by a giant wild dog. My heart is racing like a rabbit."

"I bet," he tells her, gesturing for her to sit down on one of the stools. "Let's have a couple of drinks to help calm your nerves, then you can tell me all about how my grandson disappointed you." He flashes me a conspiratorial smile, letting me know he's going to make everything all right with Mrs. Baker.

I hold up one finger to my grandpa. He has a heart condition which means he shouldn't be drinking scotch, but I won't complain if he has one. He flicks his fingers under his chin mobster-style to indicate what he thinks of my opinion, then pours two generous servings of the amber liquid.

Chuckling to myself, I make my way over to the fridge to grab a beer. After a few minutes, I take my cold Bud out to the deck and wait for the grill to heat up. Brewster is lying nearby, watching a dragonfly dive down near his head to catch a mosquito. I take a deep breath of warm summer air, happy that I get to live here in the most beautiful place in the world—and one of the last few places on Earth where a guy can be truly free.

Mrs. Baker comes out onto the porch with her cocktail and a *People* Magazine in hand. "Can you believe that Harper and Brett Kennedy are getting divorced? I'm completely devastated.

They're the perfect couple." She stares at the page she's reading, then adds, "Were."

"I don't have the first clue who they are, but if they're famous, I'm not all that shocked that their marriage is on the rocks."

"You don't know who they *are*?" She looks personally affronted by my lack of Hollywood knowledge. She shakes her magazine at me, and demands, "Haven't you seen the Helioman

movies?"

"Can't say I have." *What the hell is a helioman?*

"What about the TV show *Conspiracy*? Harper played the double agent for the CIA."

Now *her* I remember. If the woman who starred in *Conspiracy* is Harper Kennedy, wow. She has a face you won't forget. But even I know that looks alone aren't enough to keep a marriage together, especially a Hollywood one.

Mrs. Baker continues to lament the end of the Kennedys' marriage like they're close personal friends of hers, then she makes her way to the far side of the deck and settles onto a lounge chair to flip through her magazine, leaving me alone with the sound of a pair of Arctic loons calling to each other as they search for their dinner. Thank God I live in Alaska instead of in L.A. where all the phonies of the world like to congregate. Up here, we're so far removed from the entitled veneer of that world, we wouldn't know what to do if we came face to face with it. Not that we ever will ...

Afterword

A Note from Melanie and Whitney:

Thank you so much for taking the time to read Toni and Cooper's story! If you enjoyed it, please take a moment to leave a review. Reviews are a true gift to writers. They are the best way for other readers to find our work.

And if you aren't already signed up for our newsletters, please do so! This way we can keep you apprised of new releases, promotions, etc.

All the very best to you and yours,
    Whitney and Mel

About the Authors

WHITNEY DINEEN

USA Today Bestseller Whitney Dineen is a rock star in her own head. While delusional about her singing abilities, there's been a plethora of validation that she's a fairly decent author (AMAZING!!!). After winning many writing awards and selling nearly a kabillion books (math may not be her forte, either), she's decided to let the voices in her head say whatever they want (sorry, Mom). She also won a fourth-place ribbon in a fifth-grade swim meet in backstroke. So, there's that.

Whitney loves to play with her kids (a.k.a. dazzle them with her amazing flossing abilities), bake stuff, eat stuff, and write books for people who "get" her. She thinks french fries are the perfect food and Mrs. Roper is her spirit animal.

MELANIE SUMMERS

Melanie Summers lives on Vancouver Island in Canada with her husband, three kiddos, and two cuddly dogs. When she's not writing, she loves reading (obviously), snuggling up on the couch with her family for movie night (which would not be complete without lots of popcorn and milkshakes), and long walks on the beach near her house.

Melanie also loves shutting down restaurants with her girl-friends. Well, not literally shutting them down, like calling the health inspector or something. More like just staying until they turn the lights off.

Made in United States
North Haven, CT
23 December 2021

13559034R00176